12/18

A Secret
To Die For

Center Point
Large Print

Also by Lisa Harris and available from
Center Point Large Print:

Dangerous Passage
Pursued
Vanishing Point

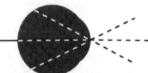

A Secret
To Die For

Lisa Harris

CENTER POINT LARGE PRINT
THORNDIKE, MAINE

This Center Point Large Print edition
is published in the year 2018 by arrangement with
Revell, a division of Baker Publishing Group.

The text of this Large Print edition is unabridged.
In other aspects, this book may vary
from the original edition.
Printed in the United States of America
on permanent paper.
Set in 16-point Times New Roman type.

ISBN: 978-1-68324-987-0

Library of Congress Cataloging-in-Publication Data

Names: Harris, Lisa, 1969- author.
Title: A secret to die for / Lisa Harris.
Description: Center Point Large Print edition. | Thorndike, Maine :
    Center Point Large Print, 2018.
Identifiers: LCCN 2018035797 | ISBN 9781683249870
    (hardcover : alk. paper)
Subjects: LCSH: Women detectives—Fiction. | Murder—
    Investigation—Fiction. | Large type books.
Classification: LCC PS3608.A78315 S43 2018b | DDC 813/.6—dc23
LC record available at https://lccn.loc.gov/2018035797

A Secret
To Die For

1

A sharp clatter jerked Grace Callahan out of the novel she was reading. She dropped the paper-back onto the empty side of the queen-sized bed, then sat up, trying to determine if the noise had come from inside the house, or outside. More than likely it was her neighbor's dog again, knocking something over. Or maybe she'd simply imagined it.

She glanced at the book's ominous cover. Next time she should stick to reading something less . . . intense when trying to go to sleep.

Not that it would matter.

Nighttime had become the hardest, especially this time of year. Seconds stretched into minutes that eventually stretched into hours. But morning never came soon enough. And then when it did come, most of the time she was still exhausted. She'd tried every natural sleeping remedy she could find, yet most of the time the middle of the night found her wide awake and unable to sleep.

Like tonight.

She heard the noise again. This time she knew she hadn't imagined it. She reached for the sub-compact Glock she kept stashed in her nightstand drawer. It was one of the fallouts of living alone. She was now the one ultimately responsible for taking care of the broken garage door opener, filing taxes, and keeping the gutters cleared.

And making sure there wasn't an intruder in the house.

Her mind started through a mental checklist as she made her way across the hardwood floor. Living alone made security automatic. Before she'd gone to bed, she'd made sure the front and back doors were locked, set the alarm, and turned on the night-light in the living room . . .

Everything Kevin used to do.

Shoving aside the thought, she opened her bedroom door and stepped out onto the upstairs landing, then paused to listen. The old clock that had been her grandmother's ticked off seconds from the living room. The air conditioner pumped cool air out of the duct above her. Water dripped from the faucet in the guest bathroom.

Nothing sounded out of the ordinary.

She took a deep breath in an attempt to suppress the wave of anxiety. She of all people should know how to deal with stress, and yet she'd still let reminders of today's date and the grief it always brought completely engulf her.

She started down the stairs for a final reassurance that she was alone in the house, then froze as the white beam of a flashlight coming from the kitchen caught her attention.

Oh God, show me a way out of this. Please.

Her finger felt for the trigger of her Glock,

but even with the weapons training her father had insisted on, the last thing she wanted was a confrontation with the intruder. She needed to get out of the house.

She slipped back into her room and silently locked the door behind her. She figured she had very little time before whoever was inside the house made their way upstairs. Which meant she had two choices. Lock herself in her closet until the police showed up, or escape.

Thanks to her father's insistence, she'd already played the scenario in her mind, making the decision easy. Grabbing her Bluetooth from the nightstand, she dialed 911, then pocketed her car keys and phone and headed for the window with the under-bed ladder her father had bought her. She'd assumed she'd use it in the case of a fire. Never running from an intruder.

Seconds later, the operator answered.

"911, what is your emergency?"

Grace slid open the window and felt a rush of air enter the room, warm even for November. "My name's Grace Callahan and someone's just broken into my house."

She gave the operator her address as she hooked the ladder onto the windowsill.

"Where is the intruder?"

"On the first floor the last time I saw him. I'm getting out my bedroom window on the second floor."

"Grace, I want you to stay on the phone with me. I have officers responding to the call now who should be at your location within three or four minutes."

Four minutes.

She didn't have four minutes. Which meant she was going to have to handle this on her own. She drew in a deep breath and tried to settle her nerves. All she had to do was get down the ladder and out of her yard, all while avoiding whoever had broken into her house.

You can do this, Grace.

The doorknob to her room rattled behind her. Adrenaline surged.

"He's at my bedroom door now," she whispered, trying not to panic. "I've got to get down the ladder now."

She slipped the Glock into one of her pajama pants' pockets, then started down the ladder. The humid night air filled her lungs.

"Grace . . . are you still there?"

"Yeah . . . I'm outside." A small measure of relief filled her as she put both feet on the ground.

"I want you to go to a neighbor's house, but stay on the line so I know where you are."

She wiped sweaty hands on her pants and gripped her weapon. "Okay."

Her neighbor to the left was an eighty-five-year-old woman who still lived alone. Across the street was a football coach who worked for the local school district. Definitely her best bet. She headed toward the backyard gate that led to her front yard.

A shadow moved to her right, just inside her peripheral vision. She swung around and aimed the gun at the armed intruder, who now stood outside the open back door of her house, a gun pointed back at her. Her mind raced for an explanation. Why had the intruder come after her when he now had an empty house to himself? She had no idea what he wanted, but she wasn't going down without a fight.

"If I go down, you're going down with me," she said, keeping her weapon steady despite the panic rising inside her.

She stepped to the left, closer to the corner of the house and the gate, and tried to memorize his features that were partially illuminated by the back-porch light. A large, burly man, well over six feet tall, dark hair, thin nose, and a tattoo on his right wrist.

"Where is the key?" he asked.

"What key?"

"Stephen Shaw gave you a key, and I want it."

Stephen? Her client?

Her mind fought to process the man's words. This was about Stephen and a key? She had no idea what he was talking about.

"Who are you?" she asked.

She'd thought whoever had broken into her

house had been nothing more than a burglar, but clearly she was wrong. And Stephen's paranoia . . . Had she been completely wrong about that as well? Stephen had never given her any real proof that anyone was after him. He had spoken only of shadows, and ghosts he couldn't catch. She'd told him she believed he was simply suffering from paranoia and tried to help him deal with the symptoms. He'd never given her anything.

"I don't have time for games," he said. "Tell me where it is."

She took another step to the left, forcing him to re-aim. "I honestly don't know what you're talking about."

"And I know you're lying."

She weighed her options. If he was determined to murder her, she'd already be dead. Which meant the information he believed she had was keeping her alive. But while he probably hadn't expected her to be armed, even if she were to shoot him, there were no guarantees he wouldn't shoot her back. Or that a bullet would stop him. Neither did she want to risk becoming a hostage. And she wasn't sure if she had time to wait for the authorities to arrive. She was less than fifteen feet from the gate that led to the front yard.

She needed to run.

Sirens wailed in the distance, distracting him for a split second and giving her the opportunity she needed. Praying the darkness would shield her, she sprinted around the corner toward the gate as a bullet pinged off the side of the house.

Her heart felt as if it were about to burst out of her chest. She glanced behind her as she slipped through the gate in her bare feet. He was behind her. She could hear him cursing as he followed her. She cut across her neighbor's front yard, trying to outrun him.

What she really needed was a place to hide.

Moving into the shadows, she dashed across another driveway, then through five or six more yards. The sirens were getting louder. All she needed to stay safe was another sixty seconds. She crossed another driveway and threw a quick look over her shoulder. He was now two houses behind her and slowing down.

She crouched behind a row of neatly manicured shrubs in front of one of her neighbors' houses, and tried to catch her breath. Someone called her name. She'd forgotten the 911 operator—her headset had fallen next to her foot when she'd hunkered down behind the last bush.

"Grace."

She picked the Bluetooth up off the ground and put it over her ear again. "I'm here," she whispered.

"I heard you talking to the intruder. Are you okay?"

The man had stopped in the middle of a driveway, trying to determine which way she'd gone.

"Where are you now?"

"About seven . . . maybe eight houses north of my house. He's armed, but I found cover behind a row of bushes."

"Do you know the man who's after you?"

"No."

"Okay. I want you to stay on the line with me. Officers are thirty seconds out."

Thirty seconds.

Just stay hidden, Grace, and you'll be fine.

"Can you give me a description of the suspect and his weapon?" the operator asked.

She glanced through the foliage, searching for him as she answered the woman's question, but the figure had vanished into the darkness.

2

Dawn had just started to lighten the horizon when Detective Nathaniel Quinn ducked under the crime scene tape. The crime scene unit and the first responding officers to the 911 call had already arrived on the scene that spread out beside the vacant strip mall. He'd used to love it when the carnival came to town. Every summer his parents would take him, letting him go on rides until his tickets ran out and he was so full of junk food he felt as if he were going to explode. But today the empty rides and deserted walkways felt eerie without the noise of excited children and the smell of popcorn and hotdogs. As if the apocalypse had come unannounced during the night.

He stepped onto the platform of the carousel where Detective Paige Morgan, his new partner, was already examining the body. They'd worked a number of cases together over the past four years he'd been in the department. She was focused and extremely good at what she did.

She was also a reminder of what had happened to his last partner.

"Sorry I'm late," Nate said. "Traffic's at a standstill on 35."

Dallas's traffic was the one thing that made him

miss the small Oklahoma town he grew up in.

Paige stepped away from the body. "It's good to have you back, Detective. You look a lot better than the last time I saw you."

"Thanks. It's good to be back on the job."

Nate knew what she was thinking. But the last thing he wanted was extra attention, or sympathy for that matter. Everyone told him he was lucky to have made it out alive. But sometimes that was the hardest part. The Hyde Hotel bombing had killed eighteen: twelve civilians and six officers. And made the scars on the back of his hands and forearms a constant reminder. Still, he'd somehow managed to convince his psychologist—and himself—that he was ready to be back. He just had to keep convincing himself it was true. Because healing the scars people couldn't see had proven to be a lot harder than healing the scars they could see.

"So how does it feel to be back?" Paige tightened the band holding her dark hair in a ponytail and caught his gaze.

Nate frowned at the question, wondering if he was going to have this conversation with every- one. It would be easier if people would just ignore that he'd been gone for three months and leave it at that. "We lost some of the best people I've ever worked with that day. It's hard to forget."

"It was a hard-hitting reminder for all of us," she said.

An unfortunate risk of the job, his psychologist kept telling him. But while that might be true, it didn't come close to erasing the grief.

"I know it must be tough," she said. "I just want to be supportive."

"I know, and I appreciate it. Really, I do. But I'm fine. And ready to put the last few months behind me."

He'd done everything the department had required and had finally been approved for active duty again. But that didn't mean he was back to normal yet. Or ever would be. He was still dealing with the nightmares and triggers.

Nate shifted his attention away from his new partner to the body lying slumped over the carousel bench. Appearing to be in his mid-thirties, the victim was wearing navy chinos and a striped collared shirt. A 9mm Colt Defender lay on the ground, inches from the man's right hand.

"Preliminary glance shows no marks on him other than the gunshot wound to the head," Paige said.

"Which makes it look like a suicide." Nate stopped next to one of the carousel horses. "Though this seems like a strange place to end your life."

"I agree. Then again, it's pretty isolated, especially at night. Maybe he had some kind of clown fetish or a thing for carousels. I don't know, but on top of that, he still had his wallet with credit

17

cards and some cash, as well as his phone."

"So we're not looking at a robbery." Nate glanced at one of the first responders. "Officer . . ."

"Bailey." The uniformed officer stepped forward.

"Who is he?" Nate asked.

The officer glanced down at his notes. "According to his driver's license, his name is Stephen Shaw. He's thirty-two years old and lives about ten miles from here."

Nate glanced back toward the exit. "What about a car?"

"Found it on the other side of the lot with a couple suitcases in the trunk. CSU is going through it right now."

"Sounds like he might have been either on his way out of town or maybe on his way home from a trip," Paige said.

"And he stops en route to kill himself?" Nate shook his head. The scenario didn't make sense. They were missing something. "Who found the body?"

"The security guard." Officer Bailey stepped onto the platform. "Said he found him about an hour ago. Realized the man was dead and called 911."

"Wait a minute. Didn't the guard see or hear anything?" Nate asked the officer. "I mean, this place is pretty spread out, but if nothing else, he should have heard the gunshot."

18

"Says he didn't hear anything."

Nate turned back to the body. "So why would this guy show up at a traveling carnival in the middle of the night, with a trunk full of luggage, and then shoot himself?"

The lights from the carousel flashed above him. Music blared as the platform jolted forward. Nate grabbed on to the pole next to him. His heart rate escalated. Paige shouted for someone to turn the ride off. A row of sweat beaded on Nate's forehead. Someone else shouted over the warped music. The department psychologist had worked with him to fight the negative thoughts. Thoughts that sometimes brought on panic attacks because he was afraid he couldn't escape.

Even when there was nothing to escape from.

He grabbed the watch in his pocket and ran his finger across the bronze back to calm himself. They were lies. Those thoughts—that it was happening again. That he—and everyone around him—was in danger. He couldn't pay attention to them. Instead he focused on his breathing. In, out. In, out. Focused to keep the panic off his face so no one knew what was going on inside his head.

But he wasn't sure that was possible. And that's what scared him the most.

The carousel slowed to a stop.

"Nate?" Paige stepped in front of him. "Everything okay?"

"Yeah, I'm fine. Did you find anything else?" he asked Bailey, diverting the conversation away from himself.

"There was a business card in his pocket." Officer Bailey handed him the bagged card. "It's for a psychologist named Grace Callahan. There's a number handwritten on the back."

"And according to his call log," Paige said, "two of the last three calls he made were to her. He left a message just after eleven, then about an hour later tried to reach her again."

"What time?"

"The second call was made just after midnight."

"Grace Callahan." Another memory surfaced, but this time minus the panic. "Strange, but I think I might know her."

"Really?"

"If it's the same person, I was good friends with her and her husband. I was in their wedding." Nate pulled up the memory. "And she studied psychology in college. If Shaw did kill himself, it makes sense that he would call his shrink first. He's about to step over the edge, calls her for some moral support—"

"But when he can't get ahold of her, he ends it."

"What about the third call?" Nate asked. "Any ID on that one?"

"We'll have to run the number," Paige said.

"Then we need to start with his psychologist,"

Nate said, handing the evidence back to the officer.

"Are you still close?" Paige asked.

"Lost touch with her and her husband years ago. You know how it goes. They were married, I was single. We both stepped into demanding jobs. Life gets in the way."

He'd heard they'd had a little girl a couple years after they got married, but that was it. He wasn't exactly one to keep up on Facebook. They'd been married over a decade by now, so more than likely had at least one or two more kids.

Nate stood over the body, working to put the few pieces they had together. "So all we really know is that he decides to break into a traveling carnival, calls his shrink, plus another number, then ends up dead."

"Maybe he was meeting someone here," Paige said.

"Grace Callahan?" Nate asked.

"It's possible. Or it makes sense that he was worried about whoever was meeting him here, and he called her for support."

"Any signs of someone else being here?" Nate asked.

"That's going to be pretty impossible to tell," Paige said.

In the middle of a carnival where hundreds of people had been, finding a unique fingerprint or

DNA was going to be impossible. But then why had Stephen Shaw come here?

"I'd like to talk to the security guard, then we need to pay Grace Callahan a visit," Nate said.

Five minutes later, Nate and Paige found the lanky guard, with thinning red hair and a slight pudge around the middle, leaning against the trunk of his car. "Mr. Peters? I'm Detective Nate Quinn and this is my partner, Detective Paige Morgan. I'm sorry to keep you waiting."

"No problem, I'm just ready to get out of here. I mean, finding a dead body . . . Let's just say that isn't exactly in my job description."

"I'm sure that must have given you quite a scare," Nate said.

"Tell me about it. I gave a statement to the other officers and told them everything I know. Which really isn't anything. I'm sorry I couldn't be of more help."

"You're the only guard here?" Paige asked.

"At night, yes. I look after the equipment. Make sure kids don't break in and trash the place."

"And yet you didn't hear anything tonight? No gunshots?"

"No, I'm sorry. I must have been on the other side of the carnival when it happened."

Nate frowned. While the man's explanation was plausible, he was having a hard time buying that he didn't hear the shot.

"Did you recognize the victim?" Nate asked,

22

continuing with his line of questioning for the moment.

"No."

"And you didn't see anyone else around tonight?"

"Not tonight. We've had a few teens looking for trouble the last couple nights. But tonight was pretty quiet."

And no doubt horribly boring.

Nate glanced up at the roller coaster towering beside them. Making the rounds in the dark in this deserted place every night wasn't a job he'd place on his top-ten list.

"What can you tell me about the carnival?" Paige asked.

"It's a family-owned business that's been around since the nineties. They set up at fairs, festivals, and even private parties all over the state. I've worked for them for a couple years now."

"What are your normal working hours?" Nate asked.

"I get here when the park closes at eleven and stay until seven when the staff starts arriving."

"But you weren't here all night, were you?" Nate asked, deciding to go out on a limb and test his theory.

"Of course I was." The man reached up and rubbed the back of his neck. "Why would you say that?"

"According to your statement, you found the body around five thirty."

"That's right."

"The medical examiner won't be able to give us an accurate time of death until he does an autopsy, but we do know that by the time you found him, he had been dead several hours. So it seems to me if you'd been doing your rounds, you would've found the man much earlier. And on top of that, the man was shot. It's hard to imagine you not hearing a gunshot. This place isn't that big."

"I—"

"He's right. If you're lying, you're only going to make things worse," Paige said. "Because, trust me, it will never work out in your favor."

Peters combed his fingers through his hair. "Listen, if my boss even suspects I wasn't here all night, he'll fire me."

Nate shot him a weak smile. "I sympathize with you, but a man is dead on your watch."

Peters kicked at the gravel with the toe of his boot. "Fine. I left right before midnight, but just for a couple hours."

"Where did you go?"

"I met a friend at this bar down the road. We had a few drinks."

"So clearly you wouldn't have heard a gunshot," Nate said.

"No."

"And if I talk to the bartender, can he verify your whereabouts?"

"Yeah. I'm a regular."

Nate handed the man his business card while Paige took a call. "We will check out your alibi, but in the meantime, if you think of anything else, please give us a call."

Paige hung up and signaled Nate. "Sarge wants us to go see the psychologist. He's sending in another detective to talk to management as soon as they show up."

"They're going to be in for a surprise." Nate headed with her toward the parking lot.

"Do you mind if we take your car?" Paige asked, heading with him across the lot to where he'd parked his Ford. "I'll grab mine on the way back to the precinct once we're done interviewing Grace Callahan."

"No problem." Nate pulled out his keys and unlocked his car with the push of a button.

"You don't mind if we stop for a coffee on the way, do you?" Paige asked as they slipped into his car. "There's a drive-thru two blocks from here."

"Coffee?" Nate headed across the parking lot toward the nearest cross street. "The last time I saw you, you said you were giving up caffeine because it made you too jittery."

Paige let out a low laugh. "You can ask my last partner about that. Apparently not drinking it makes me even more jittery."

Ashley had loved coffee too, and had started most of her days with a vanilla latte with low-fat milk and a sprinkle of cinnamon.

He shoved aside the unwanted memory of his former partner and tried to remember the other things he knew about Paige. She'd been top in her class at the academy, had led a special narcotics team before being promoted to homicide detective, and was married to an auto mechanic.

Five minutes later, he handed her a large caramel macchiato from the drive-thru window, then took the freeway toward Dr. Callahan's home.

"You're sure you didn't want one?" she asked as she took a sip.

"I'm fine, thanks."

Cutting out caffeine and upping his exercise routine had lessened his PTSD symptoms. And for the moment, he had no plans of going back to his old routine caffeine-addictive habits.

"You said you might know this woman we're going to see?" Paige took another sip of her drink. "What do you know about her?"

"If it is her, I haven't seen her for almost a decade. We went to college together, and I was close to her husband back then."

"There are a couple friends I had in college that I've thought about tracking down," Paige said, then let out a low chuckle. "Most of them, though, I'm happy to forget I ever knew."

26

"I have a few of those as well, though I've always wished Kevin and I didn't lose track of each other. Last I heard they'd moved out east, but this is where they were both from."

He could be wrong, but Grace Callahan wasn't a common name, combined with the fact that she was a psychologist. If it was her, catching up might be nice after all these years, though not the reunion he would have liked.

Fifteen minutes later, he pulled up alongside the curb in an older neighborhood with a row of small two-story houses. A woman wearing loose yoga pants and a T-shirt stood next to a red minivan that was parked in the driveway. She held a wad of paper towels in her hand.

"It might have been a while since I saw her, but that's definitely not her." Nate turned off the engine, then climbed out of his car.

"Grace Callahan?" Paige held up her badge as they approached the van.

The woman turned toward them. "No . . . I'm her friend, Becca Long. Can I help you?"

"I'm Detective Paige Morgan, and this is my partner, Detective Nate Quinn."

"Sorry about the mess." The woman took a step back from the van filled with car seats, baby dolls, and fast-food wrappers. "I brought coffee for Grace, thinking it would help, and it dumped all over the back seat. Not that anyone would notice the spill."

"Is Ms. Callahan here?" Paige asked.

"Yeah. She's inside. I came over as soon as I found out what happened, but I'm so glad you're here." She slid the door shut, then spun around to face them, apparently leaving cleanup for later. "I'm still a bit freaked out. We've been waiting for you."

"I'm sorry." Nate's brow rose. "You were expecting us?"

Becca dumped the soggy paper towels into a plastic sack. "The officer who took the initial 911 call told us they were going to send someone from the robbery unit as soon as they could."

"Actually, we're from homicide," Paige said.

"Homicide?" The woman planted her hands on her hips, clearly confused. "Wait . . . then why are you here?"

"Why don't you tell us what happened," Nate said.

"She's already given statements to the officers who responded. Someone broke into her house last night, and then the guy ended up chasing Grace down the street with a gun."

Nate glanced at the house with the brick exterior and neat front yard, a part of him hoping that the Grace he knew wasn't involved. "I think it's time we spoke with her."

3

Grace stood in the middle of her living room and forced herself to draw in a slow, deep breath. Until the authorities discovered what was going on and who had broken into her house, she wasn't going to feel safe.

She moved in front of the fireplace mantel and picked up the framed photo of Hannah on her birthday. At four, she'd been a daddy's girl and fearless of what lay ahead. It was ironic that Grace's job as a psychologist was to help people understand and calm their emotions. Today, she was the one feeling vulnerable and exposed. She forced herself to push aside the memories of that day. It had taken so long for her to put her life back together, and now it was as if someone— once again—was trying to strip it all away. But she couldn't give in to the panic. Not this time.

What key had he been looking for?

If he'd wanted to search the house while she was gone, he'd have broken in during the day. Her schedule was fairly predictable. She saw clients at the office four days a week. On Fridays, she volunteered with an organization that offered free counseling to cancer patients and their families. But as far as she could tell, he hadn't even touched anything of value. Instead he'd come at night when he could safely assume she would be asleep. If she hadn't heard him, or been prepared . . .

"Grace . . ." Becca stepped through the front door. "Hey . . . you okay?"

"Yeah. Just ready to know what's going on."

"Maybe you will. There are a couple of detectives who would like to speak to you."

Grace set the photo back on the mantel as a man in a gray suit and turquoise tie entered the room in front of a second detective. But she only saw him.

Nate?

Grace felt her breath catch as the figure from her past crashed through her memories. Football games and tailgate parties, all-night study sessions and way too much pizza and caffeine.

"Nate?"

"Gracie. Hey . . . it's been a long time. I had no idea you were back in Dallas."

He looked exactly as she remembered him, with his dark hair, strong jawline, and piercing brown eyes, and she couldn't help but smile. It had been a long time since anyone had called her Gracie.

"And I had no idea you were a detective," she said.

"Yes. This is my partner, Detective Paige Morgan."

"So, you're with the robbery unit?"

30

Nate glanced at his partner. "Homicide."

"Wait a minute . . . Why would homicide respond to a break-in?"

"That's what your friend just asked us," his partner said. "Can you tell me when the break-in occurred?"

"Early this morning, about two. I managed to get out of the house, then he came after me with a gun."

"Did he take anything?" Detective Morgan asked.

"I don't think so, but apparently he was looking for something one of my clients gave me. He kept asking about a key."

Nate held up his phone and showed her a DMV photo. "Something this man gave you?"

"That's Stephen Shaw. He's one of my clients. I've been worried about him and trying to get ahold of him all morning." She watched the shadow that crossed Nate's face and felt her jaw tense.

"Gracie, I'm sorry to have to tell you this, but Mr. Shaw's body was found early this morning."

"Wait a minute . . . He's dead?" Grace felt her knees start to buckle. She hadn't been able to get ahold of Stephen because he was dead? "I'm sorry, but I need to sit down."

"Gracie . . ."

"I'll be fine." Her legs threatened to give out as she moved toward the couch. "I'm just having trouble believing he's gone. I saw him yesterday in my office. He was stressed, but very much alive."

Nate followed her to the couch, but she barely saw him. There had to be some kind of mistake. She couldn't deal with this. Not now. She didn't have the emotional energy to deal with another death. Today of all days . . . She fought to smother the panic and the darkness pressing in against her.

Nate sat down next to her. "Are you okay?"

Grace pressed her palms against her shaking legs. "Not only did someone break into my house and threaten to shoot me, now I find that one of my clients is dead. What happened?"

"We believe he shot himself," Nate said, "but it will take some time for the medical examiner to determine the official cause of death."

"Suicide?" Her fingers pressed in harder against her legs as she worked to process the news. That wasn't possible. Stephen might have been paranoid, but he would never have killed himself.

"Like I said, we don't know for certain how he died," Nate said.

"I can't see him killing himself." She looked up at him. "He was focused on what he was doing. Determined to find a solution for some problem he was dealing with at his job."

"Do you know what he was working on?" Detective Morgan asked.

"No. I'm sorry." She clasped her hands together. *Why today, God? I can't handle more loss.*

But for the moment, she didn't have a choice.

Nate leaned forward. "Gracie . . . Are you sure you're okay?"

"I will be. I just . . ." She hesitated. She couldn't tell him how fresh death was on her mind at the moment. How much she'd lost since she'd last seen him. Because this wasn't about her. "Just tell me how I can help."

"Okay. Let's start with the man who broke in," Nate said. "Do you have any idea who he was?"

"No, though I gave a fairly detailed description to the police who were here earlier. They also dusted for fingerprints, but I'm not sure if they found anything."

"Do you know how the guy got in?" Detective Morgan sat down across from them on the matching recliner.

"One of the officers told me he came in through the front door. I have an alarm system that I know was armed, so I have no idea how he got past it."

Nate glanced at his notes. "You said he spoke to you. Please think very carefully and tell me exactly what he said."

She hesitated at the question. "He kept telling me that he wanted what Stephen had given me. A key, like I mentioned. But Stephen never gave me anything."

"So you don't know what key he meant?"

Detective Morgan looked up from her note-taking.

"No, though I've asked myself the same question over and over." Grace gripped the edge of the couch cushion, trying to steady her hands. "I can't think of anything that Stephen might have given me that seemed classified or confidential. Nothing that raised any red flags."

"That's okay. Let's switch to who Stephen was. What can you tell me about him?" Nate asked.

She automatically replayed their last conversation in her mind. A surge of guilt swelled. If she'd taken Stephen seriously, would things have turned out differently?

"Stephen had been coming to see me off and on for the past few weeks, mainly because he was under a lot of stress at work and, on top of that, believed someone was stalking him."

"You don't sound as if you believed him," Nate said.

"Honestly, I thought he was a bit paranoid." During all their sessions together, he'd never given her any kind of proof that someone had actually been watching or following him. Because of this, her focus had been to help him deal with his stress and anxiety.

"Do you know what he was afraid of?" Nate asked.

She caught his gaze, wondering if there were other things he wanted to ask her. Like why she wasn't wearing a wedding ring. Why she'd moved back to Dallas. And why there were no photos of her and Kevin on the mantel. All things she really didn't want to explain to him.

She switched her mind back to the subject they were discussing. "He told me he was worried he'd gotten involved with the wrong people."

"Do you know who?" Detective Morgan asked.

"He never gave me specifics. Just told me about several incidents when he felt that someone was following him. How he'd ordered some bug detector online because he was convinced someone had bugged his office."

"Did he find anything?" Nate asked.

Grace shook her head. "If he did, he didn't tell me."

Detective Morgan leaned forward. "Why didn't he go to the police?"

"I told him that if what he believed was true, then he needed to report what was going on. But he didn't have any solid proof, so he kept hesitating. I think he was convinced the authorities wouldn't believe him."

"And what about you?" Nate asked. "Did you just think he was being paranoid?"

"I believed he was truly afraid of something. But honestly, I didn't know if it was in his head or if someone was really after him. At least I didn't know until now. Clearly he was right and someone was after him."

But why?

Grace squeezed her eyes shut for a moment, trying to figure out what she might have missed. Stephen had come in to her office a few minutes late yesterday, clearly flustered and upset. He'd been struggling to keep things together like he did every week, but had something been different yesterday?

"What about his work?" Nate asked, interrupting her thoughts. "Do you know what he did for a living?"

"Yeah, he . . . he worked for a company as a computer security specialist—I'd have to look up the name—and was also doing some consulting work on the side for the FBI. He told me what he did was classified, but I know that he was working on top clearance security issues. Really, that's all I knew."

Nate turned to his partner. "If our victim was working with the FBI, they're going to want to be read in on this."

"Agreed. I'll call them now." Detective Morgan slipped out of the living room to make the call.

"I know there are doctor-patient privilege issues involved even after a client is deceased," Nate said, "but can you tell me more specifically why he was coming to you in the first place?"

Grace hesitated, careful with the wording of her response. "We worked on things like self-talk and relaxation techniques. Basic things that

36

helped him handle the strain of his work better."

"You said you saw him yesterday?" he asked.

"Yes."

"Can you tell me what his state of mind was?"

She stared at a spot on the couch, then pressed her finger against it. "He was extremely upset when he came in, but to be honest, most of what he said to me didn't make sense. He just kept saying that he was in too deep, and he didn't know how to get out."

"Out of what?"

"I assumed his job, though he might have had money issues. I can't be sure about that. He was always careful not to give specifics, which is why I assumed whatever he was working with—in particular with the FBI—must be classified."

"So he never specifically mentioned money issues or any other problem?"

She shook her head, wishing she could be more helpful, but she'd never pressed Stephen to disclose details he wasn't comfortable divulging.

Nate made another note. "Anything else you can think of?"

"He . . . he told me he was going to meet with his FBI handler last night and confront him with his concerns. And if the handler wouldn't listen to him, he was planning to get out."

Nate's brow rose. "Meaning?"

She shook her head. "Honestly, I'm not sure. I know this sounds a bit crazy, but I couldn't help wondering if he was planning to disappear."

"That would explain a few things. We found his car parked not far from where he was killed, and there were two suitcases in the trunk."

The initial shock of Stephen's death was beginning to pass, but not the guilty emotions that had come with it. "Do you have any idea who killed him?"

"At this moment, we can't confirm how he died, but he had your business card on him, and he called you late last night. That's why we came here."

"He called me?" Grace grabbed her phone off the coffee table and checked the call log. "You're right, but I missed it. I turn the volume off at night so I can sleep. And then with everything that's happened since then . . ."

She found the message and put it on speaker.

"Dr. Callahan . . . this is Stephen, though I guess you know that. Um . . . it's late, and I probably shouldn't be calling you, but I don't know what else to do. I'm on my way now to meet with my FBI handler, but I don't know . . . something's not right. Something big's in the works, and I don't know who to trust. And I think they figured out I'm on to them."

There was a pause, as if he was walking fast and struggling to catch his breath.

"Listen . . . I know you think I'm just paranoid, and to be honest, I hope you're right. Though I don't know which is worse. Feeling like you're crazy or knowing you're crazy. Anyway, if things turn out the way I think they might, I'm going to need you to get ahold of the Colonel. He's the only person I know who could actually stop this. Because if they use what I have, the fallout's going to be huge. I know . . . I know you think I'm acting crazy and maybe I am, but I've seen now what they can do and I don't know how to stop them."

Another pause, followed by something ruffling in the background. "There's a key to a safe-deposit box . . . Hopefully, I'm wrong about what's going on, but either way, I need you to find him . . . He can help stop this. I left everything you need to put an end to this with Oscar. I put your name on record with the bank, so you shouldn't have problems getting what's in the box. Take it to the Colonel, and please know that I'm sorry. For everything. I just . . . I don't know who else to trust—"

The message cut off.

"He left me a key." Grace stared at the phone, her pulse racing. If she'd picked up the call last night and talked to him, he might still be alive. "But I still don't understand. He never gave me anything."

"Who's Oscar?" Nate asked.

"I have no idea."

"And the Colonel?"

"I don't know that either."

She stood up, confused with Stephen's cryptic message. If whatever he had left her was so important, why had he been so vague with his directions? Why talk in code, especially if it was something so critical?

She turned back to Nate. "Why not just tell me outright what he needed me to do?"

"I don't know, but you said he'd been acting paranoid. Maybe he was afraid someone was listening in to his conversations."

She nodded. That made sense. If Stephen had been right about his phone or office being bugged, his vagueness would be justified.

But the Colonel . . . Oscar . . . What was he talking about?

Whatever his reasons were, she needed to figure out what he'd been trying to tell her.

"Okay. Was Stephen in the military?"

"If he was, he never mentioned it." Guilt continued to eat at her as she sat back down on the couch. "How could I have been so wrong?"

"You know, don't you, that none of this is your fault."

"I know. But I'd given him my private number—something I rarely do. He was so convinced his life was in danger. If I'd taken him more seriously or found a way to help him deal with what he was so afraid of, maybe he'd still be alive."

"Stop." Nate leaned forward and brushed his fingers across her hand. "You have no way of knowing if you could have prevented this."

"I just made a couple calls," Detective Morgan said, stepping back into the room. "Stephen Shaw wasn't on the FBI payroll."

Nate glanced up at his partner. "What do you mean?"

"I talked to our FBI liaison, and they don't have any record of our victim working for them."

4

Nate took a few seconds to let the news sink in. If Stephen Shaw hadn't been running security tests for the FBI, then who had he been working for? And in the process, had there been any breach in security? Or was he really crazy? All were questions that were going to have to be answered.

"How is that possible?" Gracie asked, beating him to the next question he wanted to ask. "He told me he'd been working for the FBI for the past couple months on several classified matters."

Paige sat back down on the edge of the chair across from them. "I don't know, but either he was lying to you, or I suppose it's possible that he really did think he was working for the FBI. But according to my contact, he definitely wasn't on their payroll."

Gracie stood up again, clearly flustered, and started pacing in front of the fireplace. The line of photos on the mantel behind her caught his attention. There was one he recognized of her with her parents and sister. A couple more of her were candid shots with a little girl with bright-blue eyes. But there were none with Kevin. He glanced at her left hand. And no wedding ring. Which was strange. To him they'd been the perfect couple. But he of all people knew how much could change in ten years.

"I'm sorry," Gracie said. "But I don't understand what's going on. Even though Stephen was paranoid and depressed, he wasn't suicidal. So that leaves murder. I guess someone *was* after him. Because there was no reason for him to lie to me. Maybe he wasn't really working for the FBI, but he definitely thought he was."

"We need to tackle things one at a time," Nate said. "You said you don't know anything about a key he might have left you?"

"No. I've been trying to figure out why he didn't just give me the key if he wanted me to have it." She stopped in front of the mantel, hands on her hips. "I stepped out of the room for a few minutes halfway through our session yesterday, which might have given him time to hide a key, but why all the cloak and dagger? He must have been scared. Paranoid."

"It doesn't make sense to me either," Nate said. "Which is why I think we should head over to your office now and see if we can find that key."

"Agreed," Paige said. "The robbery unit is on their way here now. I can stay and update them on what happened. They can take an official statement from you later, Grace."

"Of course." Gracie grabbed for her purse sitting at the end of the couch, along with her cell phone. "Let me just quickly tell Becca where I'm going."

A minute later, he and Gracie were headed toward his car. Fall had blown in with unseasonably warm weather. At the moment, with a slight breeze in the air, the temperature was perfect.

"This isn't exactly how I imagined reconnecting with an old friend from college," he said, breaking the silence between them. "But it's really good to see you."

She smiled back at him. "I agree. It's good to see you as well."

"How long have you been back in Dallas?" Nate caught her gaze as he slipped into the driver's seat and started the engine. The last time he'd seen her and Kevin had been a year or so after their wedding. The three of them stayed up half the night catching up. Today, though, there was a sadness in her eyes that made him wonder what had happened since he'd last seen her.

"About a year now." Gracie glanced at the ringless finger on her left hand that lay on the armrest between them. "Kevin and I divorced three years ago, in case you hadn't heard."

"No. I . . . I hadn't, but I'm sorry. I haven't exactly been in the loop these past few years."

"He left me."

He shifted the car into drive but didn't let his foot off the brake. "I'm so sorry, Gracie. I had no idea."

"It was over a long time ago. He's living back east and working for a law firm." Her words came

44

out with no emotion. As if she was telling him what she'd had for dinner last night, not referring to the end of her marriage. "I was offered a job in a local practice and decided to move back here. It's been a good change for me."

Nate pulled away from the curb and started down the tree-lined residential street. Kevin and Gracie were the last couple he'd ever imagined splitting up. He wanted to ask what had happened and who the little girl was in the photo on the mantel, but he knew it wasn't his place. If she wanted him to know, she'd tell him in her own time.

"I've always regretted losing track of the two of you," he said instead. "In college, you think you'll stay in touch forever, but then . . . I don't know what happens. Life gets in the way, and before you know it, it's years later."

Time had rushed by for him and nothing had turned out the way he'd expected.

"Kevin regretted losing track of you," she said. "He always planned to try to reconnect, but you're right. Life happens. Things change."

"Do you keep in touch with him at all?" As soon as the question was out, it struck him that he'd probably delved into something too personal. "I'm sorry—"

"No. He's got his own life now apart from mine. It took a long time for me to get back on my feet again, but I've accepted it. I just . . .

45

I think I feel sorry for him. I wanted to make things work. To try to find what we'd once had. He just couldn't do that. Maybe he's happier now. I don't know. He remarried and has a little boy."

"Wow."

Her revelation surprised him. He remembered clearly the day of their wedding. Kevin was crazy about Gracie, and had been from the first time they'd met. And Gracie had completely fallen for him as well. Back in college, she was beautiful, smart, funny, and carefree. Today, she was still just as beautiful and smart, but seemed more reserved. More distant.

"I never imagined I'd be in this situation," she said. "Divorced and single at thirty-two. Anyway, I'm really not complaining, because I know the two of you were close. I've always tried not to speak bad of him."

Nate turned onto a busy four-lane road, his surprise turning into aggravation at the knowledge Kevin had walked out on her. "I guess it's impossible to know what life is going to throw you, isn't it?"

"I've worked to carve out a good life for myself," she said. "I've got a good church, good friends, and I'm doing what I love again. I just thought you should know."

"Thank you. I appreciate it."

"Anyway, it's all in the past now." Her fingers

fidgeted with her purse strap. "If you take a left at the light, my office will be another two blocks on the right-hand side."

A part of him wanted to ask more questions, but it was clear from her voice that the subject was closed. Which was fine. He wasn't going to press. As good as it was to see her, they were both different people today than they'd been back in college. He felt sorry for her—for both her and Kevin—but once he finished with this investigation, unless he took the initiative—which he wouldn't—they'd probably never run into each other again.

Two blocks later, he turned into the parking lot of the counseling center and parked, then they headed for the older one-story building with glass doors and a brick face.

"There are four of us who have offices here," Gracie said, unlocking the door before stepping into the cozy reception area furnished with two long couches and a coffee table piled with magazines. "There's also a larger room in the back that we use for group meetings. Mine is the second door on the left."

He followed her through the small reception area to a door with Gracie's nameplate.

Gracie stopped. The door was open halfway. "Nate . . ."

He reached for his service weapon. Something was off.

47

"Stay here." He moved in front of her, then stepped through the open doorway.

A woman dressed in a black pin-striped skirt and pink blouse stood in the middle of the office that had been completely trashed.

Nate pulled back his suit jacket to expose his badge. "I'm with the police, ma'am. I need to see your hands."

"Grace . . ." She held up her hands in front of her, her eyes wide. "What's going on?"

"Nate." Gracie stopped in the doorway behind him. "This is Anne Taylor. She's the secretary for the practice."

"Sorry to have startled you." Nate holstered his weapon. "I'm Detective Nate Quinn. Can you tell me what happened here?"

"No. I just got here a couple minutes ago. I noticed the door was ajar, and when I came in . . . this is what I found."

He quickly took in the details of the office. Gracie had done all the things therapists did to try to create a sense of safety for their clients. There were a few plants, calming artwork, neutral wall colors, and several throw pillows with inspirational sayings on a comfy-looking leather couch.

But what once was a clearly organized, cozy room now looked as if it had been hit by a tornado. Books lay in a pile beneath a row of shelves. A plant lay dumped onto the floor, its dirt scattered across the beige carpet. A lamp was broken, next to a couple abstract paintings that had fallen off the wall. Whoever had broken in had done a thorough job of trashing the place.

Gracie stepped into the office and drew in a slow, deep breath. "This is unbelievable. Why would someone do this?"

"I don't know." Anne stepped up to Gracie and gave her a big hug. "Are you okay?"

"I'm not sure. I just feel . . . numb."

"That's pretty much how I felt when I first walked in here, but how did you know to bring the police? I hadn't even called 911 yet."

Gracie's gaze swept the floor, surveying the damage before she turned back to her friend. "There was a robbery at my house. We decided to come check things here—"

"What? Did they do this there too?"

"Thankfully, no."

Anne looked to Nate. "Do you believe this is connected?"

"I believe we have to consider the possibility."

Anne shook her head. "But why would someone break into your house and here? They must have been searching for something."

"That's what we think. I'm just not sure what, at this point."

"Were any of the other offices broken into?" Nate asked.

"Not that I know of. Grace is usually the first one in, but I can double-check—"

"I'll need you to wait and not touch anything. I'm going to call in our crime scene unit and see what they can find."

"Well, I'm here to help in any way I can."

Nate put in a quick call to his precinct, then turned back to Gracie. "I know this isn't convenient, but I need you to cancel your appointments, at least for the morning."

"Of course," Gracie said. "Anne, go ahead and cancel all my appointments for today."

Anne raised a sculpted eyebrow. "Including Mrs. Fitzgerald?"

"Tell her I'll work her in first thing tomorrow, and I'll bring maple bars. That should appease her."

She caught Nate's gaze and shook her head as Anne headed to her own desk to start making calls. "Long story."

"What about security in the building?" he asked.

"It's minimal. This is a counseling center, not a bank. We do have an alarm system, though I found out recently that most of the time it's not even set when the last person leaves."

"What about cameras?"

"None. But then again, security has never been an issue. There's nothing of value here to steal." Gracie walked to the middle of the room. "I've put a lot of time into this space, but every piece of furniture is secondhand. There are no electronics, and certainly nothing of value. Nothing really but a few shelves of books and my files. But even in the files, there's nothing incriminating there."

"Can you tell from an initial look if anything seems to be missing?"

"Not really. Like I said, the only thing beyond the furniture are my files. It's going to take time to figure out if any of those are missing."

She started turning in a slow circle, assessing the damage, and he tried to see the room through her eyes.

"Gracie?"

"I'm sorry. You're going to think I'm some big blubbering baby. Do you remember our plans back in college?"

He smiled at the memory. "You were going to start your own counseling service and Kevin had visions of being a partner in a law firm before he was thirty."

"We thought we could save the world." She picked up a pillow off the floor and tossed it back onto the couch. "I might not own my own practice, but I never totally lost that dream. Even when I found out you can't save everyone. And maybe I am still nothing more than a dreamer. But this place . . . for me it was a brand-new start. A place where I could make a difference again."

He'd always been impressed by her compassion. Her draw to those who were hurting. That was the Gracie he'd known back in college.

And clearly the same Gracie that stood before him today.

"You sure you're okay?" he asked.

"Yes. I just don't typically have my life threatened and office ransacked all in one day." She let out a low chuckle, breaking down some of the awkwardness between them. "I've been wishing for a bit more adventure in my life, but I'm thinking I might have to reevaluate that wish."

He couldn't help but smile. "You always were able to look at the positive side of things."

"The bottom line is this has to be connected to whoever broke into my house. There is something that strikes me as odd."

"What's that?"

"They broke in here and trashed the place looking for the key they were after. But at my house, they didn't disturb anything."

"Was there anything in Stephen's file that someone might have been able to use against him?"

"Stephen was paranoid. He was worried about the chance of his medical records being subpoenaed in a legal battle one day. He would always tell me not to write down anything personal, so I kept my notes of each session as bare bones as possible. Nothing more than brief updates and any new symptoms he was exhibiting that needed to be addressed in the next session.

My observations on how he was doing along with my clinical assessment of the situation for that week. Never anything personal."

"Is there any way the intruder could have gained access to information in those notes?"

"No. I use my own brand of shorthand for all of my notes. But even if they figured it out, I don't think there's anything in them that someone could use."

"Wait a minute." Gracie stared at the red betta fish in the corner of the room that swam undisturbed in the chaos. "I can't believe I didn't think of this earlier, but I had a client who named my betta fish Oscar. Stephen always told me that was a dumb name for a fish."

Nate crossed the room. "Maybe Oscar really does hold the key then, literally speaking."

Gracie grabbed a small net and started digging around the blue gravel, then pulled out a key with a bronze ID tag. "Take a look at this. I certainly didn't drop this here."

Nate grabbed a tissue from a box on the floor and wiped the key off. "There's the name of the bank and the box number." He held it up for her to look at.

"That bank isn't too far from here," she said.

Nate ran through their options. There were a number of laws surrounding a safe-deposit box, which included the death of a renter. Something that might delay their access to the box.

"I know this has been a rough few hours for you, but I'd like for you to go to the bank with me and see if we can find out what Stephen left you. We could get a warrant, but it will be quicker this way."

"Of course."

He was surprised at her quick response. "You don't have to do this."

"Yes, I do. I have no idea why he left this for me, but he had a reason. I owe him that much."

"No. You don't owe him anything."

"I'm okay. Really. I want to."

He was still second-guessing his request, but from the look on her face, she was determined to follow through.

Nate pulled up the bank's website on his smartphone. "The bank lobby opens at nine, so that gives us another . . . forty-five minutes."

"That's fine."

He turned back to her. "Have you ever had a safe-deposit box?"

"No."

"Here's what will happen. We'll drive to the bank. To open the box, as long as your name is on the approved list, all you have to do is walk in, sign your name, and then they'll give you the contents of the box."

"Sounds simple enough. I can do that."

"After that, we'll head to the precinct, where you can give your official statement."

Gracie started toward the door with him, then paused at the end of her desk. She picked up a five-by-seven framed photo that had fallen next to it. The glass was shattered, and the photo was of the same little girl he'd noticed back at her house.

"Gracie . . ."

"I'm sorry." She glanced up at him, then fled the room.

5

Grace fought back the tears as she stumbled from her office with the shattered photo pressed against her chest. She shouldn't be falling apart. She was stronger than this. She'd prepared herself for the emotional barrage she knew would hit her today. But all of this—the break-in, the encounter with the intruder—it was proving to be enough to push her over the edge.

She ducked into the small meeting room in the back of the building, thankfully avoiding Anne's watchful eye. She was busy on the phone canceling today's appointments with her clients. Becca had tried to talk Grace into taking the day off, if not the entire week. But she'd convinced herself that staying busy and focused on other people's problems would prove to be therapeutic for her own emotional well-being.

She sat down on the flowered couch and pulled her legs up beneath her before drawing in a slow breath. She stared at Hannah's photo. Another wave of emotion swept through her, forcing her to go to a place she didn't want to go. But as hard as she tried, she couldn't fight the grief and tears.

Back in college, she had her life mapped out, down to how many kids she'd have, where she'd be one day career-wise, even down to what Dallas suburb she would live in. Until the unthinkable had happened and her dreams had shattered like the glass on the photo in front of her, leaving her with memories she had no idea how to deal with.

She heard the click of the door opening and shutting behind her. Nate crossed the tiled floor, then stopped in front of her.

"Hey . . . you're crying." He sat down next to her on the couch. "What's going on?"

"It's nothing. Really." She wiped her cheek and turned away from his probing gaze, wondering if her best approach was to let him believe that *this* was simply a reaction to the break-ins. Because the last person she wanted involved in all of this was Nate. Involving him meant explaining why she was falling apart and everything she'd lost. Something she had no desire to do.

"Listen, I know we haven't seen each other in ages," he said, "but I think I know you better than that. Besides, you always were a bad liar."

Memories surfaced, but this time they were good. "If you're referring to my poker-playing skills, or perhaps the plastic cockroach I put in Kevin's cereal—"

"And then tried to blame me, as I remember."

"Wait a minute," she said. "For one, that was your idea, so technically you were to blame, and two—"

"You know there's no way out of this one." His

smile faded. "But this isn't just about the break-in or Stephen's death, is it?"

She blew out a sharp breath, wondering when he'd become so perceptive. "No."

He touched the edge of the frame in her lap. "Who is she?"

"I told you about Kevin and me, but I . . . I didn't tell you everything." She wiped her wet face with the back of her hand, then held up the photo. "This is our daughter. Hannah."

Saying her name out loud brought another barrage of pain with it.

"She's beautiful," he said.

She wasn't sure how much to tell him. She ran her finger across the frame. "Hannah died four years ago this month. And on top of that, her birthday is today. She would have been nine."

"Oh Gracie . . . I'm so, so sorry. I can't even imagine what that has to be like for you."

"It's made today extra hard. Then between the reminders of her death and everything that's happened . . . I'm finding it hard to deal."

"You used to tell me I was a good listener."

Another memory surfaced. She'd gotten a call from her mom, telling her that her grandfather had passed away. Kevin had to work, so she and Nate had ended up talking at an all-night diner until Kevin got off. Nate had just let her cry and talk. He'd always been that kind of friend.

"You were a good listener. And I appreciate the

offer." She glanced at the clock on the wall. "But we need to go to the bank. I need you to find out what happened to Stephen."

"We will, but right now we've got time."

She felt the long pause that followed, thankful that he didn't try to interrupt or push her. She could hear his steady breathing next to her and suddenly felt the urge to let him pull her into his arms and hold her. To reassure her that she wasn't alone. It had been so long since she'd felt safe and protected. Since anyone had held her. But just like she wasn't the same person she'd been when they knew each other back in college, neither was he. And just because seeing him again stirred up memories, that didn't mean she really knew him anymore. But her desire to trust the person she'd known years ago won out, and she took a deep breath.

"I was seven months pregnant with her when Kevin and I moved out east," she said. "He'd just received a job promotion with his firm, and I had the opportunity to work part-time at a counseling center after Hannah was born. She was born perfect and was the sweetest thing you can imagine. And honestly, she was until the day she died."

She stared at the photo, working to stave off the engulfing sadness she'd been fighting all week. A sadness that always intensified this time of year.

"This was taken on her third birthday. We went

to her grandparents' farm for the day. She was happy and funny. She always made me laugh." She handed the photo to Nate. "Her grandma gave her the stuffed elephant. She never went anywhere without it after that."

"She's absolutely adorable." He brushed his hand across her arm. "But you don't have to talk about it, Gracie. Only if you want to."

"It's okay." Because for some reason, she needed to tell him. While most of her friends were sympathetic, time went on, people moved on with their lives, and she was left trying to put together the shattered pieces of her life. It was part of the reason she'd moved back to Dallas. It was a chance to start over.

While Becca had become the exception, Grace preferred making friends who didn't know her past. It had ended up being easier than explaining over and over to everyone what had happened. And, she supposed, it had been a way to guard her heart.

"Not long after this photo was taken, she was diagnosed with leukemia, and after that, we pretty much dropped out of sight. I took leave from my practice in order to stay home with her full-time. Between doctors' visits and treatments, I didn't have energy for anything else. Including Kevin."

"I'm so sorry."

"It was every parent's worst nightmare. Having

something wrong with your child when there's nothing you can do. Watching her struggle through treatment after treatment, hospital stays, reactions to the medicine . . . And then things got better. Hannah went into remission for about six months, but then the disease came back more aggressive than before. Three months later, we lost her."

Nate winced and glanced down at the photo in his hands, then looked back up at her. "And Kevin? How did he handle her death?"

"While I grieved, I made sure I had people to talk to, but he didn't cope well with losing Hannah. He didn't talk—really talk—to anyone except his brother every once in a while, and even then, I'm not sure how much he shared. I felt so helpless. Here I was, a psychologist, and no matter what I did, I couldn't get him to open up to me."

Just like losing a child had never been on her radar, neither was divorce. She believed in "until death do us part" and had done everything she could to work things out between her and Kevin. Not that the collapse of their marriage was all his fault. She couldn't blame him entirely for what had happened, but things still hadn't turned out the way she'd planned.

"Tell me about her."

Her eyes widened at his request. Most people asked *what* happened, never getting to the more uncomfortable conversation of *who* she'd lost.

"Well . . ." Grace paused. "She loved tea parties, drawing, roses, and animals—especially horses. In fact, from the time she was four, she decided she wanted to be a cowgirl." The memories brought a smile to her lips. "I had some friends back East who taught her how to ride. Even when she was sick, there was nothing that made her happier than riding. We spent most weekends there, and when she was too sick to ride, she'd sit out on the porch and simply watch the horses."

And now she was gone.

She grabbed a tissue from the table beside her, finding it ironic that here she was, sitting on a couch at her practice, crying and needing support instead of being the one giving it. Wishing—not for the first time—it was possible to go back in time and do things over. Start at another place in time to get a different ending. Not that she regretted marrying Kevin. Without Kevin, she wouldn't have had Hannah. She just regretted what had happened between them and the empty space his leaving had left in her heart. The image of Hannah rose to the surface, and that familiar surge of emotion swept through her.

He handed her back the photo, and she noticed the raised scars on his forearm. She started to say something, but he tugged down his sleeve and covered them. Apparently, she wasn't the only one with secrets. And secrets, it seemed, he wasn't willing to share. Which meant that, for the moment, she kept her own questions about him to herself.

"I should have seen it coming and yet, you know what? I didn't. I guess I was so wrapped up in losing Hannah, I forgot to be there for Kevin. And then one day . . . he just walked out. He set his fork down after a pot roast dinner and told me he couldn't pretend that things were okay between us anymore. Told me he'd met someone else and that he wanted a divorce. He wanted to completely leave his life behind and start over. Like he could somehow just . . . forget Hannah and me."

Time might have smoothed out some of the jagged edges of the pain, but she knew she'd carry them with her the rest of her life.

"I'm so sorry." Nate leaned back against the couch. "It's hard for me to imagine how he could have done something like that. I also can't imagine how hard it would be to lose a child."

"It's been over three years since he left, and for the most part I've found ways to move on, though I don't think it's ever possible to get over the loss of a child. There's always this . . . this deep, black hole inside me. Like something's missing. And then the dates of her birthday come around, or the anniversary of her death . . . those feelings are magnified. Sometimes it feels as if I'm starting all over again with the pain and loss. Parents aren't supposed to bury their children. They say a high percentage of marriages break up after losing a child. I guess I never imagined it would happen to us. That we'd become nothing more than a statistic. But we did. And at the time, I didn't even see it happening."

She took in a deep breath while he waited for her to continue. "I find myself hardly able to breathe sometimes. I don't know why she died before me. I still feel guilty when I'm happy. Miss the memories we never created. And yet at the same time, I'm thankful for the time we had and don't regret any of it. I wouldn't be who I am today without her short time on earth."

"Thank you for telling me," he said. "I know it can't be easy to dredge up all those memories. And with all that's going on right now—especially with today being her birthday."

She nodded. But this wasn't a place she could stay. Not today, when there was so much she needed to deal with right here. Stephen was dead. Someone had broken in, threatened her life. No, she needed to stuff her grief back into its compartment. At least for now.

She glanced at her watch. "We should go. The bank's going to open soon—"

"Gracie, forget it. You don't need to do this. Not with everything you've gone through. You should be spending the day with friends and family. Definitely not this. We'll get the necessary paperwork and get it done."

"You need answers, and I can help get them for

you. Besides, not only is it a distraction I need, it puts off having to clean up the mess here and having to deal with all of this."

"Gracie—"

"Please." She touched his arm. "I need to do this. If I go home, I'll just end up eating a pint of ice cream and binge-watching Netflix."

He squeezed her hand. "You're sure?"

She nodded, surprised at how comfortable she felt talking with him. Out of all of Kevin's friends, Nate had been her favorite. He'd been funny, smart, steady . . . and today it felt as if time hadn't even passed since she'd seen him.

Except for her, everything had changed.

He glanced at his watch. "Okay, but that's it. You walk into the bank, get Stephen's stuff, and leave. I've got a team on their way here to see what they can find. With all the people who are in and out of this office, I'm not expecting much, but there could be something in your office that will help point us to the intruder."

She grabbed another tissue and nodded. "Just give me a couple minutes, and I'll be ready."

She walked into the small bathroom, stopped in front of the sink, and splashed some water on her face, trying to ward off the familiar panic she'd learned—in part—to deal with. There was something about Nate's presence that helped to center her. She'd made it through this day before, and she'd make it through again.

Five minutes later, she followed him out to his car, feeling the rising defenses she'd put into place so many times before. When today was over, she'd go home, have a long soak in the tub, and cry. And maybe eat that pint of ice cream.

Nate's phone rang and he answered the call.

"Everything okay?" she asked once he'd hung up. But she could tell by the expression on his face that it wasn't.

"No, actually. That was my partner. The medical examiner isn't done yet with his autopsy, but he's found evidence that Stephen Shaw didn't commit suicide. He was definitely murdered."

6

Nate measured Gracie's reaction as he drove them away from her office and toward the bank a few miles down the road. Murder changed everything, and made him wonder if they'd made the right decision to bring her along with him to the bank. But in order to expedite the process, he needed her. Some banks had regulations that didn't allow anyone into the safe-deposit boxes until the estate was cleared, and the last thing they needed was a delay in getting whatever Stephen had left for Gracie. In order to figure out what was going on, they needed answers.

"Are they positive he was murdered?" she asked, breaking the silence.

"Apparently there were a couple of indicators, including contact range. In most suicides, the bullet is shot from close range, producing a star-shaped wound."

"And in Stephen's case?"

"The shot came from farther away."

"So, his suicide was staged."

"That's what it looks like," he said. "On top of that, his shoulder had been dislocated."

"What are you saying?" She kneaded her hands together in her lap. "He was tortured?"

"It's possible."

He turned onto Main Street and headed into a familiar part of town. They needed to find out who they were dealing with and how all the pieces connected. What he didn't want was her entangled in the situation. Whether or not Stephen had been tortured for information, he had gotten himself into something way over his head.

That wasn't a place he was going to let Gracie go.

He stopped at another light, his decision made. "We're going to call this off. I'll get a court order to get into the box if I need to. It shouldn't be that difficult—"

"Forget it," Gracie said. "Even if Stephen was murdered, I'm not going to change my mind, Nate. I want to do this. I need to know the truth about what happened to Stephen. And in order to do that, you need answers."

"I know, but someone killed him, Gracie, and someone tried to shoot you last night. We know the two situations are connected, and that potentially puts you in a dangerous position. If someone believes Stephen gave you something—something they're willing to kill for—your life is in danger as well."

"I'll be fine." Gracie gripped the armrest as she shot him a grin. "I've got you watching out for me, don't I?"

He frowned at the compliment, not sure that

was going to be enough, considering he had no idea what they were dealing with.

"Then here's the deal. We'll go to the bank together, but then I'm going to arrange to have you stay at a safe house until we find out what's going on—"

"Forget it, Nate. I can't just live in fear and go into hiding. What about my clients? My friends? I came here to start over. Not run at the first sign of trouble."

He turned on his blinker, then passed a slow pickup. He understood her frustration, but that wasn't going to keep her safe. "Until we know what's going on—"

"I can't go into hiding and end up jumping at every shadow I see."

He glanced at her. Her blonde hair that fell past her shoulders had darkened, but her eyes were still the color of amber. He looked back at the road. She was strong. She always had been, and he was sure that all that she'd gone through over the past few years—all that she'd lost—had made her even stronger. In the end, he couldn't force her to accept protection, but he also couldn't just play down the danger.

"We'll talk about it more later. For now, just think about it. Okay?"

"If it will make you feel better, I'll think about it."

"Thank you." He couldn't help but smile. She

was just as stubborn as he remembered her.

And just as beautiful.

Five minutes later, Nate pulled into the parking lot of Stephen's bank, hoping that whatever it was that Stephen had stashed away before he died was going to give them some answers. Half a dozen cars were scattered across the small lot, but at the moment the area was quiet.

He turned off the motor. "You still sure about this?"

"Nothing's changed in the past few minutes, though I'd forgotten just how overprotective you are."

"Overprotective?"

"In a good way." She smiled, but the tension was still in her eyes. "Did you ever go into the military like you used to talk about in college?"

Nate nodded. "Four years. Marines."

"And now you're a homicide detective. I'd say that pretty much makes my case."

"I like ensuring justice wins, and while not everyone agrees with this anymore, I still believe in chivalry."

"Which is why you're insisting I go to a safe house?"

He shot her a smile back. "Just doing my job, ma'am."

"Then why do I feel like I'm about to do something illegal?" Gracie chuckled as she undid her seat belt.

Nate nudged her with his elbow. "Stephen said he set you up jointly on his account, so you're fine. We'll be out of here in ten . . . fifteen minutes tops." He undid his seat belt and climbed out of the Explorer.

He'd get her out of here and insist she go somewhere safe where he wouldn't have to worry about her while he was working. She'd put up a fight. He was sure of that, but that was okay. Kevin might have walked out on her, but he wasn't going to.

He shoved down the thought as he walked around the car. He had no desire to judge his friend. And this certainly wasn't a competition.

As he reached Gracie, who was just stepping out of the car, another car pulled into the empty space next to them. Nate glanced at the driver and felt his pulse quicken.

"Gracie . . ." He stepped between her and the opening car door, pulled out his service weapon while pushing her back into the Explorer, and turned around, but he wasn't fast enough. The driver was already out of the car, shooting a Taser into his back. Nate collapsed, helpless, as the electricity coursed through him, while a second man grabbed Gracie.

He fought to stay focused despite the intense pain shooting down his legs. He couldn't give in. Couldn't let the pain stop him from keeping Gracie safe. But every muscle in his body seemed

71

frozen, and he couldn't respond to what his mind was telling him to do.

The man dropped the Taser and zip-tied his wrists, then opened the back door of the Explorer. "Get in the car."

Nate struggled to get his legs under him, and the man grabbed his arm, pulled him up, and shoved him into the back seat. A tattoo on the man's wrist peeked out from his suit sleeve as he pulled Nate's gun from its holster, then searched his pockets for the car keys. There was nothing Nate could do to stop him. Another few seconds and he would regain his strength, but what then?

"What do you want?" Nate forced out the words while staring at the blurred dome light of his car above him.

"Stay down, or I'll shoot both of you."

Nate tried to move so he could find Gracie, but he couldn't see her. Panic coursed through him. This wasn't some random mugging. These guys knew exactly who they were targeting. Stephen had been murdered, and now they were after Gracie and whatever was in that safe-deposit box. Shots fired in front of the bank would get someone's attention, but at this point it didn't matter. He couldn't do anything, and Gracie wasn't armed.

Where was Paige?

He heard one of the men talking to Gracie.

Ordering her to show him the bank key. His mind raced. As long as they needed her, she'd be safe. She could signal the guard, stall until backup arrived. She'd be okay.

Please let her be okay, God.

The man tossed Nate's gun onto the front seat, then closed the back door.

What had he been thinking? He should have gone with his gut and never allowed Gracie to get involved.

His captor slid into the driver's seat and started the car. "Here's how this is going to play out. You're going to stay out here while my partner goes inside. I've got orders to shoot you if you do anything stupid, so if you're thinking of being a hero or something . . . think again."

They were taking a huge risk, immobilizing a police officer in front of a bank with the expectation of walking inside with a hostage. But they'd worked to cover their bases. If she refused to play, they'd kill him. If he refused to play, they'd kill him. Someone was determined to get what was in that box, and he was out of options.

"You know you'll get years for this," Nate said, frantically working to undo the zip tie. The pain had begun to ease, but his brain still felt fuzzy.

"No I won't. I'll be long gone before they start looking."

"Do you even know what's in that bank box?" Nate continued, looking for a way to throw off his captor. "I hope it's worth it when you go down for murder one."

"Shut up."

"How old are you?" Nate asked as the man pulled out of the bank parking lot. "Twenty-four . . . twenty-five? Why throw your life away for this? The contents of a safe-deposit box. Because I'm right. There's no way you'll get away with this."

"This is far bigger than me. Far bigger than either of us."

"If that's true, then whoever you're working for won't mind you taking the fall when this goes bad."

"Shut up."

What was so important that they would risk taking hostages, including a police officer? Nate tried to make sense of what was happening, but there was only one clear thought in his head. Stephen Shaw hadn't been paranoid.

7

Grace glanced back at Nate's car one last time before heading toward the bank. Last night she'd stayed up late reading a thriller about a woman being stalked. Today, it was as though she was living inside the nightmare.

"Keep moving." The armed man who'd pulled her away from the car gripped her elbow too tight.

"You'll never get away with this." She forced down the terror of the past few hours. "What happens if security notices you have a weapon? He'll have the cops here in a matter of minutes. You'll never get out."

"I'm not going to need a weapon. If you try anything stupid—if you do anything at all that catches someone's attention—we'll shoot the detective back there. Is that enough motivation for you?"

She wanted to tell him that she didn't care what happened to Nate. That she didn't know him. But she wouldn't gamble on Nate's life by trying a bluff that failed.

"Here's what's going to happen," he said. "You're going inside the bank with me. If you do anything at all to make the employees inside suspect even for a second that something is wrong, the detective is dead. If you do anything to catch someone's attention, he's dead. And if that's not enough motivation, I have no problem shooting you as well."

She glanced at him and studied his face, ensuring that she memorized his features so she could give a description to the police when this was over. Assuming there was going to be an end to this. Thirtysomething, Caucasian, an inch taller than her five foot seven. His short, sandy hair had been jelled and spiked . . . jeans and a blue button-down dress shirt . . . and he carried a slim messenger satchel.

"Did you kill Stephen?" she asked Spike as they approached the glass front doors.

"Forget about Stephen. Get out the key."

"It's in my purse," she said, digging through the side pocket until she found it, willing her hands to stop shaking. "But you still haven't told me what you want."

"What I want is for you to shut up." He stopped about ten yards from the doors to the bank and caught her gaze. "Because you have one job, and one job only. You're going to walk into that bank with me and sign in, and when I've gotten what I want, you'll be getting me out of here without any trouble."

"Do you even know what's inside the box?"

"It doesn't matter what's inside."

She could tell by the twitching of his lip and

the beading of sweat across his forehead that he was anxious. More than likely this had been a spur-of-the-moment plan after torturing Stephen for information. But that didn't really matter, because they still held the advantage. It might have been something they'd talked about as a plan B, but clearly they thought they'd be able to walk in, open up the box, and waltz out with no one being any wiser.

The sun streamed in through the windows as they stepped inside the bank. In the air-conditioning, the temperature felt a good ten degrees cooler. Grace glanced around the lobby where there were six or seven customers, including a young mother and her small children, and a security guard standing in the far corner of the large, open space. A wave of nausea swept over her. How in the world was she supposed to go through with this like nothing was wrong?

She debated her options. She could try to signal to the security guard or one of the tellers, but then what? The guy had a gun. He could turn this into a hostage situation where someone got killed, not to mention what they'd do to Nate if she didn't do what they told her.

No. She couldn't do that. For the moment, she was going to have to play along and pray Nate had a plan of his own. What she couldn't think about was what was going to happen when they left the bank and this guy didn't need her any longer. She could identify him and they wouldn't want to have any witnesses.

A female employee wearing a gray suit and blue shirt greeted them with a too perky smile. "Can I help you?"

Grace fingered the key and felt her mouth go dry as she read the woman's nametag. "Shannon . . . hi . . . I, uh, need to get into a safe-deposit box."

"Of course. Your name?"

"Grace Callahan."

"And the box number?"

"Nine sixty-nine."

"No problem. If you'll just give me a second, I'll find your card."

Grace stood in front of the counter, heart racing while they waited. Spike stood close enough that she could smell cigarettes on his clothes and spearmint gum on his breath. She took a step to the left as one of the front doors to the bank opened again. A man with a briefcase walked in and proceeded straight toward an open teller.

Nate would find a way to escape from the man holding him and rescue her. She trusted him. Knew that he would do anything in his power to save her. But how could he? The last time she'd seen him, he'd been shoved into his car by a guy with a gun. She swallowed hard.

She had no idea where his backup was.

Her captor started drumming on his thigh with his fingers. Another outward sign of anxiety.

Maybe the employee helping them—Shannon—would notice something was wrong. There had to be a way to signal her that Grace was here against her will. That the man standing next to her was a complete stranger trying to steal whatever was in that box.

"What is she doing?" he asked, stuffing his hands into his pockets.

"I don't know."

She stared at the door Shannon had gone through, willing the employee to sense her thoughts.

He's got a gun.

She screamed inside her head at Shannon.

He's got a gun.

He forced me to come inside with him.

Nothing happened. Music continued playing in the background. The teller across the way kept talking to the man with the briefcase. The security guard still looked bored.

When she was a kid, she and her best friend used to send mental messages to each other to see if they could read each other's minds. Like what they were going to wear the next day or what to pack in their lunches. Telepathy had never worked for them, and it wasn't working now.

"Box 969, right?" the woman asked as she returned with a smile, clearly unaware of what Grace was thinking.

"Yes. Is there a problem?" Grace asked.

"I am so sorry. Would you mind sitting down and waiting for just a few more minutes? I'm having problems finding your card, though I'm sure it was simply misfiled. I'll be back with you in just a minute."

Spike pressed in beside Grace. "Please do. We're in a bit of a hurry."

"It's nothing that can't be quickly resolved. It will just take a moment, I'm sure, and again, I am sorry."

Grace glanced at the door. "Of course. Thank you."

She sat down on one of the empty chairs, while Spike paced in front of her.

Shannon was talking to another employee. Had they found a discrepancy? Did they know somehow that Stephen was dead? What would Spike do if something went wrong? Would the already volatile situation escalate to a full-blown hostage crisis, putting the lives of everyone here in danger?

I need a way out of this, God, and I have no idea how to fix it.

"What did you do?" Spike asked, sitting down next to her, causing her to momentarily shove away her own list of questions.

"What do you mean?"

"This was supposed to be simple." He leaned in toward her. "Walk in. Get the stuff. Get out. Something's wrong."

80

"I have no idea. Stephen set this up. Not me. I didn't even know about the key until this morning."

How had this happened? Stephen was dead, and now she was being held hostage in a bank, forced to remove the contents of a dead man's safe-deposit box. Yesterday, Stephen had rambled about how he believed his life was in danger. Clearly, she should have taken him more seriously.

"Do you know what's in the box?" she asked.

"I already told you it doesn't matter. My job is simply to retrieve the contents."

"Maybe it does matter. Who are you working for?"

"Shut up and stop asking questions."

He stood up and started pacing again.

"Ma'am . . ."

Grace stood back up as Shannon called to her. "Yes."

"I'm sorry for the delay. If you'll just sign here."

She walked up to the desk slowly with Spike right beside her. The security guard was on his phone. Two women laughed on the other side of the room, while most of the other customers went about their business in silence. There had to be a way out of this. Someone who would notice that something was very wrong. But no one acted like there was anything out of the ordinary happening.

81

Grace picked up the pen, trying not to shake. It slipped out of her fingers and dropped to the ground.

"Sorry." She reached down and picked it up, scribbled in her name, then let out a short breath.

The woman signaled one of her coworkers. "James will take you to your box."

Spike elbowed her in the ribs.

"Can we go together?" she asked.

"Of course."

They followed James down a short hallway to a room with dozens of rows of safe-deposit boxes. He took her key and used both it and another one to unlock the box, then set it on the table.

"Feel free to take as long as you want." James's smile widened as he started to leave. "I'll be right outside if you need anything."

She stared at the box, desperate for a plan, while Spike opened it a moment later. She needed to find out what was inside. Because whatever was in this box, Stephen had died for. And because if she didn't find a way out of this, she had no doubt that they would kill her as well.

"Take a step back." Spike opened up his messenger bag and set it on the table.

Grace hesitated.

"Do it."

She nodded, then feigned twisting her ankle in her low-heeled boots. She reached for the table and, in the process, flipped the box onto its side, letting the contents spill out onto the floor.

"Sorry."

"You fool."

Most of the contents of the box fell onto the floor. She slid her foot over a flash drive and reached down, scrambling to help pick up items while trying to memorize what they were.

Maps, pages of computer code, several flash drives . . .

What had Stephen stumbled across? Why did he want her to have it?

"Stop. Stay back." Spike kept his voice at a whisper, but the anger in his eyes was evident.

She complied, but not before she'd slipped the drive into the top of her boot, praying he hadn't noticed. If he discovered what she'd just done . . .

"Is everything okay?" James's voice sounded from the other side of the door.

Spike signaled for her to answer as he shoved the papers into his bag.

"Just fine." Grace's voice cracked. "I dropped some of the papers. We'll be out in a minute."

Spike finished picking up the contents, then closed the bag. "We're leaving the bank now. Together."

Grace glanced at the door. "You don't need me. You've got what you want. Let me stay here. Please."

She knew what they'd done to Stephen. If she

left the bank with this man, she'd end up being another casualty. But would not doing what they said put Nate's life in further danger? Her resolve wavered.

"Do I need to remind you what will happen to the man sitting in the car with a gun to his head right now if you don't do what I tell you?"

She shook her head. "No."

"Then you go out first. And smile."

Her stomach clenched. Whatever was in that box wasn't worth their lives. She had no choice but to do what he told her to do. At least for now.

Thirty seconds later, Grace walked through the open glass doors and into the bright morning sunlight. Spike's fingers closed around her arm, once again squeezing too tightly. To a bystander, it would look as if he was her husband or boyfriend.

She looked toward the spot where Nate had parked, but his car was gone. And from what she could see, there was no sign of police backup. Any hope she'd had vanished.

She tried to pull away from Spike. "You've got what you want. Please let me go."

He pressed his weapon against her side. "If you were expecting a rescue, you're going to be disappointed. You'll be coming with me now."

No . . . no . . . no . . .

Where is Nate?

"At least tell me where we're going."

"Or what?" Spike laughed as a black sedan pulled up alongside them. He shoved her into the back seat, then slid in beside her. "You don't exactly have anything to bargain with. I have the contents of the safe-deposit box. Which means I don't need you anymore."

Fear sliced through her. She should have fought harder from the beginning. Should have caused a scene at the bank.

Spike slammed the door behind him, then banged on the headrest. "Let's get out of here."

She wasn't done yet. "The authorities will find you. They'll have your faces on every channel by the evening news."

The driver glanced up at the rearview mirror. "Keep her quiet, will you?"

"Pull over up ahead, and I'll take care of her. There's an alley on the right."

The driver pulled into the narrow passageway and stopped. Spike dragged her out of the car. She'd pushed them too far. Not that it probably mattered. They were going to get rid of her no matter what she said. They'd never intended to let her go. To let either of them go.

Spike pulled her behind the car, zip-tied her hands in front of her, then shoved her into the trunk. A second later, he shut the lid, leaving her in pitch darkness.

8

Nate glanced at the clock on the dashboard as his captor headed through traffic away from the bank. He was thankful that the majority of the effects from the Taser had passed. But three minutes had also passed since they'd grabbed Gracie. These guys knew what they were doing. Probably former military, and definitely well trained.

Another ten minutes max and Gracie and her captor would emerge from the bank. Somehow, he had to find a way to take control of the situation and get back to the bank before that happened. But at the moment, he had no way to get backup and no way to ensure Gracie's safety.

He'd managed to sit up, but his hands were still secured behind him. Unclenching his hands and turning his wrists so they were facing inward had given him a half an inch or so of slack, but it hadn't been enough. He needed to get his thumbs out first. Once he did that, he should be able to get free.

Nate's skin was getting raw from trying to slide his hands out of the ties, but he ignored the pain. Over the past couple minutes, a plan had begun to formulate in his mind, but he had to find a way to escape without getting Gracie hurt. The guy in his front seat—who he'd nicknamed Tat—was on the phone and watching him in the rearview mirror. From what he'd been able to determine from the situation, Tat had been ordered to drive him away from the bank, while the other two men would take Gracie in their car. Nate's gun sat out of reach on the front passenger seat. If he got loose, he'd only have a second to subdue the man. But hopefully that would be all the time he needed.

He tried to listen to the conversation, but all Tat did was answer yes and no a couple times. Not enough for Nate to pick up the other side of the conversation.

"Where are we going?" he asked Tat when he was done on the phone.

"Don't think that concerns you at this point."

Nate frowned. As far as he was concerned, it did involve him. Especially if they were planning to dump his body somewhere. At the moment, though, he didn't really care what happened to him. Gracie was the one he needed to rescue.

Flashes of trauma surfaced. His heart hammered. Adrenaline surged. He tried to stop the panic, but the claws of his past only dug deeper.

His counselor had tried to get him to combat the lies. Lies that told him he could have prevented Ashley and the others from dying. Lies that told him he was at fault. True or not, he didn't know how to shake the demons haunting him. And now Gracie's life was in danger. He couldn't let it happen again.

The zip tie dug into his wrists as he twisted them, but he ignored the pain as he worked to break free. Seconds later, he managed to slide out his left thumb, then his right. Another moment later, he was out of the zip tie.

He didn't wait to weigh the consequences. He grabbed his gun from the front passenger seat before the driver could react.

"Keep your hands on the wheel and keep driving." Nate scanned their surroundings. "There's a mall parking lot fifty feet ahead of us to the right. Pull the vehicle over and park, or I promise, I will shoot you."

"You're making a mistake. If I don't respond to their next call, they'll shoot the girl. And besides, no matter what you do, you can't stop what's already been put into motion."

"Just do it." Nate pressed the gun against the back of the guy's head, tired of the cryptic messages.

The man hesitated, then flipped on his blinker and pulled into the mostly empty lot.

"There's a row of parking places to your left. Park there, then shut off the engine."

The man followed his directions, shifted the car into park, and cut the engine.

Nate grabbed his handcuffs out of the pocket in the back seat with his free hand. This wasn't over yet.

"With your left hand on the steering wheel,

you're going to hand me the keys first, then your gun, and then you're going to put both hands on the steering wheel."

Instead of complying, Tat thrust his hand between the bucket seats, skimming Nate's face with the butt of his gun, then bolted from the car.

Nate yelled at the guy to stop, then chased him as he took off across the parking lot toward a group of kids. The man still had his weapon, which meant a mall full of shoppers could quickly turn deadly.

Thirty yards to their left, a woman was loading her purchases into her trunk, oblivious to what was going on.

Nate was gaining on him. "Stop now!"

He knew he couldn't risk a shot. His only option was to physically stop the man. And he had to stop him before he got to the woman. Another ten feet . . . five.

Tat stumbled over a curb, breaking his stride and allowing Nate to gain the final few feet he needed. A second later, he tackled him to the ground. Tat's gun went off, shattering a car window.

The sun beat down on them as Nate quickly confiscated the gun, then put the guy in handcuffs. A crowd began to form, but what he needed was backup.

"Next time you might want to try something a bit more creative than zip ties. Now I want you to tell me who you are and what the plan was."

He hauled the guy up, wishing he had his partner or his phone, or preferably both. He needed to get back to the car and then to the bank before Gracie left.

"I don't have to tell you anything. Besides, by the time you get back to the bank, they'll be long gone."

"Well, when you're up on murder charges, I'll be sure to tell the DA that you refused to cooperate."

"That won't happen. I didn't kill anyone."

"I'm not sure I believe that. You seemed awfully eager to shoot somebody."

A police car pulled into the lot, heading directly toward them. Nate signaled for him to stop.

"What's going on? 911 just got a call."

"Detective Nate Quinn," he said, pulling out his badge. "I need you to transport this man to my precinct and process him until my team can question him."

"Yes, sir."

"You'll never find her," Tat yelled at him as the officers escorted him to the squad car. "She's expendable. Just like Stephen was. Just like you are."

Nate ran back to his car, ignoring the man's threats. What had he been thinking, asking Gracie to go into the bank? Whatever they'd wanted, the stakes were apparently high enough for the murder of a security expert.

Nate slipped into the driver's seat, grabbed his phone where it had fallen on the floor, then put in a call to Kelli at the precinct, who did the majority of the technical legwork for their squad.

"Kelli," he said when she answered. "I need a BOLO put out for a black sedan in connection to a probable kidnapping situation." He pulled out of the mall parking lot, his lights flashing on top of his vehicle, as he gave her a description of the men.

"What's going on, Nate?"

"Things went south. They ambushed us at the bank. One is inside the bank with Gracie. The other one Tasered me."

"What did you do? Walk in on a robbery?"

"I told you, it was an ambush. I got one of the men subdued about six blocks from the bank and have local LEOs delivering him to the precinct. I'm headed back to the bank now, but I'm not sure I can walk in there without putting Gracie's life at risk."

"I'll inform the bank manager of the situation."

"Where's Paige?"

"She got held up but is on her way now. I can have additional backup there in less than five minutes."

He glanced at the dashboard clock. "I'm not sure we have five minutes."

Nate sped down the road, heading back to the

bank. If they left before he got there, finding her in this city was going to prove almost impossible. There were too many variables. Too many places for them to go, and they still had no idea who was behind this. What they did know was that this was much more than a murder. But what, he had no idea. Nothing made sense.

I need a miracle, God.

He slowed down and pulled into the bank parking lot, searching for the black sedan he'd seen pull up next to them.

The vehicle was gone.

"Nate . . . what's going on?"

"She's not here, Kelli. The car's gone."

"Maybe they left her and she's still inside."

He banged on the steering wheel. He'd lost her. Unless Kelli was right, and she was still inside. But they both knew that the chances of that were slim. And if she wasn't inside, how in the world were they supposed to find her?

"Paige is a minute out," Kelli said. "Go inside and see if she's there. Get them working on the video footage to see if we can get a license plate on their car."

He ran into the bank. A security guard stood in the back corner, several customers were at the teller booths. Was it possible that no one noticed what had happened to her?

"Can I help you?"

He turned to the twentysomething blonde and

held up his badge. "I'm Detective Nathaniel Quinn. A woman came in a few minutes ago with a man to get something out of a safe-deposit box. I need to know if they're still here."

"I'm sorry. I don't know, but Shannon . . ." She signaled to a coworker. "Can you help this gentleman?"

Shannon seemed just as perky. "What can I do for you today, sir?"

Nate tried to squelch his impatience. "A woman, early thirties, light-brown hair, came in fifteen minutes ago with a man to get something out of a safe-deposit box. I need to know if she's still here, or if she's already left."

"I'm sorry, but they're gone. Is there a problem?"

"There is, actually. The man she came in with was holding her against her will. How long ago did they leave?"

The woman's eyes widened. "Um . . . a minute . . . two tops. Do you want me to call security?"

"I've got backup on their way. What I need now is security footage from when the bank opened until now. Both inside and outside."

"Of course. Come with me, and we'll go see the manager. She can make that happen."

"Hurry."

He glanced at the clock in the corner of the bank as they headed toward the manager's office. Another minute had passed. Every minute spent in the bank meant Gracie was another minute farther away.

Melissa quickly introduced Nate to Sondra Parks, explaining the situation to the brunette in her late forties. Nate told her exactly what he needed, then got Kelli back on the line. "Kelli, I need you to see if you can track Grace Callahan's cell—"

"I just got a call from Paige, and I'm already on it, but there isn't a current signal. Looks like either the phone went dead, or they took out the battery. But wait a minute . . ."

Nate felt his panic grow. So tracking her phone wasn't going to be an option? This couldn't be happening. They'd used her for what they needed. And if they didn't need her anymore—

"I think I've got something." The bank manager leaned forward, then pointed at the screen.

"Stay on the line for another minute, Kelli." Nate glanced at the screen in front of him.

Grainy footage showed Gracie walking to the car with someone holding her arm. They walked across the parking lot, then climbed into the black sedan. His heart raced as the footage showed the vehicle pulling out of the parking lot and heading left onto the main street. "See if you can zoom in on the license plate, then freeze the footage . . . there."

Nate let out a sharp breath. They had the license plate, but where had they gone?

He read off the license plate number to Kelli, thanked the manager, then headed out of the bank to the parking lot. "Track any 911 calls placed in the last thirty minutes. Then search street cams . . . license plate readers . . . there's got to be a way to track her. They couldn't have just vanished."

"I'm doing everything I can. But wait a minute, Nate . . ."

"What have you got?"

"Okay, I've got the last location of her phone, but without the ability to track it, that doesn't give us much."

It might not be enough, but at least it was a start. "It will steer us in the right direction."

"What can you tell me from your end?"

"We've got her leaving the bank at 9:16," he said. "They were heading north. Add your location and map it out."

"Okay . . . They're headed northeast."

He pulled out of the parking lot and headed that direction. He thought he was three to four minutes behind them, but even that was a guess. And until the security cameras tracked her, he would have no idea if they were still on 428 or not.

He drove through the area, keeping the line open with Kelli, looking for the sedan. Why was it that every other car was a black sedan?

"Nate . . ."

"I'm still here."

"An alert just came through via one of the city's plate readers. I've got a cross street, four blocks from your location."

"Give me the address."

She gave him the street names. "Paige has just arrived at the bank."

"See if she can find out anything else there." He made a left and continued toward the location. "Is there any way to follow that sedan live?"

"I wish. All I can do is try to catch them on the traffic cams, but it's not going to be easy."

At least it was a start. It wasn't foolproof by any means, but technology had allowed authorities to capture fugitives and kidnappers by reading license plates, then passing on up-to-the-minute data to local police.

"Nate . . . I found them again . . . They just turned left at the second stoplight ahead of you."

"I'm on my way."

He raced down to the four-lane intersection. Traffic might be somewhat lighter now that the official rush hour was over, but there was always congestion in the city no matter what time of day. He weaved in between a couple slower cars, fighting the urge to honk his horn.

"I'm making the turn now."

"Wait . . . I've lost them again. Just give me a minute."

He slowed down, not wanting to waste time having to backtrack.

"Okay," she said finally. "Take another left at the next street."

He flipped on his blinker, following Kelli's instructions.

Where are they taking you, Gracie?

Unlike with Ashley, he still had a chance to stop this. But he was going to have to find her first.

"Do you see her?" Kelli asked.

He searched the lane in front of him as well as the side streets. "No . . . I don't have her yet. Where is she?"

"Give me a second, Nate."

His breaths became shallow. They'd narrowed it down, but it wasn't enough. He needed to pinpoint her location. "Where is she? I need something."

There was a long pause before she answered. "I'm sorry, Nate, but I've lost her."

9

Grace lay in the pitch-black darkness of the trunk, struggling to force back the panic. It was so dark she couldn't even see her hand in front of her face. The panic threatened to engulf her, but she knew she couldn't give in to it. Panic would make her react emotionally instead of rationally, and she needed a clear head. She took in a breath, counted to three, then released the breath for another three counts.

Relax, Grace. You're going to find a way out of this.

Breathe in, one, two, three.

Breathe out, one, two, three.

A memory surfaced. A few months ago, she'd seen a news report about a woman who'd been kidnapped. She'd somehow managed to pop the trunk from the inside with the emergency latch and escape from her captors. That could work. If she could find the latch, she could open the trunk once the car slowed down, then jump out and run. Once she was free, she'd worry about what would happen after she got out.

She ran her bound hands along the edge of the trunk, searching for a release switch.

Nothing.

Darkness pressed in around her, bearing down

on her lungs like a physical force. The latch had to be here. Somewhere she'd read that it was required by law for all newer cars, but where was it? She took in another slow breath. The most logical place was where the trunk lid met the car body at the center.

Please, God. Please. It has to be here somewhere.

She fought to focus. She knew God didn't always answer prayer, and that sometimes bad things happened to good people. She'd lived in that dark place of unanswered prayers when God didn't say yes. And on one level—when she was looking at the situation as a psychologist—she understood why.

But that wasn't always enough to take away the pain and emptiness of loss.

Or the constant reminders.

She felt the car slow down.

She searched the darkness for the latch, then caught something glowing in the dark. That had to be it. She felt again for the latch and pulled on it. A second later the trunk lid popped open, allowing sunlight to stream into the trunk.

There was no time to think about the armed driver as she struggled to climb out of the vehicle with her bound hands. The car moved forward. Her ankle twisted as she hit the pavement. She stumbled, barely catching her balance before she started running. She ignored the pain shooting up her ankle. The car skidded to a stop, taillights on, then backed toward her. She needed a plan, but for right now, the only option was to run and get as far away from the men as she could.

To her left was a neighborhood filled with a long line of single-family homes with rear alleyways. She had no idea what had happened to her phone, but if she could find someone at home and call for help . . .

Choosing the shortest distance—her hands still bound together in front of her—she darted toward the first yard as fast as she could. They weren't going to stop looking for her until they'd killed her.

Like Stephen.

She could see him now. Imagine his dead body, single gunshot to his head, lying lifeless in some nameless place. The image wouldn't leave her alone as she darted toward a gate and into a backyard toward the back alley where she prayed she could hide. If they found her, she would be next. The thought terrified her. She'd worked with clients who were dealing with PTSD. Patients who'd faced their worst nightmares of abuse and violence, and who were now simply struggling to survive.

But no one had ever tried to take her life.

She ran toward the nearest house and banged on the back door. The house looked empty, so she kept running down the narrow road, three, four, five houses . . . She needed to put as much distance between her and the men as possible before she stopped again.

She glanced behind her. The black sedan passed on a cross street, slowed down, then put on its brakes and reversed. She pressed her back against the wooden fence, trying to stay in the shadows. Her heart pounded as she stood, frozen. She counted the seconds. Five . . . ten . . . fifteen . . . The brake lights went out and the car kept moving.

Which meant they hadn't seen her. Still, she was far too exposed and out in the open. She slipped through a gate, then crossed the backyard of the next house before banging on the door.

Come on . . . come on . . .

No one answered, and she couldn't wait. She ran back out of the yard and glanced both directions before running to the next house. It wasn't going to take them long to figure out where she'd gone. And while getting someone else involved was a risk, she needed a phone.

An older man with a white beard opened the door. "Can I help you?"

"I'm sorry . . . I need to call 911. Please. I know this is going to sound crazy, but I was just kidnapped and managed to get away, but they're still after me—"

A woman's voice called out from somewhere in the house. "Marty . . . who's at the door?"

"Please." Grace held up her bound hands, praying he wouldn't think she really was crazy and turn her away. "If I could use your phone."

The man glanced outside toward the back fence, wasting precious seconds. If they found her again now . . .

"Please."

"Hurry up and come in."

He shut and locked the door behind her, then turned back to her in the middle of a kitchen that was decorated with bright yellow sunflowers. He took a pair of scissors from a drawer and snipped the zip tie around her wrists.

"You said you need a phone?"

"I need to call 911," she said.

"Come with me into the living room. I think the phone's in there."

An older woman stepped into the kitchen wearing a loose-fitting, floral-print dress.

"The girl's in trouble, Jill. Where's the phone?" the man asked.

"I'm not sure. You had it after breakfast . . . What's going on?"

"I promise I'll explain everything," Grace said, "but please hurry."

Grace moved toward the front window and glanced down the street. A man jogged past the house, but there was no sign of the men who'd taken her.

"Here it is," the woman said.

Grace wished she had Nate's number. Instead, she called 911 for the second time in less than twenty-four hours.

Her hands shook as she punched in the numbers.

"911, what's your emergency?"

"My name's Grace Callahan. I was kidnapped and just managed to escape from the trunk of a car." She was surprised at how calm her voice sounded. Like everything that had just happened was a bad dream. If she could wake up, it might all be over, but her throbbing ankle and trembling hands told her different.

"Where are you now?" the operator asked.

"Just a minute." She turned back to the man. "I need your address."

She put the phone on speaker and let the man give them the address.

"Retired Marine Corps Gunnery Sergeant Marty Phelps here, ma'am. She ended up at me and my wife's house."

"Mr. Phelps." The operator's voice helped calm her. "I want you to make sure the house is locked, then stay away from any windows and out of sight. I'm sending the local police to your location now, but Grace, I want you to stay on the line with me."

"Okay."

"I need to know if you're still in danger."

"I don't think they know where I am, but

they're out there looking in the neighborhood."

"How many men were in the car?"

"Two," Grace said. "And at least one of them was armed."

"Were you hurt at all during the escape?"

"No. Well . . . just my ankle, but it's fine."

"Can you describe the vehicle you were taken in?"

"Yes . . . it was a black, four-door sedan. I think it was a Chevrolet."

"Do you know how much time has passed since you escaped?"

Grace glanced at a pendulum wall clock. It seemed like it had been hours since she and Nate had arrived at the bank, but it was only nine forty. Barely forty minutes since she'd seen Nate. Not more than five since she'd escaped from the trunk.

"About five minutes, but I also need to let you know that I was with a Detective Nate Quinn when we were attacked and separated. I don't know what happened to him, but you need to find him."

"Grace, I'm going to need to put you on hold for a minute, but I want you to stay on the line. Officers have been dispatched and are on their way to your location right now."

"Thank you."

Grace set the phone down on the coffee table in front of her.

"Name's Marty, like I told 911, and this is my wife, Jill."

Her gaze shifted to the shotgun he'd just grabbed out of the closet. "Grace Callahan," she said, "and I'm sorry. Sorry for getting you involved in this. I just . . . I didn't know where to go."

"You did the right thing. I'm retired military, and trust me, when I say I've seen everything, I mean it. The Persian Gulf in '88, then later the Gulf War in Iraq. We'll get you out of this."

She managed a smile. "I guess I picked the right house."

"Yes, you did." Jill closed the blinds just enough so they could look out, but hopefully no one could see in. "Do you know who's after you? Ex-boyfriend? Ex-husband?"

"Nothing like that. It's . . . it's complicated, and will probably sound crazy. I had something that some very bad people wanted, and now I'm a liability."

"What else can we do?" Marty asked.

"I don't know . . ."

She stood up again and started pacing. She couldn't think. Her mind seemed to be frozen. She needed to talk to Nate, but she had no idea where he was. Or if he was even alive. Fear seeped through her. What had she been trying to prove by insisting on going with him to the bank? That she could somehow bring justice for Stephen's death?

Unlike the pieces of her own life that she hadn't been able to control.

The wall clock ticked the seconds. Time seemed to be creeping by. She listened for the sound of sirens, but there was nothing. She needed a distraction. There were photographs of birds hanging on the wall. A row of family photos with groups of kids smiling at the camera.

A familiar ache engulfed her.

What happened to living happily ever after? To families staying together? To kids who outlived their parents?

"You said you hurt your ankle, and you're definitely favoring your left foot." Jill's voice pulled her back to the present.

"It's nothing. I just twisted it jumping out of the car."

"You should get off of it. I've got an ice pack in the freezer for emergencies. I'll get it. And if someone does try to get into this house, they won't get far. Marty was a drill instructor and an expert marksman—"

"That was three decades ago, Jill."

"And you are just as tough today as you were back then."

A moment later, Grace took the ice pack and towel and nodded her thanks. She pulled off her left boot, sat back down, and pressed it against her ankle. The cold shot up her leg.

"A black vehicle just parked about three houses

down on the other side of the street," Marty said.

Grace dumped the ice pack beside her and moved to the window where she could peek through the blinds. She felt an adrenaline rush. One of the men was walking down the street toward them. They were still out there, circling in on her. But there was no way for them to find her, was there?

"That's them," she said.

"Where are the police?" Jill asked.

"Grace?" Marty handed her the phone she'd set down on the coffee table. "The operator's back on the line."

"I think the men are coming," she said to the operator.

"Can you give me a license plate number and a more detailed description of the car?"

Grace peeked through the blinds and squinted. "They parked down the street, it's too far away. I don't think I can read it."

"Wait a second . . ." Jill stepped out of the living room, then returned with a pair of binoculars. "Try these. We do a lot of bird watching."

Grace peered through the lenses as the man walked down the sidewalk.

Did he know where she was?

She turned back to the car.

"Okay, I've got the license plate number," she said, then read off the plate. "How long until the police are here?"

"They're ninety seconds out."

Ninety seconds suddenly seemed like an eternity. The men were already here. She couldn't expect complete strangers to defend her with their lives.

She stared back out the window. That was the driver, but where was the man who'd gone into the bank with her?

"There were two men in the car," Grace said. "Where's the other one?"

She ran into the kitchen and pulled back the curtain, looking out at the backyard. The yard was empty.

Movement to her left caught her eye. The back gate swung open in the wind.

She hadn't shut the gate.

A shadow crossed the yard. He was there, not more than twenty feet from where she stood in the kitchen, a gun in his hand as he headed for the back door. Grace moved back against the wall, trying to slow her breathing, and looked at the door handle, praying they'd remembered to lock it.

Marty stepped into the kitchen.

Gracie held a finger to her lips and nodded toward the backyard. A second later, the door handle rattled. Marty motioned for her to move away from the window, held up his gun, and aimed it at the door.

10

Nate pressed down on the accelerator as he sped down the busy four-lane thoroughfare, searching for the black sedan. If Kelli lost them, tracking Gracie down was going to be difficult, if not impossible.

"Nate . . ." Kelli was back on the line. "A 911 call just came through from Grace."

His heart raced. "What happened?"

"She escaped the kidnappers and managed to take cover in a residence, but we have reason to believe that the men have found her again. We've got patrol cars on their way right now to intervene."

"What's their ETA?"

"Roughly ninety seconds. Homeowners are Marty and Jill Phelps, and from your GPS, it looks like you're currently three blocks south of her location." Kelli gave him the address.

He pressed on the accelerator and made a sharp U-turn.

"I'm on my way now," he said.

"Hold on, Nate. As far as we know, both men are armed. Wait for backup."

She was right, but he wasn't sure there was time.

He turned the corner and saw the black sedan parked at the end of the street.

"I've found the vehicle," he said, driving past, "but it looks empty."

Where were the men?

Nate parked against the curb two houses down from the address Kelli had given him, quickly evaluating the situation. One of the men he recognized from the bank was standing at the front door of the one-story house. Backup wasn't going to get here quickly enough, especially if the man's intentions were to breach the house. And where was the second man? He scanned the street, but there was no sign of him.

He approached the house via the driveway, his own weapon raised. "This is the police. Put your hands in the air and stand down, or I will shoot."

The man hesitated, clearly caught off guard. If the man managed to get into the house, the situation could change drastically. And there was still no sign of the second man.

"Put your gun down now," Nate repeated.

Sirens wailed in the background, giving him the advantage he needed.

"You're about to be surrounded, so if you're smart, you'll do what I'm telling you."

Nate caught the conflict in the man's eyes. Another five seconds passed before the man slowly set his gun on the ground and put his hands in the air.

Fifteen seconds later, two squad cars squealed

to a stop in front of the house and four officers rushed from the vehicles.

But this wasn't over. Not by a long shot.

"Detective Quinn?" one of the officers shouted as he pulled out his firearm.

"Have your men go around back and spread out," Nate shouted. "There's a second armed assailant still unaccounted for."

One of the officers followed his signal and took their suspect into custody as Nate headed for the house. He needed to see Gracie for himself and make sure she was okay.

He banged on the door, then took a step back. "Mr. Phelps? This is Detective Nathaniel Quinn. You can open the door now."

An older man with a shotgun opened the door six inches, still hesitated.

"Nate?" Gracie stepped up behind the man. "We're okay. But the second man was at the back door . . . He heard the sirens and ran east down the alleyway."

"We've got officers out there looking for him now," Nate said, stepping inside the house. "We'll find him."

Her face was pale, but other than that she looked okay.

It could have ended so differently, God.

He told one of the officers to take statements from the owners, then turned back to Gracie. She rushed toward him, and without thinking, he put his arms around her and pulled her against him.

"I don't know who these people are," she said, "but I thought they'd killed you."

"Looks like I'm not the only one who managed to escape."

She looked up at him with those big eyes of hers that somehow managed to do something crazy to his heart. "How did you get away?"

"Long story, and a big miracle, but all that really matters right now is that you're okay. But I'm so sorry. I never should have taken you with me to the bank."

"Stop. I'm fine, and besides, this wasn't your fault. I insisted on coming with you."

"Maybe, but if anything would have happened to you . . ."

He took a step back, unprepared for the surge of emotions at almost losing her. And then the subsequent feeling of finding her again. The familiar panic threatened to engulf him, but he fought it. He couldn't let anything happen to her. Even if that meant locking her up in some safe house until all of this was over.

But neither could he make this personal.

He drew in a quick breath. "You're not hurt, are you?" He glanced at the ice pack lying on the couch and noticed she was only wearing one boot.

"It's nothing. I twisted my ankle when I jumped out of the trunk of the car, but it barely hurts."

"That's how you got away?"

Another wave of anxiety sliced through him. If she hadn't gotten away . . . If they hadn't managed to track her down . . . He pushed away the string of dark thoughts threatening to strangle him.

"I didn't exactly have a lot of options," she said. "And all I could think about was what they'd done to Stephen. And that they had killed you too."

He tried to gauge her demeanor. She seemed calm, but he knew how shock tended to mask reality. When all of this did hit her, it was going to hit hard. Knowing that she was dealing with great loss even before the harrowing events of the past few hours made him want to whisk her away from all of this. But for now, he still needed her help.

"As you can see, I'm fine," he said. "We'll get the paramedics to look at you as soon as they arrive, then get you to the precinct. We're going to need to take an official statement from you."

"Of course."

"Detective . . ." One of the officers caught his attention. "The paramedics just arrived."

"Any sign of the second suspect?"

"Not yet, but I'll let you know the moment I hear something."

Gracie grabbed his arm. "What about the contents of the safe-deposit box? We need to know what was in that box, because they're planning something."

"Did you see what was in it?"

"Just a glimpse. There were some maps of the US, printouts of computer code, and several flash drives . . . Wait a minute." She dug into the side of the boot she still had on. "This was in the box."

"How'd you manage to get that?" he asked, slipping it into his pocket.

"It had to be a God thing. I don't think he saw me take it, but he definitely got everything else. I'm sorry."

"You have nothing to be sorry about. And we're going to find whoever's behind this."

Paramedics showed up at the front door. Nate called them over to the couch before turning back to Gracie. "I want to hear everything that happened, but in the meantime, stay here with them, and I'll be right back."

He waited another few seconds while the paramedics took over, then headed outside, where an officer was putting the handcuffed man into a squad car.

"Did you find anything on our suspect?" Nate asked.

"A set of car keys and a wallet. Nothing else."

"No papers or flash drives?"

"Nothing."

Nate glanced down the street at the black sedan. "What's his name?"

The officer handed him the man's ID and the car keys.

Brandt Gunnison. White male. Thirty-eight years old.

"Until our second suspect is found, don't take your eyes off her," Nate said.

"Yes, sir."

Nate took the keys, then ran across the street toward the black sedan.

He unlocked the car and scanned the front and back seats, careful not to touch anything. CSU would search the car later, but for now, he needed to know if they'd left the contents of the box behind.

Nothing.

He moved on to the trunk, shivering at the reminder that Gracie had been locked up in it. If she hadn't escaped, they probably would have found a way to dispose of her body and he'd never have found her. He sucked in a quick breath. But that hadn't happened. He forced his thoughts back to the second man as he walked toward the house. He must still be in possession of the items they'd stolen.

But where was he?

His phone rang. It was Kelli.

"There was a hit on the license plate of the car they were driving. It was reported stolen this morning."

"Another probable dead end, then. I'll be

coming back to the precinct as soon as we wrap up here." Irritated, Nate hung up and stepped inside the house.

"How's your ankle?" he asked Gracie, moving next to the couch.

"It's fine." She smiled up at him, fatigue in her eyes. She had to be exhausted. "I told you it was nothing."

"You're lucky," he said.

"It wasn't luck. Like you said, it was a miracle."

He smiled. "Touché."

"What about the contents of the box? Did you find it?"

"Not yet."

"She's good to go." The paramedic stood up. "Looks like it's just a mild sprain. Nothing seems to be broken."

"Can you walk?" Nate asked.

"Yes. Like I said, it's really not a big deal. Plus, they gave me a couple of painkillers just in case it starts hurting."

"Good, but there's been a change of plan." He knew she wasn't going to like what he had to say, but he was certain his boss would back him on this one. "I want you off the radar, which means I'm putting in a request to get you placed in a safe house until we figure out what's going on. Until we know what's behind this, it's too risky—"

"Too risky?" He caught the flash of anger in her eyes, but he really didn't care if he made her angry. He wasn't going down that road again.

Gracie frowned. "I can help. I want to help."

"She's right, Nate."

Nate turned around. Paige had just stepped into the house. He frowned. He didn't have the energy to fight them both, but neither was he going to take a gamble with Gracie's life. "You're supposed to be on my side, Paige."

"You can't expect me to stay locked up in some safe house," Gracie said, clearly not finished arguing with him. "I can't just sit around and do nothing."

"In case you've forgotten, those men broke into your house, shot at you, then kidnapped you and stuffed you into a trunk . . . I think that's enough for one day." He pulled out the flash drive she'd given him and held it up. "And on top of that, as far as we know, they are still searching for you. And we don't even know who these guys are or what their connection is to Stephen's murder."

"Nate . . . look at me." She stood in front of him, then reached up and let her fingertips graze his arm.

He tried to ignore her touch as he caught her gaze and felt himself begin to slip under her spell. He shook his head. He couldn't feel anything toward her. Especially not now.

"Nate?"

"What?"

"In order to figure out what's going on, you

need me. There might be something I know that can help you."

Nate worked to settle his irritation. She was being irrational. Both of the women were being irrational, actually, and he was letting this get personal. There was something about Gracie that made him want to protect her. She seemed vulnerable and yet strong. But the worst part was that it had him digging up lots of old memories he didn't know how to shake.

Paige stepped in beside him. "Will you give us a minute?" she said to Gracie.

Gracie nodded.

"She's right, you know," Paige said, pulling him aside and keeping her voice low. "I realize she's an old friend and that you want to keep her safe, but we need whatever information she might have about Stephen."

"I know that, but whoever's behind all of this murdered a man last night, then kidnapped her," he said.

"She's not Ashley, Nate."

His frown deepened as the past fought to raise its ugly head. "I know that."

"She knew the victim and has information that could help. I know you're worried about her, but this is bigger than your fears. You can't let your personal feelings get in the way."

His jaw tensed. "I understand that."

"You don't look convinced. Why is this different

than what we've done before? We use confidential informants all the time."

"Because—" He fought to come up with a reason she wasn't going to refute and throw back at him.

"Because it's personal and you care about her," Paige said, answering her own question before he could respond.

"She's an old friend, Paige. Nothing more."

"We can debate the truth behind that another day, but for now, you're going to go with the decision. Or as much as I don't want to, I'm going to report that you're not ready to be back on active duty."

He caught her gaze and realized she wasn't playing games.

"If you let what happened affect how you do your job—"

"It isn't and it won't," he said.

His anger simmered beneath the surface. He wanted to tell her that she was totally out of line in calling him on this. That she had no right to bring up his past. Except he knew she was right. Which made him even angrier. He didn't want Gracie involved, because no matter how hard he tried to fight it, he had made it personal.

He glanced across the room where one of the paramedics was talking to Grace. They might have been close a decade ago, but neither of them was the same person now. Knowing what

119

she'd gone through the past few years made him sympathize with all she'd lost, but he didn't know her anymore and didn't owe her anything. She was a person of interest in a murder investigation. Nothing more.

"You're right," he said. "We'll take her down to the precinct. She can talk with victim services, then we'll have Sarge interview her."

"You don't want to do it yourself?" Paige asked.

"There's no reason I need to be the one doing the interview." He glanced out across the front of the house. "We've got two suspects to interrogate."

11

Nate headed into the precinct toward their unit's bullpen with Paige, his frustration growing. Maybe he was just out of practice after so much time off, but playing hardball with their first suspect had yielded them nothing. And now they had only one more chance with the second suspect, which meant they'd better get it right this time.

"Detectives?" Kelli signaled them with a wave of her hand. "You're going to want to see what I found out."

"What have you got?" Nate grabbed a mini Snickers from Kelli's ever-present candy bowl, ripped off the wrapper, and popped it into his mouth.

"I found it odd that I couldn't come up with much of anything on Winters and Gunnison. So after a bit of digging, I discovered that their licenses are fake. Both of them."

Nate tossed his wrapper into the metal waste-basket next to her desk and frowned. "That would explain a lot."

Kelli held up the bagged licenses. "And it explains why I can't find anything on your suspects."

Nate took the bag from Kelli and held the

licenses up to the light. Instead of the official microprint, continuous lines circled the Texas state seal and the flag. He groaned in frustration.

"Can you find out their real names?" Paige asked.

"I'm running their fingerprints, but it's going to take time. I do have something, though. CSU found Winters's fingerprints on Shaw's phone. So we know he had contact with our victim."

Paige took the offered file. "Any way to tie him directly to the murder?"

"Simply finding prints at the scene—"

"—is meaningless." Paige finished Kelli's sentence.

"Exactly." Kelli sat back in her chair and shifted her gaze to Nate. "Now, on a more positive note, I haven't had a chance to officially welcome you back."

He shot her a smile. "I'm glad to be back. You did good today."

"Thank you." She reached behind her chair, then handed him a square white box. "This is a welcome-back caramel chocolate-chip cupcake. There are more in the break room, but I was afraid if I put them all there, you'd never get one."

He peeked under the lid and grinned. The woman never missed a birthday, anniversary, or any other reason to celebrate. "There's no way to convince you *not* to retire next month, is there?"

Kelli cocked her head. "Makes me wonder if

people are going to miss me, or just the goodies I bring in."

"Without a doubt, it's you and your superhuman technical skills we're going to miss the most," he shot back. "But that's just ahead of your amazing caramel chocolate-chip cupcakes."

Kelli laughed. "Good answer. I'll keep you both updated on what I find."

"Thanks, Kelli." Nate started to walk away, then paused and turned back to her. "By the way, do you know where Grace Callahan is?"

"She's still in the briefing room with Kirkbright. Sergeant Addison is planning to take her official statement as soon as they're done."

"Thanks." Nate didn't miss the irony as they headed toward interrogation. He had a feeling Gracie wasn't going to react well to having to bare her soul to another shrink. Though on the other hand, she might not mind. She'd been through a lot, and he was sure she could use someone to talk to. The department's counselor would no doubt do a much better job than he'd done this morning.

He stopped in front of the interrogation room, then pulled the cupcake out of the box. "Do you want half? I have a feeling whatever she left in the break room is already long gone."

Paige shook her head. "Thanks, but my morning coffee contained all the sugar I need for the day."

"If you're sure," he said, taking a bite. His

stomach growled, reminding him he'd missed breakfast. One of Kelli's cupcakes would have to do. "So how do you want to run with this one?"

"We already told the first suspect we can charge him with kidnapping at a minimum," Paige said, "which should have been enough to get him to cooperate when we told him he was facing murder charges. Except it wasn't."

The man they'd just questioned had stalled for a couple minutes before invoking his right to counsel. He'd still serve prison time, but they hadn't ended up with the answers they needed.

Nate licked off a piece of frosting before it fell. "Here's what I'm trying to figure out. You don't just wake up one day and decide to Taser a cop, kidnap a woman, then drag her into a bank to steal the contents of a safe-deposit box. Gracie told me one of them said this was bigger than them. As if it didn't matter if they were caught. And I got the same impression."

"Agreed. Which means we need to find not only who's behind this but who or what their target is."

"Exactly." Nate took another bite of the cupcake, his mind working to put together what little they had. "What if they're a part of some . . . some hacking group? Stephen was apparently a computer genius who thought he was working for the FBI, then finds out he's not. Once tech finds out what's on that flash drive, we might have some more answers."

"You think we're looking at some kind of cyberattack?"

"It's my working theory. I don't know a lot about how those kinds of things work, but there are always people creating malware and viruses in order to attack businesses and investment and pharmaceutical companies. And that's what your average computer geeks do. Makes you have to ask why whoever's behind this needed to hire someone with Stephen's level of expertise."

"Meaning the stakes could be high enough for murder."

Nate popped the last bite of cupcake into his mouth. "Exactly."

Five minutes later, he dropped the virtually empty file folder onto the interrogation table, hoping his bluff was going to work to get them what they needed. Mark Winters—or whatever the man's name was—avoided his gaze, giving him a moment to study the man sitting across from him before speaking. Narrow face and tense jawline, plus a tat on his wrist. Interrogating a suspect always worked better the more information they had, but for now what they had was going to have to be enough.

"Mark Winters, I'm Detective Quinn and this is my partner, Detective Morgan." Nate set a cup of coffee onto the table in front of the man, then took a step back.

"I . . . thanks." The man stared at the offering, clearly thrown off by the gesture.

Paige pulled back the chair across from the man, then sat down. Nate took another breath, shoved his hand into his pocket, and fingered his watch. He wanted to yell at the man. Insist he tell him who he was and who he was working for, but that approach had already been tried. His gut told him he needed to take the opposite approach. They might not know who these guys were working for yet, but the first interrogation had flopped, and he had no intention of losing this one.

Nate chose his words carefully. "I'm going to cut to the chase. Right now, you're looking at a minimum of two to ten years in a state prison for kidnapping. Of course, it'll only take the DA about thirty seconds to look at the police report and up that to aggravated kidnapping. On top of that, the state of Texas has sharp penalties for assaulting law enforcement."

Paige glanced at Nate. "That could easily double his time."

"Easily. Which means things are not looking good for you right now. But we want to give you a chance to explain exactly what happened."

Winters folded his hands on the table. "I don't have anything to say."

"I'd think twice about not cooperating if I were you." Paige tapped on the file folder in front of her. "We need to know who is behind this operation and who they're targeting. You do that and I'll make sure the DA knows you're working with us."

Sweat beaded across the man's balding forehead. "I was hired as security. Nothing more. And I didn't exactly ask questions. I don't even know who hired me."

"Here's one problem," Nate said. "We're not just talking about kidnapping and assaulting a police officer, which is bad enough on their own. A man was murdered this morning. And that man's death is connected to the kidnapping of Grace Callahan, which means you're connected to his death." He nodded at Paige, who slid a photo of Stephen Shaw's body across the table. "And the other problem—at least for you—is that we have your fingerprints on his phone. So we know you were with him."

Winters turned away, eyes boring into the opposite wall as he drummed his fingers against the table.

"We found his body at a carnival. The coroner just confirmed it was not a suicide, but that Stephen Shaw was murdered, which makes kidnapping look insignificant in comparison. You're connected to the crime. That alone could get you life in prison."

"I didn't kill anyone."

"But we know you were there. At the carnival. With Shaw."

He ran his finger around the cup. "I was there, but I didn't kill anyone."

Nate buried a smile. If he could get Winters to defend himself, he might be able to turn him.

"Then what did you do there?" Nate asked, taking the chair next to Paige.

Winters leaned forward. "I was hired as muscle. To scare the guy—Stephen. That was it."

"Now you're making sense," Paige said. "You're a big guy. Six three . . . four?"

Winters shrugged.

"And let me guess," Nate continued. "Two twenty . . . no, I'd say closer to two fifty. Yeah, I could see why someone might hire you as their muscle."

"What does it matter?"

"I know what guys like you who are hired to do odd jobs do," Nate said. "Security, if that's what you want to call it. Muscle the clients a bit. Your boss wants someone bumped off, but doesn't want his hands dirty, so he pays you to do the dirty work."

"I didn't kill him. When I left, Shaw was alive. I do the job they ask me to do, get paid, and I don't ask questions. I don't know what happened to him."

"Maybe," Nate said. "But here's what I know. The medical examiner is going over Stephen Shaw's body right now. You'd be amazed at what they can discover." He glanced at the clock on the wall, then back at Winters. "In a few hours, we'll know exactly what happened. I know a lot about the process because my father was a coroner. He used to tell me that his job was to communicate the story of the person he was working on. And discovering the cause of death is often the first thing he'd do. It's like a puzzle, interpreting body tissues and fluids in order to discover the series of events that led to their death. It's pretty amazing what they can learn about a body, the moments leading up to their death, and not only how they died, but who did it."

Winters squirmed in his seat. Nate hoped the man had watched his share of crime shows on television. On every TV crime show, every murder is solved in forty minutes with a handful of high-tech forensic clues. In reality, things never happen that swiftly, but if he could spin the truth and use it against their suspect, it'd be worth a shot.

Winters shoved away the photo. "I told you I didn't kill anyone."

"But you know who did," Paige said.

"No."

He was lying. Nate could see it in his eyes. Who was he covering for?

Kelli's voice came through the wireless earpiece he'd slipped on before starting the interrogation. "His real name is Edwin Perkins. His record shows a few misdemeanors, including possession of a forged license three years ago."

Which made the second offense a felony.

Nate studied the man's face. So Winters—Perkins—really was way over his head this time around. And from the way he was sweating, he knew it. "Like it or not, you've just landed in a place I'm going to assume you didn't think you'd be.

"Because here's the thing, Edwin." Nate leaned forward. "We know you were at the crime scene. How long do you think it will take for the ME to connect the murder to you? We've got your fingerprints on the victim's phone. They've already tested you for gun powder residue. All it's going to take is putting two and two together."

Winters rubbed the back of his neck. "It . . . it wasn't supposed to end this way. They promised me we wouldn't get caught. That they'd thought of everything."

"That's a pretty hard thing to promise." Nate sat back in his chair, patient for the moment to let the conversation play out. Push too hard and he'd lose any ground they'd gained. "Just tell us what happened."

"I was hired by a man named Jenkins."

"Do you know his first name?"

"No. Just Jenkins. But I heard him mention something called Rogue a couple times."

"What is that?"

He shook his head. "I don't know. As far as I know, though, Jenkins is behind everything. The meeting with Shaw at the carnival, the break-in at that woman's house, her office, and the bank fiasco."

"And you were supposed to do what?"

"Make sure everyone . . . cooperated."

"The Taser was a nice touch," Paige said, glancing at Nate.

"It was never supposed to end this way."

"Yet it did. And now this Jenkins—who is supposedly behind all of this—is free, letting you take the rap." Nate leaned forward again. "What is he planning?"

"I don't know, except that it's bigger than you are. Bigger than any of us."

Nate paused. Stephen had said pretty much the same thing. What was this guy Jenkins planning?

"What do you mean, 'it's bigger than you are'?" Nate tapped on the photo of Stephen's dead body.

"He . . . he wouldn't tell me, and I didn't ask. All I know is that it has something to do with computers. Probably some kind of malware to steal government data. Something damaging. That would be my guess anyway. I was just in it for the money."

"We're going to bring in a sketch artist. And we're going to want a full statement from you."

"Fine."

"Good job." This time Sarge's voice boomed in Nate's earpiece. "But I need you both out here now."

Nate nodded at Perkins. "We'll be back."

Jonas Addison, the sergeant in charge of their unit, was waiting for them on the other side of the

131

door, wearing one of his signature ties. Today's was covered in gold handcuffs.

"What have you got?" Paige asked.

"I'll arrange for the sketch artist, but I just got a call from Stephen's workplace. I want the two of you to go down there. His boss says she knows who killed him."

12

Thirty minutes later Nate pulled into an empty parking spot in front of a multistory office complex, then exited the car with Paige. He fingered the watch in his pocket as they headed toward the glass doors at the entrance. He'd passed Gracie on the way out of the precinct. She'd finished talking to the victim counselor and was headed to give her statement. He shouldn't worry about her, but he did. He'd caught the fatigue in her eyes, along with the sadness. She'd lost so much, and he hated that they were having to drag her into all of this today.

"There's always this . . . this deep, black hole inside me. Like something's missing."

". . . this deep, black hole inside me . . ."

He stopped replaying their conversation. He might not talk about it, but he felt the same thing. It wasn't up to him to fill in the holes of her heart. So why did a part of him want to?

"Nate?"

He glanced at Paige as they headed up the long sidewalk.

"Your phone's going off."

"Sorry." He pulled it out of his pocket and scanned the message. "Kelli just sent a text with a more detailed background check on Stephen Shaw."

"And?"

"She came up with something interesting. Apparently, Stephen really was brilliant. No run-ins with the law, but it looks like while he was in college he got involved in hacking. He was able to analyze and deactivate a piece of malware that had been written to steal credit card numbers from the payment system of a department store chain."

"If he started off as a white hacker, it would explain his focus on security."

"But I'm not sure his motives have always been pure. At least not lately," he said, reading through the rest of the message.

"What do you mean?" she asked, stopping in the middle of the sidewalk.

"Kelli checked his financial records. There've been a number of recent, large deposits into his bank account."

"That could go along with the job on the side. What we don't know is who was paying him."

"That's the question. She's looking into that. Gracie said he thought he was working for good guys," Nate said.

"I know, but I'm finding that hard to buy," Paige said as they started back down the sidewalk. "If the guy was a genius, you'd think he'd know exactly what he was doing."

"Maybe, but head knowledge doesn't always compute to an abundance of common sense.

Besides that, a lot of security research is done by bypassing security and showing that a system can be breached. I'm assuming the ethical line isn't always easy to see."

"So Stephen thinks he's working for the FBI—or at the least claims that's what he's doing—but he's really involved in working for the bad guys, building some kind of malware?"

"All that fits."

Thirty seconds later, they stepped out of the perfect Texas fall temperature into the sterile, air-conditioned high-tech lobby. Following directions from Stephen's boss, they walked past white walls, a red-and-gray seating area, and rows of modern art, and headed straight for the elevator.

Inside, Nate pushed the button for the thirteenth floor.

"You know Gracie," Paige said, as the elevator started up. "Do you think she's holding up okay? She's gone through a lot today."

"She's always been strong." He started to share what Gracie told him at her office, then stopped. That wasn't for him to share. "If she can help us in this investigation, we'll be that much closer to finding out what's going on."

"The two of you used to be friends?"

Nate frowned. More than likely this was the real reason Paige had brought up the subject. "We were. A long time ago."

"There just seemed to be this . . . this chemistry

between the two of you," Paige said. "Made me think she'd be perfect for you. You need a good woman in your life."

"Please don't tell me you're one of those partners who's going to try to set me up with all your single friends." His frown deepened. "Besides, she's just an old friend. Nothing more."

The elevator lights flickered for a few seconds.

"Whatever you say," Paige said, staring at the ceiling. "I just think it's a bit coincidental that you're the officer who covered Stephen Shaw's murder, and that led you to her. A bit of fate involved, maybe?"

Nate shook his head. "I don't believe in fate."

"Call it what you want. But I think it's romantic."

Romantic?

He dismissed her implications. Ashley had always been trying to set him up with one of her friends until he finally told her to back off. If Paige was going to turn out to have a similar agenda, he was going to put his foot down. His last relationship had ended when he found out that the woman he thought he might one day marry suddenly started trying to control every aspect of his life. In the end, it had shown him not only what he didn't want, but what he did want as well. Which meant that until the right person came along, he was content to focus on his career. The bottom line was that there was something unsettling about the thought of getting involved with an old friend's wife, even if the guy had been a jerk and walked out on her.

The elevator jolted to a stop, pulling him out of his thoughts. He glanced at the floor number. Nine. He waited for the doors to open, but they didn't. Strange. Paige stared at the metal doors, her face a shade or two paler than when they'd gotten on.

The elevator started moving again.

"Must have been some kind of hiccup," he said.

"This is why I always take the stairs."

Two floors later, the elevator stopped again. Nate pressed the open button. Nothing.

"Nate . . ."

He stared at the lit panel. "I'm sure it's nothing."

"This doesn't seem like nothing to me."

Another thirty seconds passed. Paige was right. Something was wrong.

He pulled out his phone. "Wonderful. No signal."

He glanced at the emergency button and hesitated. He'd give it another thirty seconds. Paige hadn't moved from the corner of the elevator.

"You okay?" he asked.

"Of course."

"You don't look okay."

"Just for the record, I hate elevators," she said, jamming her finger against the button for their floor. "But that piece of information never leaves this tiny box."

He watched her punch the button again. "You know that's not going to make us get there faster."

"Like I said, this is why I take the stairs. That's how you get there faster."

"So . . . you have some kind of elevator horror story from your childhood?"

"When I was twelve, I got stuck in one of these for two hours in the middle of summer. Alone." Paige leaned back against the wall, staring at the doors. "Never realized I was claustrophobic until I couldn't get out of that metal box."

Another half minute went by.

"You think this is a coincidence?" he asked.

"The fact that I hate elevators, and our elevator is possessed?"

"I was thinking more along the lines that we're stuck in an elevator on our way to do an interview with someone who claims to know who our killer is."

"Oh, that." She leaned against the wall, taking deep breaths. "You really think it could be connected?"

"I have no idea."

It was clearly a reach. This was probably nothing more than a coincidence, but still . . .

He reached for the emergency call button as the bottom of the elevator dropped. His shoulder slammed against the wall.

"Nate."

The elevator stopped a second later. Nate managed to catch his balance before sprawling across the elevator floor.

"You okay?" he asked, righting himself.

Paige braced herself against the wall. "For the moment, but now I have another reason to hate elevators. How many floors up are we if the brakes fail?"

"Don't even think about falling."

But that was easier said than done. They'd just been at eleven. The elevator felt like it had dropped at least one floor. Paige stayed glued to the wall. "How hard would it be to hack into one of these things?"

"I have no idea. I should never have brought it up." He opened the door to the elevator phone and picked up the receiver.

He dialed the number printed on the inside of the door and waited for someone to answer.

"Something's definitely wrong." Paige jammed her finger against the emergency button again and again.

The lights flickered and went out, leaving them in total darkness.

"Hello . . . this is Frank with security." A man's voice boomed through the phone. "Sorry, folks. There seems to be a glitch in the system, but there's nothing to worry about. Hang in there, and I'll have you out in a few minutes. I promise."

" 'Nothing to worry about,' he says. Never

thought I'd die because of a glitch in the system," Paige murmured.

"We're not going to die."

"If this box drops again . . . if the emergency brake or whatever is holding us up here breaks and we drop a dozen floors, then yeah. We'll die. There was this woman riding an elevator at New Year's when it dropped five stories and—"

"I have a feeling our odds of death via an elevator are far less than, say . . . getting struck by lightning," Nate said, trying to lighten the conversation.

"Not funny."

The elevator jolted again, but this time it went up rapidly, then stopped.

There was a ding and the doors opened.

Half a dozen people stood in front of them as they walked out. A woman wearing a pink suit and high heels rushed across the tile toward them.

"Detectives . . . I am so, so sorry about the elevator. I don't know what happened, but are you both okay?"

Nate looked to Paige for an answer.

"We're fine," she said, pressing her shoulders back.

"Nothing like this has ever happened since I've been here," the woman hurried on. "Can I get you some water? Or coffee?"

"No, thank you," Nate said. "We have an appointment with Stephen Shaw's boss."

"Of course. She's expecting you."

A minute later they were ushered into a large office with windows overlooking an incredible view of downtown in the distance.

"I heard what happened on the elevators. I hope you're both all right." A woman who looked to be in her early forties stepped across the room and held out her hand. "I'm Marge Potter, Stephen's boss. I called management myself to ensure that our technicians look into the situation immediately."

"We're fine, Ms. Potter," Nate said, speaking for both of them. "Thank you for calling."

"Of course. But please . . . call me Marge." She pointed to the two chairs in front of her desk and motioned for them to sit down. "We just got the terrible news about Stephen. He was well liked around here, and I can't believe he's dead." Marge sat down across from them, then held out her hands. "I can't stop shaking."

"I know it must be quite a shock," Nate said. "We're here because we were told you know who killed him."

"I don't know exactly who killed him, but I do think I can help."

"Can you explain?" Paige asked.

"I can do better than that." The woman dug into her desk drawer and pulled out a plastic bag filled with smashed electronic pieces. "I can show you. Stephen's office was bugged."

141

"Bugged? Did he know it?"

"He's the one who discovered it. He came into my office last night, furious. Apparently, he'd bought some kind of bug detector that finds hidden cameras and bugs."

"And this is what he found?"

She nodded. "He told me he'd take care of it, but when he didn't show up for work this morning, I started getting nervous. When I saw a report on the news about a murder, I just . . . I knew it was Stephen."

"Do you know who planted the bugs?"

"No, and I don't think he did either, but it makes sense to me that whoever planted these bugs killed him. I don't know specifically what they were looking for, but our company deals with security, so we take any breach of our own security extremely seriously."

"What exactly was his job description?"

"As I said, our company deals with security, primarily cybersecurity. We work with all kinds of clients to protect them from email hacks and viruses and also to ensure that they have secure storage on their cloud service. The bottom line is that we design security portfolios for our customers to guarantee their protection in the digital world. Stephen was in charge of coming up with new, innovative security solutions. He sometimes monitored a client's defenses by breaking into their system, enabling us to give them a thorough briefing on ways they could better protect their company's data."

"What kinds of companies seek out your services?" Paige asked.

"We work with everything from small businesses to banks to Fortune 500 companies. Anyone who is concerned about cybersecurity. Because of this, you can understand the importance of this breach of our security not becoming public knowledge. To be honest, it was why I hesitated coming to you, but in the end I felt as if I didn't have a choice."

"You did the right thing. Do you know anything about Stephen working on the side for someone else? Possibly for the government?"

"Like what?" The woman let out a slow chuckle. "The FBI or something?"

"Actually, yes."

"You're serious."

"Very."

Her smile vanished. "Not that I know of, but I suppose it's possible. He worked a lot of hours here, though. Not sure he'd have the time to work a second job. But I don't exactly know what the guy did during his free time. He was friendly and all, but for the most part he didn't associate with his coworkers off the clock. And the stuff he did . . . to be honest, as crazy as it sounds, he was smart enough that I could see the FBI coming to him. And I suppose that could explain why someone would want to bug his office."

"How had he been acting lately? Anything you noticed out of the ordinary?"

"Definitely jumpy, which wasn't normal for Stephen. Just yesterday, for example, I was in the break room and he spilled coffee all over the counter while pouring a cup."

"Did you ask him what was wrong?"

"He mumbled something about being followed, but then he said forget it. That he hadn't been sleeping well lately, and the lack of sleep and too much caffeine must be affecting him."

"Was that like Stephen?"

"To be paranoid? Not at all. He was very level-headed. Very focused. But it was as if something had spooked him lately. And that was before he showed me these things."

"Was there anything else that stood out to you? Any enemies he might have made?"

"No. That's what makes all of this so strange. I just can't imagine someone trying to kill him."

"What about friends and family?" Paige asked.

"I honestly don't know. I never heard him talk about family."

Nate slipped the bag of electronics into his coat pocket, then handed her his card. "We'll take these in and have them processed. I'll also send a team to sweep his office to see what else they can find. And if you think of anything else, please give me a call."

Marge shook their hands, then walked with them to the door. "Thanks so much for coming. Please let us know if there's anything else we can help with."

Nate headed toward the elevator, then stopped when he realized Paige wasn't following.

"Do what you want, but I'm taking the stairs."

Nate frowned as they started down the stairwell. How had she roped him into taking a dozen flights of stairs? "So you've decided that whole elevator scenario wasn't a coincidence?"

"The bad guys are probably hackers as well, so this would have been a piece of cake."

"Don't you think that might be stretching things a bit?" he asked.

"Where elevators are concerned, I prefer to err on the side of caution." She looked back at him. "Now we know that Stephen was smart enough to be approached by the FBI, or at least his boss thinks so. And even though he believed he was working for them, the FBI claims not to have any knowledge of him."

Nate turned the corner and started down another flight. "It's always possible that the FBI is lying. I'm sure there are a dozen reasons why they wouldn't want us to know who was working security for them."

How were they supposed to solve this crime if both the bad guys and the good guys had something to hide?

13

Grace tapped her pen against the table in a corner of the second floor in the precinct's interrogation room, stretched her back, then started rubbing her neck. She needed a break from staring at the yellow legal pad the past thirty minutes—and simply thinking too much, for that matter—but she also wanted to make sure she didn't leave anything out of her statement. She might have been too late to keep Stephen from being murdered, but she could do everything in her power to bring his killers to justice.

A chill swept through her, and she pulled her sweater tighter around her shoulders, realizing how blessed she was to be alive. She still had no idea what Stephen had stumbled into, other than the fact that it had gotten him killed. And now she'd somehow gotten tangled up in the same web. It was a situation that terrified her.

She glanced through the doorway into the open room where several of the detectives were working at their desks and let her mind shift to Nate. She hadn't planned to share with him about Hannah or even Kevin, for that matter. And yet for some reason talking to him about her losses had seemed . . . natural. It was hard to believe she hadn't seen him for so many years.

Back in college it felt as if she could tackle anything and come through unscathed. Then over the years of being a therapist, she'd watched other couples and individuals walk down painful roads, all the while congratulating herself that her life was nothing like theirs. It had taken Hannah's death for her to face the fact that no one was immune to the heartbreak of devastating loss.

That's where she was today. Hanging on to reality by a thread as she worked to keep her emotions stable until she could find a moment alone to deal with her own haunted memories. But she couldn't delve back into the past. Not now.

Paige walked into the room and set a cup of coffee on the desk beside her. "Thought you might need a pick-me-up. Nate dropped me off, then went to grab lunch for us. I hope you like barbeque."

"Sounds great. Thanks." Grace took a sip of the rich brew, then held it up. "This is a lifesaver. I'm starting to feel cross-eyed."

"I'm guessing you didn't get any sleep last night." Paige leaned against the edge of the desk, her eyes filled with concern. "How are you doing?"

"Please don't tell me you're going to start worrying like your partner." Grace shot her a smile. "I'm shook up, I'll be honest, but I'll be fine. I've already spoken to the victim counselor, and she offered me the same advice I'd give one of my patients."

"Which is?"

"That one of the best things you can do after a traumatic occurrence is to take action and do something that can in turn help to overcome the fear and vulnerability. So that's what I'm doing."

"You're exactly right."

"I won't let myself end up feeling like a victim." She took another sip of coffee and focused on the warm sensation. "Finding Stephen's killer is helping me challenge that sense of vulnerability."

Because she'd gone that route before. Caught in the role of a victim, and while she legitimately might have been one, it wasn't a place she was going to let herself stay. Not this time.

"Just remember that knowing what advice to hand out doesn't automatically make it easy to put into practice," Paige said. "Trust me. I know from experience with this job. And you've gone through a lot over the past twenty-four hours."

"I know. But I'll be okay. We need to find whoever's behind this."

"Have you come up with anything you think might help?"

Grace looked down at the notes she'd organized into a makeshift spreadsheet on the yellow pad. "I've been trying to remember everything I know about Stephen. Things he told me during our sessions that might be a key to figuring out what he was working on, as well as a list of family and friends, which, unfortunately, I don't know much about. He was quite reserved, and even in our sessions rarely shared anything about his personal life. He was there primarily to work through his anxiety issues."

"Apparently, he had reason to be anxious," Paige said. "We just returned from talking with his boss, and someone had bugged his office."

Grace tapped her pencil against the desk again. "That would fit. He was certain someone was following him. Like they knew in advance where he would be. And it explains why he left such a cryptic message on my phone."

"Do you know if he had a girlfriend?"

"No girlfriend that I know of, but he does have a sister here in the Dallas area. Kelli's trying to track her down. I figure there might be a chance she knows who the Colonel is."

"That's a good place to start. His boss didn't know much about his family either." Paige pulled up a chair and sat down next to her. "Can I ask you a question, totally personal and off topic?"

Grace cupped her hands around her drink and sat back. "Of course."

"I know it's none of my business, but from what I understand, you and Nate have a . . . history?"

"A history?" Grace let out a low laugh. "Not romantically, if that's what you're implying. He

149

and my ex-husband were close back in college, and we were friends. But it's actually been years since I last saw him, so when he showed up at my door today . . . well, it was quite a surprise, though it was good to see him. I can't believe so much time has passed since I saw him last. We totally lost track of each other, which seems almost impossible in today's social-media-saturated world."

"I was just curious. He's not exactly one to spill his feelings, and I guess I worry about him. Especially with all he's gone through these past few months."

Grace took another sip of her drink. "Now can I ask you about that?"

"Sure."

"This isn't any of my business either, but what you just said might be the answer to something I've been wondering about. There's something different about him. Granted, it's been a long time since I've seen him, but it's like he's been through some kind of trauma. He tried to hide the scars on his arms, but I'm guessing they're connected somehow."

"You know about the hotel bombing three months ago?"

"Of course. Several police officers were killed along with a number of civilians."

"That was his team. He lost his partner and several other close friends that day. And he was

150

left with those scars on his arms. Today's his first day back on the job. He took the losses pretty hard."

"Wow." Grace sat forward in her chair. "I had no idea."

"It's been a rough recovery for him, both physically and emotionally."

"That explains a lot, actually. We were pretty good friends back in college. I remember how protective he was back then, but today . . ." Grace let out a huff of air. "At least I understand where he's coming from now."

"It's been a hard comeback for him. Part of me isn't sure he's ready to be out in the field, but he'd never admit it. And he's been officially cleared for active duty. On the other hand, maybe being back on the job is exactly what he needs. I heard rumors that being off was driving him crazy. He was spending most of his time working out at the gym."

So she had been right. She wasn't the only one with secrets.

Kelli, the squad's tech guru Grace had met earlier, stepped into the room, putting an end to their conversation.

"I have some information you're going to want to hear." She stopped next to them.

Nate walked into the room with a bag of takeout and joined them.

"You're just in time," Kelli said. "I finally

tracked down Stephen's sister. Her name's Jenny Wright, and she lives in Garland."

"Do you have her address?" Paige asked.

"I texted it to both of you," Kelli said. "I just went through the video Stephen's workplace sent over."

"And?" Paige said.

Kelli quickly pulled up some video footage on the computer at the other end of the desk. "I'll need to see if the two of you can identify him, but a man matching the description of the driver from the bank was on it, in the lobby and outside Stephen's office. And get this. The time stamp matches the time you were stuck in the elevator."

"That's definitely him," Nate said.

Paige frowned. "He would have needed help, but it looks as if the computer system of the elevator *was* hacked."

Grace set down her sandwich. "Wait a minute . . . your elevator was hacked?"

"Long story short," Nate said, "apparently he wanted to get those bugs back before we showed up and found them, so he tried to slow us down."

"But Stephen had already found them," Paige said.

"It makes sense," Kelli said. "I delivered the bugs you brought me to one of our analysts, so we should know more soon, but I do know that some of them have microcircuit encoders that both compress and record information."

"They couldn't afford for us to get that information," Nate said.

"In the meantime, we need to go see Stephen's sister."

Grace avoided Nate's gaze. "Let me go with you to talk with her. I know what it's like to receive news that someone you love is gone. It's not going to be an easy call, but we need her. She might have information about who the Colonel is."

"I don't think that would be—"

"I know if it was me, I'd rather have someone who knew him asking me questions, rather than the authorities," Grace said, jumping in before Nate could state his list of reasons she shouldn't go. "You need her to talk, but she needs someone who understands. Besides that, I know it isn't uncommon for officers to take family, friends, or clergy with them to make a death notification. I've had to do it in the past for one of my clients. Let me help. Please."

"She's pretty persuasive," Paige said, looking at Nate.

Nate started pulling out the sandwiches and waffle fries. "I'm starting to remember just how persuasive she can be."

"Funny, guys." Grace frowned. "I'm sitting right here."

"Fine," Nate said. "The two of you can make the call—"

"I'm going to need you to do it," Paige said, digging into the bag of food. "I spoke with Sarge a couple minutes ago. He wants someone to follow up with the medical examiner."

Grace tried to read Nate's expression but came up blank. She could tell he wasn't happy with the situation.

"Fine." He popped a fry into his mouth. "You go see what the ME has for us, and Gracie and I will go as soon as we finish lunch."

An hour later they were walking up to the front door of Stephen's sister's house, and Grace still wasn't sure how he felt. He'd been quiet for most of the ride—distant, really—making her question her request to come along. It was clear he'd have preferred she stay back at the precinct. But it was a little too late for that now. And unfortunately, what Paige had told her had left her with more questions than answers about him. She wished she felt comfortable enough to bring up the subject of the bombing with him, but she didn't. The only thing she did know for sure was that what happened that day had clearly changed him. There was definitely that overprotective vein he'd always had, but it was far more than that. She could sense he was on edge, an underlying result of the PTSD he'd probably yet to deal with.

"Thanks for letting me come," she said as they stopped in front of the red door. "I know you probably don't understand, but I just . . . I need

154

to help. I'll stay in the background, I promise, if you need me to."

"I'll probably be glad in the end you were here with me," he said, knocking firmly on the door. "I've always hated these calls. If you'd like to be the one to tell her about her brother, feel free."

"Okay."

An awkward silence followed until a woman much older than Grace expected opened the door.

"Jenny Wright?" Grace asked.

"Yes?"

"Jenny . . . my name is Grace Callahan and this is Detective Nate Quinn. I'm a friend of your brother Stephen."

"Stephen?"

"Would you mind if we come in for a moment?"

She hesitated before nodding and letting them step in behind her into the living room with a blue flowered couch, matching armchair, and sheer blue curtains.

She motioned them onto the couch, then sat down on the armchair across from them. "I'm sorry for the mess. I worked overtime yesterday and haven't gotten much done this morning."

"No worries," Grace said, wishing now Nate hadn't left the informing up to her.

"Something's happened to him, hasn't it?" Jenny asked.

Grace tried to swallow the lump in her throat. "I'm truly sorry to have to tell you this, but your brother was murdered last night."

Jenny pressed her hand against her mouth as she fought to process the information she'd just been given. "He's dead?"

"We're so sorry for your loss."

Jenny shook her head. "I . . . I don't even know what to say. What happened?"

"We're still trying to put everything together," Nate said, "but it appears he was working for the wrong people and stumbled upon something he shouldn't have."

Jenny grabbed a tissue from the side table next to her and blew her nose. "I . . . I knew something like this was going to happen."

"What do you mean, Ms. Wright?" Nate asked.

"It's Jenny. Please. And . . . I don't know. Nothing specific," she said. "He told me a few months ago that he'd started working on some top-secret project. Something he couldn't talk about. He told me that lame joke of how he'd have to kill me if he told me what he was really doing. And yet, I knew by the tone of his voice that there was a nugget of truth there. And apparently I was right."

"I'm truly sorry, ma'am," Nate said.

The woman turned to Grace, her eyes now brimming with tears. "You said you knew him?"

Grace nodded. "He was under a lot of stress with his job. I worked with him to help manage his anxiety."

"You were his psychologist?"

"Yes."

"I called your office not too long ago. He'd given me your card. Told me how much you'd helped him. He thought I could use a professional to talk to, but in the end, I backed out."

"That was how we were able to track you down."

"I'm his only family left. Our parents were older when they had him. Seventeen years after having me, so you can imagine they were quite surprised."

"I know this is difficult, but would you mind if we asked a few questions?" Nate asked.

"I'll help in any way I can. Even though I'm a lot older than he was, we were fairly close. Of course, it's not always been easy to maintain a relationship. Mainly because he either lived too far away, or because he spent most of his time working. And as you might expect, Stephen was never much of a communicator."

"When's the last time you spoke with him?" Grace asked.

"A week or so ago. He called me. We saw each other every couple of months. It's been nice to have him nearby. He comes by every once in a while and we have dinner." Jenny pressed the back of her hand against her mouth again. "I just can't believe he's gone."

Nate handed her another tissue. "What can you tell me about him?"

"Stephen was pretty complex. On one hand, he was your typical computer geek. He was really into superhero movies and comic books. Always went to those comic con festivals in costume, and he had all of these crazy ideas of saving the world in real life as well."

"And on the other hand?" Gracie asked.

"He had this really sweet, unexpected side. He spent time volunteering his technical skills with a local after-school program." Jenny grabbed a lone throw pillow from the floor next to her and pulled it against her chest. "Can you tell me how he died?"

"He was . . ." Grace hesitated. Why did saying things out loud always make it seem more real? "He was shot early this morning."

"And we're trying to find out who might have done it," Nate said. "Do you know of any enemies he might have had?"

"Stephen might not have had a lot of friends, but enemies? No. I just can't see that. I mean, he spent his days glued to a computer screen. He didn't go out enough to make enemies."

"Do you remember him talking about someone who went by the name 'the Colonel'?" Nate asked. "Maybe back when he was in college?"

"The Colonel. Now that sounds vaguely familiar. I remember he had a few friends. They were all geniuses on the computer. There was an old buddy he had that ended up in the army. I can't remember what his real name was, and I'm sure he wasn't really a colonel, but they all had nicknames."

"Was Stephen still in contact with any of his old friends?" Nate asked.

"I couldn't tell you that. He graduated so long ago. I do remember that he was a part of some computer group that called themselves The Shadow Masters. He thought it was cool. Honestly, I thought it was silly, though now . . ."

"Do you know any of their real names?"

"I'm not sure, but I could probably find out." She glanced toward the adjoining room. "This was the house we grew up in, and he's still got a lot of junk here. I keep telling myself I'll get rid of it one of these days. Now I'm glad I didn't." She drew in a deep breath. "Anyway, I wouldn't be surprised if there weren't some of his yearbooks here. If you'll just give me a minute, I'll look."

Jenny stepped back into the room a few moments later and set a short stack of yearbooks on the table. "I was right, though I haven't looked at them in years."

"I'm sure this will help," Grace said.

"Now, I'm not sure exactly what you're looking for, but I might be able to find a photo of the three of them together." She picked up one of the books, then opened it to the index before flipping through the pages. "Here they are. My brother, Carl Macbain, and Eddie Sumter. I think

I remember Stephen telling me Eddie died a few months ago in a car crash. As for Carl Macbain . . . I honestly have no idea where he might be now."

"Do you remember if either of them went by the Colonel?" Grace asked.

Jenny studied the photo, then tapped her finger on one of them. "Carl. I'm sure of it. He was engaged to . . . what was her name. Madeline Claire, I think. And I believe her maiden name was Waybright. I remember she had such a pretty name, though she went by Maddie. They married after graduation and settled in the area. Of course, that was a long time ago. He joined the military, so he could be anywhere by now."

"Do you know anything else about Carl?" Grace asked while Nate texted a message on his phone.

"No. I'm sorry."

"We probably should go now." Nate stood up and dropped his phone into his pocket. "But we appreciate your help."

"Of course."

"Can I call someone for you before we go?" Grace asked. "I hate to leave you alone."

"Thank you, but I'll be okay. At least for the moment. I think it's going to take a while for this to sink in."

Nate handed her his business card. "If you need anything, or think of anything else that might help, please give me a call."

Jenny nodded. "Of course."

Grace stepped back out into the Texas sunshine with Nate and they headed toward his car. "Thank you for letting me come. I know you didn't want me to."

"It's not that. It's just . . . I'll just say that you definitely knew how to handle that." Something in his voice softened. "Far better than I do. This has always been the most difficult part of my job. Informing a family that their loved one is dead."

"Something like that is never easy."

Nate's phone dinged and he pulled it out. "That was fast. Kelli is still looking for Carl Macbain—a preliminary search came up with nothing—but she did find his wife. She works at a diner not too far from the precinct."

"I don't mind coming with you."

"Not this time," he said, heading toward the car. "Sergeant Addison said he has a few more questions for you, then he'll make sure you get home. He's also promised a detail for your house until we know for sure you're safe."

She opened her mouth to argue, then stopped when she caught his expression. The tone of his voice was all business, as if he were making a conscious play to push her away. But wasn't that the way it should be? Just because they'd once been friends didn't mean he owed her anything in this situation. After today she'd be out of his life again.

14

Nate breathed in the scent of sizzling burgers as he stepped into the twenty-four-hour diner behind Paige. Even at half past three, the place was crowded with customers.

"Excuse me." He approached the counter and showed the hostess with a tired smile his badge. "We need to speak to one of the employees here, Madeline Macbain."

The woman set her pile of menus on the counter. "We've got a Maddie who works here, but her last name is Waybright."

"We'll need to speak with her." Nate scanned the room, wishing they'd found a photo of the woman.

The hostess tapped a stack of menus against her hand. "The boss isn't going to like it. The place is crazy busy right now."

"It's important we speak to her," Paige said.

The hostess let out a sharp huff, then took off across the diner. So much for service with a friendly smile.

A minute later, she returned with a woman in her early thirties, with dark hair and brown eyes, looking as if she'd already worked a double shift.

"Detectives Quinn and Morgan," Paige said. "We're looking for Madeline Macbain."

"That's me . . . but it's Waybright now," she said, hesitating. "I legally changed my name back after a divorce, but please don't tell me there's a problem with my case."

Nate shook his head. "We're not here about your case, we just need to ask you a few questions about your ex-husband."

"It's important," Paige said. "We just need a minute or two of your time."

Maddie glanced behind her toward the bustling diner. "In case you didn't notice, time is something I don't exactly have right now. Things are a bit busy, and I can't afford to lose this job. It's the only thing keeping food on the table for me and my daughter."

"We don't want to be difficult," Nate said, "but we'd rather you didn't have to come down to the station to do this. It's important—"

"So this isn't a request." She frowned, then turned to one of her coworkers. "Get Nancy to cover for me for a few minutes. I'll be right back."

They followed her to an empty table in the back corner of the room and slid into a seat across from her.

"What has Carl done this time?" She leaned her elbows against the table. "Is he in trouble with the law or something?"

"No. We just want to talk to him in connection to an investigation. He's a person of interest, not a suspect." Nate rested his palms against

163

the table. "When's the last time you saw him?"

"I don't know. I've barely spoken to him in almost a year. Not since I gained full custody of our daughter. And to be honest, I really have no desire to see him again. He comes to see Danielle every couple months, but besides phone calls, that's it."

"We need to find him, and right now you're the only lead we have."

"Good luck with that. Carl doesn't exactly want to be found. He lives on some isolated piece of property east of here—somewhere near the Louisiana border, I think—and he purposely stays off the grid, so I'm not surprised you couldn't find him."

"Do you know how we can track him down?"

"All I have is a phone number, but he'd kill me if he finds out I gave out his personal information, especially to the police." She hesitated. "I don't mean that literally, Carl's never been violent, but you know what I mean. It's a private number our daughter uses to call him. Most of the time his phone isn't on, and I think he only has a phone so he can talk with Danielle. I can't guarantee he'll answer a random number."

"How old's your daughter?"

"She's seven. And the one good thing that came out of my marriage. Sorry." Maddie glanced at her watch. "My mom is supposed to pick Danielle up in a few minutes, but she's always running late. Seems to be the theme of my life now. That was the problem in our marriage, to be honest. Carl never had time to deal with life. Like carpool, doctor appointments, homework, making sure she ate healthy."

Nate hated that they'd dragged up a raw point in her life. But they needed to find Carl. "You've never been to his place?"

"No. Like I said, I know it's east of here on some isolated property, but that's it."

"There is one more question we need to ask," Paige said. "Do you remember an old friend of his, Stephen Shaw?"

"Shaw . . . yeah. I recognize the name. I know they were friends back in college, and I met him a few times. They were both conspiracy believers. Carl was always talking about things like Roswell, the JFK assassination, and Elvis is still alive. You can imagine what it was like when the two of them got together. They both had their own theories on everything. I never took either of them seriously. I think it's part of the reason Carl now lives off the grid. He's preparing for the end of the world."

"Is he some kind of . . . prepper?" Nate asked.

"You could call him that. Thirty acres of woods is the perfect place for it."

"What about other friends?"

"I suppose he has a few. Some of his old buddies from the military. A few from college like Stephen."

A little girl with pigtails and a backpack ran up to the table.

"Danielle . . . Hey, sweetie. This is my daughter, Danielle."

"Who are you?" she asked.

Nate held out his badge for Danielle. "We're detectives. What do you think about that?"

"Cool."

"I think it's pretty cool," Nate said. "I get the chance to help people."

Danielle frowned. "And arrest people. My mom's not in trouble, is she?"

"Of course not." Nate shot her a smile. "We visit a lot of people for our job, mainly to ask questions. It doesn't mean the person is in trouble."

Danielle didn't look convinced. "Then my daddy's in trouble?"

"He's not in any kind of trouble either. We just need to talk to him about a friend of his."

"Daddy doesn't like a lot of people, but if you go see him . . ." She glanced at her mom. "Maybe I could go with you?"

Maddie tousled her daughter's hair. "You're going to see him next month, remember, sweetie? And then Daddy's coming to Dallas for Christmas Eve."

Danielle leaned in closer to Nate. "You know my daddy?"

"I haven't met him yet, but I am hoping to see him soon."

166

Danielle dumped her pink backpack on the table, then pulled something out and handed it to him. "I don't see him much anymore, but maybe . . . Will you give him this if you see him? I drew this at school today for him."

Nate took the folded paper. "Can I take a look at it?"

When she nodded, he unfolded the paper to unveil a ballerina all in pink.

"Wow . . . you're quite an artist."

"That's what my mom always says, but she has to. She's my mom."

Nate chuckled. The girl reminded him of his niece. Cute, but with plenty of sass. "Let me ask you this. Are you a dancer too?"

"Ballet. I'm going to be in a recital." Danielle pursed her lips. "You'll give it to him, won't you?"

"As long as it's okay with your mom."

Maddie nodded. "Of course. What do you say to the detective?"

"Thank you."

"You're very welcome. It's not a problem at all."

Danielle leaned forward. "He won't ever tell my mama this, but he gets lonely out there on his land. I need you to tell him I miss him. I know he's busy working and I can't see him right now, but I still miss him."

"I'm sure you do. I'm . . . well, let's just say a

lot older than you, and I don't get to see my dad that much. He lives in California and I miss him too."

Maddie squeezed Danielle in a hug, then kissed her on the forehead. "Grandma's running late, but she'll be here pretty soon. Can you go sit in the front with Paula while I finish talking with the detectives? I'll be by to pick you up before dinner."

Danielle grabbed her backpack and swung it over her shoulder. "You won't forget to give him my picture, will you?"

"I definitely won't," Nate said.

"And no cookies from Paula," Maddie said.

Danielle rolled her eyes. "Yes, ma'am."

Danielle shot Nate a broad smile, then scooted off toward the front of the restaurant.

Paige nudged him with her shoulder. "Looks like you made a friend."

"She's adorable."

"Yes, she is," Maddie said. "She has juvenile diabetes and a serious sweet tooth. But sometimes that's an easier battle to fight than the one with her father. I . . . I know he loves her. He just . . . he doesn't know how to show it."

"Looks like she's got you to keep her grounded," Paige said.

"I hope so."

"Is there anything else you can think of that might help?" Nate asked.

"No. Not now. I'm sorry." Maddie ripped off a page from her order pad and scribbled a number on it. "You can try to call him, but I can't make any promises."

"Thank you." Nate handed her a business card. "And if you do think of something—or if you hear from him—please give us a call."

A minute later, Nate stepped outside the busy diner, glanced at the slip of paper, then punched in the number. He let it ring a dozen times before hanging up. No answer. No voice mail. More than likely it was a burn phone.

"I'll keep trying, but it looks like Maddie was right," he said, heading for the car.

"You're pretty good with kids," Paige said, slipping into the passenger seat.

"My sister and her husband have three. Two boys and a girl a year younger than Danielle. I spend as much time with them as I can." He started the car, then pulled into traffic. "What about you? Do you and Doug plan to have kids?"

"I don't know. If we do, only one . . . two at the most. And I'm not even sure I'm going to do that. Juggling a full-time job and motherhood . . . well, let's just say I'm not sure how it would work."

"I think you'd make a great mom."

"No. I make a great aunt. I spoil my brother's kids when I see them twice a year, but then I get to send them home. It's the perfect combination. And so much easier. I don't have to worry about bullies or social media or them getting sick. I've seen too much in this job. The world is just too scary for this generation."

"That's why the world needs more mothers like you."

His mind shifted to Gracie as he called the number a second time through the car's hands-free system. Her daughter had been about Danielle's age when she'd died. How did a parent even begin to cope with something like that? He couldn't imagine the loss she had to have felt. And then losing Kevin on top of that?

"Nate . . ."

"Sorry. I was thinking." He shifted his thoughts back to the phone call. "He's still not answering."

"He's got no reason to answer a strange number."

"Wait a minute." Nate turned on his blinker, then made a U-turn.

"What are you doing?"

"Maddie said he wouldn't answer if it wasn't a call from his daughter's phone. Let's make it a call from Danielle."

Nate found an open parking spot in front of the diner and pulled in before jumping out of the car and heading back inside. Danielle was still waiting next to Paula near the front of the restaurant.

Nate grinned at her. "Hi again, Danielle."

"Did you forget something?" she asked, jumping down from her chair.

"We need to talk to your mom again."

Danielle pointed to the other side of the diner.

Nate and Paige and Danielle walked back to where Maddie was bussing a table. "We'd like permission to call Carl from Danielle's phone. He's not answering."

"Okay . . . Danielle, can you give them your phone? The only numbers in the contacts are mine, my mom's, and Carl's. His speed-dial number is three."

"Thanks."

Nate punched the number.

"Danielle?"

"Mr. Macbain . . . my name is Detective—"

"Where did you get this number?"

"I'm here with your ex-wife, and it's very important I speak with you."

"Is my daughter alright?"

"She's fine."

The line went dead.

Nate frowned. "I think it's time we brought in the local sheriff."

15

Nate stood in front of the whiteboard they'd set up in the noisy bull pen, with a photo of their victim, mug shots of their suspects, and the timeline they'd pieced together. So far it seemed all they had was a collection of misaligned clues, leading to a possible security breach they'd yet to identify. All tied to the murder of one man.

"We might be looking at two murders," Paige said, stepping up beside him with a bottle of water.

"What do you mean?"

"Kelli just gave me what she found on Eddie Sumter, the third guy in the yearbook picture. He died seven months ago. The ME ruled it as a suspicious death, but his findings were inconclusive and no arrests were ever made."

Nate set his hands on his hips and turned back to the board. "Okay, let's assume for a minute there's a connection between Eddie and Stephen's murder. What if before Stephen they worked with Eddie?"

"Kelli's working to get Sumter's bank account information to see if we can find a connection there." Paige took a sip of her water.

"What about the sheriff?" Nate asked. "Has he had any luck with Macbain?"

"He just called. So far Macbain isn't responding, and they're not even sure he's on the property. And as for Macbain himself, it's strange what we're finding . . . or rather what I'm not finding. There's very little about him out there. In fact, it's almost as if he didn't exist beyond the typical motor vehicle records, voter files, and property tax assessments, which are pretty hard to get rid of. On a personal level, for example, there's nothing out there on him. No social media, period. No search engines, including Google, chat rooms, or images. Not even an email address . . . It's as if the man doesn't exist. And this time we're not talking because of a fake name and license."

Nate turned back to the board, wanting to make sure they hadn't missed anything. "Then we need to go over what we do know about him again. Why did our victim feel it was so important we speak with him? Let's see if we can come up with another way in."

"Okay . . ." Paige pulled the rolling chair from her desk and pushed it in front of the board. "We already know he's divorced with a daughter, and from what we both saw at the diner, I don't believe there's much contact between Macbain and her. Looks like it was a nasty divorce and the wife gained full custody. He lives alone in some kind of eco-friendly house with solar panels and a well. He was honorably discharged after eight years with the army where he worked as a cyberterrorism specialist. After that, he pretty much disappeared and his trail goes cold."

"That seems odd. That's got to be a pretty huge switch. Going from a tech expert to living off the grid?"

"I thought the same thing."

"Nate?"

He turned around at the sound of his name and felt his heart tremble. "Gracie . . ."

He took a moment to study her big eyes staring back at him. He shifted his gaze and took in her black jeans, blouse, and jacket. He was still convinced she hadn't aged a day since college. There was something calming about her presence, despite everything that had gone between them. She was someone he wanted to spend the afternoon catching up with. Someone he wanted to get to know again. He pushed away the thoughts.

"Sorry," she said. "I didn't mean to interrupt. I just finished giving my statement, and came to tell you both goodbye before I headed out. It was good to meet you, Paige, and Nate . . . maybe we'll reconnect again someday."

"I'd like that," he said, at a sudden loss for words.

"Do you mind staying a few more minutes?" Paige asked. "I'd like to know what you think about this Carl Macbain . . . the Colonel. Psychologically speaking. The guy used to be a techie and now lives off the grid."

"Of course. Anything I can do to help."

Nate frowned as Paige motioned for Gracie to grab an empty chair.

"What you're saying actually makes perfect sense." Gracie avoided Nate's gaze. "There are actually thousands of people doing what Macbain is, and they leave their 'normal' lives for just as many reasons. There are people who worry about the economy and political arena. People who want to live simply, without anyone telling them what to do. And it's becoming more and more common."

"How do you know so much about living off the grid?" Kelli asked.

"My father was one of those men born in the wrong century. As soon as I graduated from college, he and my mother did what he'd been dreaming of for as long as I can remember. They sold everything they had and bought over three hundred acres of land in Montana. They live in a house they built themselves and are cut off from the rest of the world for a chunk of the year when the snows come. He—admittedly more than my mother—loves it."

"I'll bet it's beautiful up there, but wow. I can't imagine living there year-round, in that cold and snow." Paige shivered. "I think I'd rather live on a deserted tropical island. Of course, I'd have to have Wi-Fi and—"

Nate chuckled. "You wouldn't make it a week, Paige."

"Thanks." Paige scowled at him. "Back to the topic at hand. The sheriff also confirmed that Macbain comes into town every once in a while for supplies. But he isn't fond of visitors. He's had a few run-ins with trespassers and an ongoing feud with one of his neighbors. We have no reason to get a search warrant, and we can't force him to talk with us. And like I said, at this point, they can't even be sure he's there."

"I'm not surprised they weren't welcomed on his property," Gracie said. "It fits his profile. Men like Macbain move off the grid to avoid encounters with the law, and everyone else, for that matter."

"What's our next move?" Nate asked. He didn't like the idea that Gracie was involved in the conversation, but at the moment he didn't have a choice. "We've got a man murdered, some kind of major security breach about to take place, if our guess is right, and Carl Macbain, our only lead, is unreachable."

Gracie grabbed the arms of her chair and caught Nate's gaze. "Let me call him."

Nate frowned. Hadn't they already discussed her *not* getting involved? "Excuse me?"

"It might be a long shot, but let me try. I knew

Stephen, and Macbain might talk to me because of that connection. It might be the one open door we have."

Nate's jaw tensed. "You're supposed to be on your way home."

"Maybe, but I can't just sit at home after everything that's happened."

"Yes, you can—"

"Nate . . . Let me try to talk with him. Nothing can happen to me sitting here in the precinct while talking on the phone. I've spoken with the victim counselor, and she can verify that I'm fine, if that's what you're worried about."

"I'm not worried about that, I just . . ." Why was he always searching for excuses to protect her? "We have no idea who all is involved in this. You were kidnapped this morning and barely escaped with your life. I can't let that happen again. We don't know anything about this guy other than the fact that he lives off the grid. He won't respond to our calls or the sheriff's, which doesn't sound very stable to me. And after talking with his ex-wife, I'm pretty sure she'd agree as well."

"While all that's true," Paige said, "she has a point, Nate."

Great. Two against one again.

"All I know is that Stephen trusted him," Gracie said. "And you need him in order to figure out what's going on."

Paige handed her a cell phone and the number. "Call him. Maybe you'll get further than either of us."

Gracie nodded, avoiding Nate's gaze as she punched in the numbers, then put the call on speaker. The phone rang a dozen times, then went dead.

"Let me try one more time," she said.

The second time it rang five times before someone picked up.

"Mr. Macbain?" she said.

"I don't know who you are or how you got this number, but I don't want you—"

"I'm a friend of Stephen Shaw." She jumped in before he could say anything else.

Nate was expecting Macbain to hang up. Instead, there was a long pause on the line before he said anything. At least she'd gotten his attention. "Who is this?"

"I'm a friend of Stephen's. Grace Callahan."

"Are you with the police department?"

"No. I knew Stephen. He told me to call you."

"If Stephen needs to talk with me, he can call me himself."

She looked up at Nate, who nodded. "I'm sorry to have to tell you, but Stephen . . . Stephen was murdered early this morning."

Macbain gasped. "What happened?"

"Stephen was in trouble. I don't know what's going on, or who killed him, but I think there's going to be some kind of dangerous security breach somewhere. He said that you were the only person he knew who could stop what was going to happen."

"What did he mean by dangerous security breach?"

"I'm not sure. Possibly some kind of cyber-attack. That's why I'd like to meet with you in person."

Nate shook his head vigorously, but she ignored him.

"He's really dead?" Macbain asked.

"Yes."

"What did he tell you about me?"

Gracie handled the question like a pro. Her information might not have come from Stephen, but she didn't miss a beat. "I know you live in east Texas. That you were married and have a daughter named Danielle. I know the two of you went to MIT and have been friends since then. That you were in the army . . ."

Let it be enough, God. Please . . .

There was a long pause. "Come in the morning. I'll talk with you, but no cops. And no games."

"I'll need your address."

Paige handed her a pad of paper and pen and she scribbled down the address.

"Thank you, Mr. Macbain. I'll be there."

The line went dead.

Nate felt his anger simmer as he grabbed the

phone off the desk. "You will not be there in the morning. What were you thinking?"

"Nate . . . Grace just nabbed us our only lead. We need her."

"Why should we agree to his terms? Why would he agree to talk with you in the first place?"

"Because I'm not the police. I'm a friend of Stephen's."

"I still don't like it."

"I don't like it either," Paige said, "but it's the only way in, Nate. We have nothing to arrest him for, no search warrant. If it's the only way we can get him to talk to us—"

"There has to be another way."

"I'm open to suggestions, but at the moment, we're running out of time and ideas."

Gracie stood up. "Can we talk for a moment? In private?"

He led her toward the empty break room, his anger still simmering.

"Listen," she said, once the two of them were inside. "You've made it perfectly clear you don't want me involved in any of this, and I understand. But I'm a big girl, Nate. I can handle this. And we both know, at this point you need me."

"We can find another way in. The FBI's getting involved, which means at some point, Macbain is going to be forced to cooperate. But the bottom line is that we don't know anything about this guy, and on top of that, you've been through a

180

lot today. I can't ask you to get involved in this."

"You can't, or won't? Because in case you didn't notice, I'm not your former partner."

A sudden deafening silence filled the room at the trump card she'd just pulled out.

"Ashley has nothing to do with this—"

"I'm sorry." She took a step back and pressed her lips together. "I shouldn't have brought that up. But Nate, I'll be okay. Let me do this. I need to do this."

He struggled to press down his anger. "How did you know about Ashley?"

"I asked Paige to tell me what happened. I'm already involved in this, and I want to help. Macbain was Stephen's friend. He's offered to talk with me. We can't afford to pass this up."

"And if something goes wrong? If it turns out to be some kind of trap?"

"He's smart enough to realize I won't really be alone. Right?"

He stared past her out the window. Clouds had begun to form in the sky. While the last couple days had been warm, cooler temps would be coming soon. How was he supposed to deal with her?

"Maybe, but I still don't like this. I'd have no way to ensure your safety."

"That's just it." She brushed her hand across his arm before pulling away. "I've learned there are no guarantees in life. There's nothing you or anyone else can do to ensure nothing goes wrong. That's why sometimes we have to take risks and do hard stuff. And I'm telling you, I'm okay with that."

"Nate . . ." Paige stood in the doorway of the room. "We could send her in with a wire and have a team ready to move in if anything goes wrong."

He let his mind run through the scenario. How had they gotten to the point where they were considering bringing in someone with zero field experience?

"Do you have a better idea?" Paige asked.

He glanced at his partner. "We could send someone in undercover. Someone who's had training—"

"He'd know," Gracie said.

Nate turned to her. "What do you mean he'd know?"

"This guy was military. You don't think he'd know if a cop walked onto his property?"

"So I'm supposed to send you in against this guy we literally know nothing about."

"Stephen wouldn't have told me to talk with him if it was going to risk my life. Macbain can help, and we've got to gain his trust."

"She's got a point," Paige said. "Again."

"I'll wear a wire—or whatever it is you use these days—so you can hear everything," Gracie said. "But this isn't going to end in a shootout.

I'm not going in to interrogate him. Just to see what he might know about Stephen. That's it. Nothing more."

"We can hook her up with a wire, if that will make you feel better, Nate, but she'll be fine."

He was overreacting and he knew it, but he couldn't stop the panic reeling in his gut. "Your role is simply to gain his trust, so he will agree to talk with me."

Gracie nodded.

"I'll need your phone."

"My phone?"

Twenty minutes later, Nate stood in front of Gracie, still certain he was going to regret what they were planning to do. He stuffed down the remaining irritation from knowing Paige had told her about Ashley. Because both women had been right about one thing. Gracie wasn't Ashley. She was simply going to get them in to talk to Carl Macbain. As soon as she did, they'd both go back to their own lives.

"This is what you'll go in with tomorrow. We don't actually use old-fashioned wires very much anymore." Nate handed her iPhone back.

"So . . . this is my wire? My phone?"

"It's also the perfect cover. And pretty cool, actually. Everyone has a phone, so he won't think anything about it if he happens to see it. We use an app running in the background that's undetectable. It sends us your audio through your iPhone to whoever we need it broadcast to."

"Okay . . . it sounds complicated."

"Not at all," Paige said. "And we'll organize to have backup ready in case you need it. Not only will the audio let them know if they need to get involved, but the conversation will be recorded as well."

"Don't I need a code word in case I get in trouble?" she asked.

"You want a distress word?"

She smiled up at him and shrugged.

"How about 'monkey'?" he offered.

The word slipped out before he had a chance to think. He'd forgotten the nickname until just now. Another memory surfaced. She had loved coming along when he and Kevin went indoor rock climbing. She'd always been faster than both of them, and somehow the nickname Monkey had stuck.

But that was a lifetime ago.

"How am I supposed to work that into a conversation?" she asked.

He laughed for the first time all day. "I have no idea, but knowing you, you'll find a way."

16

Grace studied the car's GPS at just past eleven the next morning, then told Nate to take the next left on the gravel road that was lined with pine and oak trees. "Looks like Macbain's place is about two miles ahead on the right."

"If you want something isolated," Nate said, "this is definitely the place to buy property. You wouldn't have a neighbor for miles. Not sure I could handle the isolation."

"Maybe not, but you have to admit it is beautiful out here."

She snuck a glance at his profile, still surprised he'd actually agreed to go along with the plan for her to talk to Macbain. Because clearly, he hadn't been happy about it from the very beginning. She knew he would have much preferred for her to stay at home with police protection outside her front door. She'd also noticed how he'd become really good at keeping her at arm's length. Their conversation since leaving the precinct this morning had been friendly, yet noncommittal. Nothing too serious, and definitely nothing personal. But how could she blame him for guarding his heart? Hadn't she done the same thing over the past few years?

The entire trip here they'd talked about everything from their favorite foods to movies to books, and in the process, she remembered just how much they used to have in common. The past decade had mellowed him, but in a good way. He'd grown spiritually, and their conversation had revealed things about him that made her wish for a chance to get to know him again.

She pushed away the desire. Her heart might have healed with a few scars in place, but the thought of dating again left her with an uneasy feeling in her stomach. Becca had set her up twice on blind dates, and both times she'd walked away promising herself to never agree to another setup. At least not until she met the right person on her own. And Nate definitely wasn't that person. All he probably saw in her was a divorcée with baggage, including a truckload of grief and loss.

"Would you want to live out in the middle of nowhere, like this place?" Nate's question pulled her back to the present.

"I told you about my father's property up in Montana and how he pretty much tries to live off the land. So I've seen what it's like firsthand. And I'll have to say I'm with you on this one. I can stay a week or so with my folks, but beyond that, I miss civilization."

Nate laughed. "What does your mother think?"

"She threatens to move to Florida every winter, but I can't imagine them living anywhere else." She glanced at the GPS again. "Stop here."

Nate slowed down in front of the six-foot woven-wire gate. "Are you sure? We should still have another half a mile till his gate."

"I need to drive the rest of the way alone." Grace unbuckled her seat belt, waiting for his reaction. "Carl Macbain is both tech savvy and paranoid about the government, which means he's probably going to have security cameras on his property. If I show up with a police escort, he'll know. Paige is right behind us. You can wait with her, and if I need you, you won't be far."

"Gracie, this wasn't a part of our agreement—"

"Maybe not, but you know I'm right, even though you're worrying and still hoping to come up with a way to talk me out of it."

"I never said that."

"You didn't have to. But Carl Macbain is a recluse, not a serial killer."

"Actually, we don't know that."

"Funny. And now you sound as paranoid as the man behind the fence."

"You can say what you want," he said, putting the car in park, "but I still don't like this. Look what happened when we went to the bank."

"I'm fine, and I'll be back soon. I promise."

"You still need to try to get him to agree for me to come in."

She shot him a grin. "Worried you're going to miss out on all the excitement?"

"Hardly. I just want . . . I want you to be safe."

"I will be, Nate."

"Do you have your phone?"

She patted her jacket pocket. "Yes."

"What's the distress word?"

"Monkey. Now stop worrying. I'll be fine."

"There is one more thing," Nate said.

"What's that?"

"I almost forgot." He pulled something out of the center console. "This is a picture his daughter Danielle drew. She misses her father and asked me to give it to him if I saw him."

"I can do that."

He squeezed her hand before getting out of the car, leaving her shaken by the jolt of emotion his touch left. "Just be careful, Monkey."

Grace slipped into the driver's seat, put the car in gear, and headed down the gravel road lined with woods on both sides. A minute later she came to a gate that stretched across a driveway lined with shrubs and tall pines that blocked her view of the house. She slipped her canvas bag over her shoulder, exited the car, then headed through the open gate and up the long drive. She'd tried to hide her fear from Nate. Fear that something would go wrong. That she hadn't completely weighed the consequences of her actions. She drew in a breath of fall air. The temperature had dropped to the low seventies as predicted. The property was edged with heavy woods on either side, with no-trespassing signs every twenty feet or so and, she was sure, hidden cameras. She couldn't help but wonder what would happen if someone decided to ignore the warnings.

She counted her steps until she got to sixty, then stopped. Ahead, she could finally see the house. The structure itself was simple, with solar panels on the roof and a complex gutter system. Apparently totally off the grid.

Macbain met her at the end of the drive with a Rottweiler leashed on one side and a rifle on the other. She swallowed hard. The dog she could handle—maybe—but the rifle? She hadn't expected that, though she should have. Of course he'd come armed.

"Grace Callahan?"

"Thanks for agreeing to see me."

"Sorry for the frosty welcome. I've had a few threats by trespassers who aren't exactly stopping by to be neighborly."

The guy is definitely paranoid. "What kind of threats?" she asked, praying he didn't let go of the dog's leash.

"Does it matter? I'll just say there are people who think I'm a bit crazy living out here like this and like to remind me of that."

"I'm not sure why. I think it's beautiful out here. And as long as you aren't bothering anyone, who cares." She paused, needing to find a way to connect with him. "My father moved up to

Montana and built himself a place off the grid. He's never looked back. I got used to a garage full of water, toilet paper, and peanut butter."

"Really?" The confession seemed to surprise the man. "My ex-wife thinks I've lost it."

"My father sees it as a way to save money and was able to retire early. Besides that—" she let out a soft laugh—"whether something happens or not, he'll never run out of anything."

"I've got a year's supply of food, everything from sugar and salt to rice and beans, a solar oven, heirloom seeds, water, medical supplies. A house that's self-sufficient, between the woodstove, solar panels, and rainwater collection system. I even have a composting toilet and shower. Because the day will come when everyone is going to wish they'd been prepared."

"My father used to say you were a survivalist if you know the shelf life of a can of Spam but have no idea how long you've had an open jar of mayonnaise in the fridge. And let me tell you, he fit the bill." She studied his demeanor. He seemed calm and relaxed.

"My wife used to laugh at me when I had to make a run to the store when we were down to a dozen packages of toilet paper. But I'm telling you, one day that stuff's going to be worth its weight in gold."

She started to ask him about his weapons, then stopped. Her father had a .22LR rifle, a .223 for hunting, and plenty of ammo, but he never talked to people about that collection. She'd found their connection. Which meant she'd pushed enough for the moment.

She studied his face. Except for his long beard, he appeared pretty clean-cut, and neatly dressed. Something she hadn't expected. After talking to him on the phone, she'd imagined him to be rougher around the edges.

"Did you build the house yourself?" she asked.

"Every square inch. But you're not here to talk about my prepping habits."

"No, I'm not."

"How did Stephen die?"

"He was murdered."

"How?"

"He was shot, but the police aren't sure at this point who did it. When's the last time you saw Stephen?"

"We go all the way back to college, though it's been, I don't know . . . probably five . . . maybe six months since he called me."

"So, you didn't really stay in touch?"

"I lost touch with a lot of people after I moved out here. I'm not a big fan of the internet and social media, and that includes emails and phone calls."

The edge was back in his voice. She had a feeling he was ready for her to get to the point, then get off his property.

"Listen, I know you drove all the way out here to talk to me," he said, "but I really don't have anything else to say. I agreed to speak with you because you told me you were a friend of Stephen's, but I haven't seen him in years, so I'm not sure how I can help."

"I am—was—his psychologist, but I'd been worried about him. He was in over his head on some kind of project he got involved with."

"Something connected with his murder?" he asked.

She nodded.

"Look. I am sorry he's dead, but I don't know what I have to do with this."

"He told me to come see you."

His gaze narrowed. "Why would he say that?"

"That's what I need to find out."

His dog pulled on the leash and started whining. Macbain took off the leash and gave a command. Immediately the dog headed for the house.

Grace paused, then pulled her phone from her pocket. "This is the last message I received from Stephen. I need you to listen to it."

"I don't know if—"

"Please."

He nodded and she let the recording play.

"If things turn out the way I think they might, I'm going to need you to get ahold of the Colonel. He's the only person I know who could actually stop this. Because if they use what I have, the fallout's going to be huge. I know . . . I know you think I'm acting crazy and maybe I am, but I've seen now what they can do and I don't know how to stop them."

"What's he talking about?"

"He worked with computer security, so I'm guessing some kind of computer malware he was working on. But that's why I'm here. Two nights ago, someone broke into my house. They were looking for something Stephen gave me."

"What did he give you?"

"The key to a safe-deposit box where he'd put evidence of what he was involved in."

"And were you able to get what was inside it?"

She shook her head. "I only saw some of it. There were some maps and flash drives, but long story short, the bad guys got everything but one drive I managed to snatch."

Macbain ran his fingers through his hair. "What exactly are you asking me to do?"

"Here's what I know. Stephen was into computer security, but also had experience as a hacker. We know that the two of you worked together back in college. He clearly believed you could help with what he was involved in."

"But you don't know what it was."

"I don't. But if you'll agree to talk to the investigating detective, it might help. His name is Nate Quinn and I promise you can trust him."

Macbain folded his arms across his chest and

stared at the ground. "You need to understand that normally I don't let people on my property, and I definitely don't let cops on my property."

Grace frowned. She needed something. Some kind of leverage to get through to him. She glanced at Macbain's gun that he'd propped up against a tree.

Nate was going to kill her, but it was worth a try.

"You target practice?" she asked.

His gaze narrowed. "Spent the morning shooting, why?"

"I'll make a deal with you. Best out of five. I win, you help us. I lose, and I'll walk away."

"You're kidding, right? You don't look like much of a sharpshooter."

"Maybe not, but we need your help, so I'm willing to do what it takes."

"How about with a bow and arrow?" he asked.

She watched as he studied her expression. "Fine."

"Then follow me."

He headed toward a more secluded part of the woods surrounding the house. Nate was not going to be happy about this. But that didn't matter at this point. She had to win this bet.

Macbain stopped at a clearing where a bow rack hung secured to a tree and took down a bow and an arrow.

"Ladies first."

"That's our target?" she asked, turning to the other end of the clearing about sixty yards away.

"It might be a little rustic, but I made it myself out of recycled lumber."

"Looks like it'll do fine." Grace hesitated, wondering how she'd ended up in the middle of the woods with a complete stranger whose only connection to her was a murdered client. And on top of that, wagering a ridiculous bet that she had to win.

"A fifty-pound bow, might be a bit heavy for you," he said, handing her the bow.

She ignored the comment and concentrated instead on the task at hand, remembering what her father had taught her. She had no idea that shooting with him on her last visit to Montana would prepare her for a moment like this. Sturdy grip on the bow, but not too tight . . . She aimed at the target, then let go.

The arrow hit the top left of the target.

She frowned.

Macbain let out a low laugh. "My turn."

Grace hesitated, then handed him the bow.

His pierced the target an inch to the left of the bull's-eye. He was definitely a good shot.

"My turn again," she said.

"You might want to quit while you're behind."

She made sure her stance was balanced. Feet shoulder-width apart and perpendicular to the target. Align the target, use the shoulder muscles, slowly pull the arrow back. Index finger above the arrow, middle and ring finger below it.

She released all three fingers at the same time.

Bull's-eye.

She quickly pulled another arrow out of the quiver, let it fly, then pulled out another and another in rapid succession. She lowered the bow.

She'd managed to find her groove. All but one had hit the bull's-eye.

It took Macbain a few seconds to find his voice. "Where did you learn to shoot like that?"

"Deer hunting with my father. He didn't have any sons, so I was his camping buddy. Hunting buddy . . . climbing buddy . . . you name it."

"Most people stick with rifles and shotguns."

"Bows are silent, for starters. On top of that, you can run out of ammo, but you can always make another arrow."

He stared at her, clearly unsure how to take her. Grace held his gaze. "What about our deal?" she asked. "Either you beat me, or you agree to talk to my friend."

"Our original deal was no cops."

"Fine." She handed him back the bow. "My father also used to say that one's integrity was of far more value than one's possessions. Though there's one other thing I forgot about."

"What's that?"

Grace pulled out the picture Nate had given

her. "This is from your daughter. She gave it to the detective who went to see your ex-wife. He promised he'd give it to you. She misses you."

Macbain unfolded the page. "Do you have kids?" he asked.

"I had a daughter."

"What happened to her?"

"She died from cancer when she was five."

"I'm sorry."

"Me too." She drew in a deep breath and prayed for wisdom. "I don't know exactly what's at stake here, but there's more to think about than just yourself—"

Grace jerked around at the sound of a gunshot. The hairs on the back of her neck stood on end as she tried to ascertain where the shot had come from.

"What was that?"

"Remember when I told you I've been having trouble with a neighbor?" Macbain grabbed her arm. "I'm hoping you're not about to meet him."

17

Nate stood at the gate listening to the audio transmission of Gracie's conversation with Macbain. Did she really think he'd wait a half mile away while she talked to a crazy hermit? He was betting on Macbain coming outside to talk to Gracie, away from any surveillance screens he'd have inside the house. But even being this close didn't stop the gnawing anxiety in his gut. What in the world had inspired her to hinge his interview with the man on an archery bet? Winning wasn't going to get her off the hook, as far as he was concerned. He never should have brought her here and let her go in alone. Hadn't he already learned that lesson? She was strong, he knew that. But strong didn't always win.

"She's really gotten under your skin, hasn't she?"

Nate glanced at Paige, who'd waited with him along with a third car for backup in case things went south. "She's vulnerable, after everything that's happened."

"Vulnerable is the last word I'd use for her."

Maybe.

He pressed his finger against his earpiece and focused his attention back on the audio coming from Gracie's phone.

"I had a daughter." Gracie was talking again.
"What happened to her?"

"She died from cancer when she was five."

"I'm sorry."

"Me too . . . There's more to think about than just yourself—"

The crack of a gun echoed in the distance.

Gracie said something he couldn't understand.

"We're going in now," Nate shouted. "You two split up and take the perimeter. Keep your radios on. We need to know where that shot came from."

Nate started running down the long drive. Had he heard the distress word? No. He was sure he hadn't. Which meant he was probably overreacting. It was hunting season, and no doubt these woods were filled with deer, quail, and turkey. But he wasn't taking any chances.

A branch snapped beneath his foot. He turned to the left as an explosion ripped through the trees in front of him. He could feel the heat burning the hair off his arms. He wiped the beads of sweat from his brow and started running toward the burning house. Gracie was in there. He had to save her . . .

A second later it was all gone.

He stopped in the middle of the drive. Silence surrounded him. He was imagining things. There was nothing there. No explosion. No fire. Nothing.

Nate's radio buzzed. "Looks like the shot came

from a couple of teens target shooting. Everything's fine."

Everything was fine. Maybe, but he needed to be sure.

"Wait for me at the gate," Nate said. "I'm going in to talk to this guy."

He ran the rest of the distance to the porch of the small wooden cabin. Forget what Macbain had said about trespassers on his property. He was finished playing games.

A man came around the side of the house with a rifle aimed at him. "Who are you?"

"Detective Nathaniel Quinn." Nate aimed his own weapon back at the man before holding up his badge with his other hand. "Put the rifle down now."

"It's okay, Nate," Gracie said, stepping out from behind Macbain. "You heard the shot?"

"I just got the report that it was a couple teens out doing some target practice near your land," he said, still holding his gun steady. "Put your weapon down so we can talk."

Macbain hesitated another second, then leaned his rifle against the porch railing. "Those boys are always causing trouble. Shooting BB guns at my dog. Setting off fireworks. Local law won't do anything about it, let alone their parents."

"I'm sorry about that, but as you know, that's not why I'm here."

Macbain glanced at Gracie and frowned. "She

did win our bet—though something tells me you already know that. I still don't think I'm going to be any help, but I'll give you five minutes, then I want you both gone."

Five minutes. Nate frowned. Nothing like good ol' southern hospitality.

"When's the last time you heard from Stephen?" he asked, reholstering his weapon.

Macbain shoved his hands into his pockets. "I lied earlier. Stephen called me last week."

"What did he want?"

"He was scared. Told me how he thought he was working for the FBI, but then he realized that the people he was working for weren't using the information he was coming up with to stop hacking. Instead, they were using his programs to gain access to classified information and steal login and password credentials."

"Why call you?"

"He needed some advice. He had no idea what he'd gotten into or, for that matter, how to get out. He also thought they might try to recruit me. He didn't have any proof yet—for any of it—but he said he was getting close. Sounds like maybe he found what he was looking for."

"And was murdered for it," Gracie said.

Nate studied Gracie's expression. She seemed fine, but he wanted her out of here. For the moment, though, he was going to have to take advantage of Macbain's seemingly cooperative mood.

"What kinds of computer stuff did you do together when you were back in college?" he asked.

"Mostly a lot of dumb pranks, like flipping computer screens and rearranging the keyboard so it couldn't be typed on properly. We realized from the beginning that as fun as hacking was, we didn't want to end up in prison, so we made sure we never stepped over the line. But Stephen was always light-years ahead of me. He was brilliant when it came to coding and solving security issues, which was his specialty. He'd find the vulnerabilities for companies and fix them." Macbain turned to Gracie. "You mentioned there were some maps in the box you saw. What kind of maps?"

"What do you mean?"

"Was there anything distinct about them? Markings, gridlines . . ."

"I didn't see much, but the country was divided into three colors, I believe. Most of it was two colors, and there was another color at the bottom."

"Give me a second." Macbain headed up the porch stairs and into the cabin. A second later, he returned with his computer and the dog. "Bear, sit."

Bear immediately sat.

Macbain punched in a website, then flipped the screen so she could see the photo he'd pulled up. "Like this?"

"Yeah, exactly like that. What does it mean?"

"I can't be a hundred percent sure, but in putting all this together, it actually might make sense."

"What do you mean?" Nate asked. The man's demeanor had changed. No longer was he focused on getting them off his property. He was actually working with them.

"We know Stephen got involved with the wrong people," Macbain said. "Someone who was exploiting his expertise to find vulnerabilities in security systems. We also know it was something that would have a huge fallout if implemented. Why else would these people risk murder charges? I believe what you saw was a map of the electric grid. What if Stephen was hired to find a vulnerability in one of the national grids with the intent of taking it down?"

Nate let out a low whistle. A cyberattack would have its own set of serious repercussions, but taking down the grid . . . "Explain to us how something like this could happen."

"The simplest way to explain it is that the electric grid for the US is made up of a very complex network of power plants and transmission lines, with most of it privately owned. Most people probably assume there is only one national power grid, but there are actually three main grids that are interconnected and cover the United States. The Eastern, Western, and Texas."

"Texas has its own grid?" Nate asked.

Gracie let out a low chuckle. "What else would you expect? This is Texas."

Bear picked up a ball from the porch and brought it to Macbain.

"On top of that," Macbain said, taking the ball out of the dog's mouth and throwing it across the yard, "parts of the grid are actually shared with Canada and Mexico."

"What happens if a section of the grid goes down?" Nate asked.

"Most of the time, nothing serious. Everyone knows that it's common for sections of the grid to go out temporarily, primarily because of severe weather, but that's not the only reason." Macbain set the computer on the wide porch railing. "Back in 2003 there was an outage across a large section of the United States that was caused by a software bug. In this case there were thousands who didn't have power for a couple of days, because what should have been a manageable localized blackout ended up cascading into a widespread power outage."

"I remember that," Nate said. "What other reasons would the grid go out for?"

"In 2013 there was a sniper attack on a substation in California that caused $15 million in damage. The engineers were able to reroute the lines and keep the power on. But you can imagine what might have happened if they hadn't been able to fix it. The government is continually working to protect the grid from cyberattacks. Their major concern is that even if security is breached, the grid continues with critical functions."

"Which is what Stephen thought he was helping to ensure," Gracie said.

"That would be my guess. What experts are worried about is not just a hack but a cascade effect that could potentially take down the entire grid."

Nate glanced out across the yard as Bear retrieved the ball before running back toward them. "Guess that's why you live here?"

"It's always been a part of my motivation. Because it will happen one day. Criminals target various infrastructures, not just here, but in Europe as well. Power grids, water supplies . . . taking down the grid would automatically destabilize— perhaps even destroy—the US economy. And what makes it scary is that some of these hackers are actually backed by other governments or even some terrorist organizations. There is compelling evidence that if only nine of the fifty-five thousand substations went down, we'd be talking coast-to-coast blackouts for at least eighteen months."

"Eighteen months would devastate the country," Gracie said.

Bear stopped in front of Macbain, ready to continue their game. His owner wrestled the ball from the dog's mouth, then threw it back across the yard.

"But while there's been a push to physically secure the substations, cyberattacks are a constant threat. And my guess is that if anyone could come up with a way to find vulnerabilities, that person would have been Stephen."

"So you really believe he thought he was working for the FBI?" Nate asked. "He didn't know he was working for the other side?"

Macbain shook his head. "Stephen was no black hacker, and I find it hard to believe he'd knowingly do something like that."

"What would be the motivation behind something like this?" Gracie asked.

Bear dropped the ball halfway back, then ran after a squirrel.

"Money, which is why cybercrimes are what you normally see," Macbain said. "Today, data theft goes way beyond just your credit card. Information is hacked from social media sites like LinkedIn and Twitter and sold to the highest bidder. There's also money to be made off of hacked medical records. Stolen IDs can be used to submit fake insurance claims."

"But the electricity grid. We're talking about something that will completely change our way of life," Nate said. "How long are we talking?"

"That depends on a lot of things. They might simply find a way to temporarily shut down the grid like in the Ukraine. But if they found a way to actually destroy the components that run the grid, we'd be looking at a completely different situation. Months, if not years, of downed power."

"So how do we stop this from happening?" Nate asked.

"The only thing I can think of is if Stephen came up with a security patch that would fix the vulnerability he found."

Gracie looked hopeful. "Maybe the patch is on one of the flash drives from the safe-deposit box. Maybe that's what Stephen wanted me to have."

Nate turned back to Macbain. "And if the patch isn't on one of the flash drives . . . could you write one?"

Macbain laughed. "Not by myself. Stephen was the genius. I was always just his sidekick. At MIT, the three of us worked on one serious project and created a worm. It was similar to the Stuxnet worm released a few years ago that seriously damaged Iran's nuclear capabilities. We eventually stopped working on it and promised each other we wouldn't finish it."

"What could it do?" Nate asked.

"If you know anything about Stuxnet, you know that the worm didn't damage the computers themselves, because they were not its real target."

"What do you mean?" Gracie asked.

"Stuxnet was built to go beyond simply stealing

information from its targeted computers. It went straight to the control systems of factories, chemical plants, nuclear power plants—"

"And electrical grids." They'd already brought the FBI in on this, but what if they couldn't stop the threat? "Could this worm, if modified, take down the grid?"

"It's possible. And if he wasn't working for our government and that information got into the wrong hands . . ."

He didn't have to finish his sentence. They all knew what the outcome could be.

Macbain's brow furrowed. "There was this fourth guy."

"What was his name?" Nate asked.

"Donnie Banks. He was smart, but was always a bit of a loner. He hung out with us a few times, but never quite connected with us."

"Did he know about what the three of you were working on?"

"He probably had an idea. And he was jealous. The three of us were getting awards and he couldn't quite measure up. I can see him involved on the wrong side of something like this."

"Do you know what happened to him?"

"Honestly, it's been years since I even thought about him. I think he floated from job to job for a few years, then I lost track of him. Last I heard he was living in Houston, but that was several years ago."

Nate frowned. The clock was ticking and they still didn't know exactly what they were up against.

"Come back to Dallas with us," Nate said. "Clearly Stephen thought you could help stop this. If you could work with our techs to find out what Stephen was working on, maybe you could find out what his solution was."

Macbain looked at his watch. "I'm sorry, but your five minutes is way over, and I have no desire to get involved with your people or the FBI—"

"Stephen believed you could stop what they are doing," Gracie said. "If the people who killed him have his work, the authorities are going to have a hard time stopping them."

"You don't get it, do you? I don't hack anymore, good or bad. I spend my time working on upping the production of my solar power, and I've just started beekeeping. That's it."

Nate hesitated, then pulled out the one card he still had. "I met your daughter yesterday. I'm the one she gave the drawing to."

Macbain frowned. "Don't go there."

"I also understand she's a diabetic," he continued.

"I said, don't go there."

"You do realize what will happen if the grid goes down?" Nate said.

"I don't need to answer that again."

"Is your ex-wife prepared?"

"Hardly. Like most of America, she lives in a house run by electricity, drives a fully computerized car, and relies on her smartphone."

"Which means your daughter will be right in the middle of it," Gracie said. "ATMs won't work, the banks will stay closed, and once cash becomes worthless, which it will, people will have to barter in order to survive. There will be no cell phones and no way to communicate. What happens to the police and firefighters at that point? What happens when the electricity goes out? There will be no fuel, and no water, which means no flushing the toilet and no clean water. Law and order will break down. It's going to be chaos."

"Of course, people like you will be fine," Nate continued before the man could argue again. "At least for a while. You'll have food. But for how long? What if the grid is out for six months . . . a year . . . eighteen months? Can you last that long with what you've got right here? How much jerky, dried fruit, and MREs do you have?"

"And what about Danielle?" Gracie said, desperate now. "Those who rely on lifesaving medications won't be able to get what they need because pharmacies will be stripped bare."

"Stop."

Bear tore around them, then dropped the ball in front of his owner. Macbain picked it up and

210

squeezed the ball between his fingers. Nate studied the man's body language and caught the tension. It was too bad life wasn't as simple as a dog's world where there was nothing more to do than play catch and run across the open field chasing squirrels. Whether either of them liked it or not, they needed Macbain, and they had to find a way to convince him to come back with them.

"Whoever is behind Stephen's death might not have what they need at this point," Nate said, "but I'm sure it won't stop them from figuring out the rest of the puzzle. We've got to find a way to stop this."

Macbain let out a sharp breath. "Even if I wanted to help you, I'm not sure I could."

"Stephen wouldn't have told me to come see you if he didn't believe you could do something," Gracie said.

Macbain threw the ball again for Bear to chase.

Nate tried one last time. "Come with us back to Dallas."

"Fine. But I'm only doing this because of my daughter."

18

Gracie had fallen asleep in the passenger seat next to him, while Macbain snoozed in the back on the long drive to Dallas. Nate gripped the steering wheel, willing his body to relax. The past two days had pushed him emotionally, and the events that had triggered flashbacks hadn't helped. At least despite the possible far-reaching effects of the case, Gracie was safe, and they'd managed to convince Macbain to return with them. The FBI was being brought in to meet with them first thing in the morning, which was going to change the dynamics of the case. Whether for good or bad, he didn't know, but he wasn't going to worry about that today.

Gracie groaned softly beside him and opened her eyes.

"Hey, sleepyhead," he said.

She tugged on the seat belt and leaned back against the headrest. "Sorry I fell asleep. I didn't realize how tired I was. I think I'm still in a bit of a fog."

"You haven't exactly gotten a lot of rest lately."

She shot him a sleepy smile. "No, I haven't."

"I know today hasn't been easy, but you've been a trouper. And in the end, it turned out to be worth it."

"Admitting I was right again?"

"I don't think I'll answer that question."

She stared out the window and laughed. "Well, I might end up sleeping the next twelve hours after everything that's happened, but I needed to be here."

She had needed to be here, and she'd been right again. Now he was just ready for all of this to be over. The soft glow of the city lights that were coming on shone in the distance. It would be dark soon, but their work had only just begun.

"Have you ever thought how much we rely on electricity?" he asked, not wanting to imagine what would happen if someone was actually able to take down the grid. "Cell phone chargers, air-conditioning, the internet, refrigeration or heat in the winter . . ."

The list of things that would be affected was endless.

"My father always talks to me about what will happen," Gracie said. "Every Thanksgiving he gives the same speech to the family, wanting to make sure we're ready in case we have to live off the grid. I guess I never thought it would really happen, but after all I've seen the past couple days . . . I think I might have been wrong."

"It's unnerving, if you ask me."

Because it wasn't just the lights that would go out in a society completely dependent on electricity. Companies would shut down, along with critical services like telecommunications, banks, emergency responses, and water supplies.

Nate glanced in his rearview mirror, monitoring a pickup coming up fast behind them. He took his foot off the accelerator as he went around a curve. If the driver was in that much of a hurry, he could go ahead and pass them.

But instead of passing as the road straightened out, the vehicle zoomed up within inches of their bumper.

"Gracie . . . Macbain . . . we've got a problem."

"What's going on?" Gracie turned around to look out the back window as the pickup smashed into the back of Nate's vehicle.

Nate gripped the steering wheel, determined to keep his vehicle from running off the road.

"Both of you . . . get down."

The back window shattered. Nate pressed on the accelerator. He had no idea who was behind them, but they'd clearly stumbled into the hornets' nest that had gotten Stephen Shaw killed and now wanted them stopped. Or dead.

The truck slammed into them a second time as Nate fought to keep his car on the road.

"Gracie . . . I need you to contact dispatch on my phone, then put it on speaker. And in the meantime, hang on. I'm going to try to outrun him, but this guy means business."

"Give me a sec . . ."

"This is Detective Quinn en route to Dallas

with two civilians," he said once they'd been connected. "A vehicle is trying to run us off the road and they're armed, and I need you to send backup immediately."

He quickly gave the dispatcher their location, hoping they could get there quicker than Paige, who was at least twenty minutes ahead of them.

The woman's voice came over the speakers. "I'm sending backup to your location now. Can you get me a plate and description of the car?"

"If you can speed up, I should be able to read it," Macbain said from the back seat.

Nate pressed on the accelerator. Macbain read off the numbers on the plate while Gracie passed them on to the dispatcher.

Nate searched for options as the other vehicle again began to narrow the distance between them. If he'd been alone or with his partner, he could take more of a defensive stance and try to end this, but with both Macbain and Gracie involved, he wasn't going to risk their lives any further than they were already being threatened. And on the narrow, curvy road, there was nowhere else to go.

"Nate . . ."

"I see it."

"What's going on?" Macbain asked.

"There's an embankment to our right with the lake below and nothing but a guardrail to stop us."

If the truck shoved them off the road, they'd end up in the water.

"Can we outrun them?"

"I'm trying."

The road made another sharp turn. The pursuing vehicle hit the tail end of their car. Nate felt the tires skid beneath them.

"Hang on!" he shouted.

The car smashed through the guardrail and flew down the embankment. Seconds later, Nate felt the impact as the car hit the lake and immediately began filling with water as it floated away from the bank.

He undid his seat belt and reached for Gracie, who was struggling with her own seat belt. "Are you okay?"

"I can't get my seat belt off."

He caught the panic in her voice. The water rushing through the car felt like ice. With the back window shattered, they had a few seconds at the most to get out of the car before it sank beneath the surface.

"Move your hands, let me try."

She nodded as he pushed on the release button. Nothing.

God, please . . . we need a miracle.

Hypocrite.

The word that flashed through his mind after his prayer took him by surprise. He didn't remember the last time he'd actually prayed. The word was true. Why was it that most people called out to God only when their lives were on the line? Like he was some genie in a bottle just waiting for their latest request.

He pushed on the release button again and this time it came undone.

Nate grabbed her hand and started pulling her out the back window.

Where was Macbain?

The car was filling up fast, and there was no sign of him.

Fighting the current, Nate managed to pull her out of the vehicle and toward the surface, but there was still no sign of Macbain. Nate tightened his grip on Gracie's hand. The other man must have made his way out of the back window as soon as they'd hit the water.

Something slammed into him and he lost his grip on Gracie. He swam to the surface and searched the dark water for her.

"Gracie?"

She had to be here, but he couldn't find her. One second she had been right beside him. The next second, she was gone.

God, no. I can't lose her . . .

By now the car had filled with water and was sinking. Nate drew in a lungful of air and dove down into the murky water. She had to be here somewhere. She couldn't just vanish. But it was too dark to see. Fear swallowed him. Fear that

217

Gracie and Macbain hadn't surfaced. Fear that he couldn't save her. But she'd just been here.

God . . . you let my team and twelve other people die in that explosion. Let me find Gracie. You owe me that much. Please. It can't end that way again.

His lungs felt as if they were about to burst as he headed once again for the surface. He treaded water, searching for her. She'd made it out of the car with him. She had to be nearby.

"Gracie! Macbain!"

He turned in a slow circle, but darkness had already settled above the lake. Something bobbed in the water to his left. His heart raced and he swam toward it. A plastic bottle. He smacked the top of the water with his hands in anger.

"Gracie! Where are you?"

A pair of car lights hit the water from the shore, illuminating a slice of the darkness.

He didn't want to leave her here, but he needed help.

He started swimming for the shore.

An older man helped pull him out. "Are you all right? We saw a car go over and called 911."

"I'm fine, but there are two more people out there. I can't find them."

"Help is on its way, but you're far from fine. You've been injured."

He followed the man's gaze to a gash on his shoulder. Blood had soaked his torn shirt and ran down his arm, dripping onto the ground, but

218

he felt nothing. Strange. He must have cut it on the rear window of the car, but at the moment he didn't care. All he cared about was finding Grace and Macbain.

"How far out is your vehicle?" the old man asked.

"I'd guess twenty feet. Both of the other passengers got out. I just don't know where they are." He started back for the shoreline. "I need to go out there—"

"You can't. You've lost a lot of blood."

"That doesn't matter."

"He's right."

He turned to see his partner behind him. "Paige?"

She didn't wait for him to argue. "What happened?"

"We were run off the road. Gracie and Macbain are still out there. I lost them . . ."

Paige immediately started shouting orders. Sirens screamed in the distance as more law enforcement and an ambulance arrived.

"We're going to find them, but I need you to let them work."

"No." Nate stumbled as he headed back toward the water. "I need to be out there looking for her—"

"You need to stand down, Nate." Paige grabbed his arm and turned him around. "That's an order. You're injured."

"I don't care. I just want to find her."

"So does everyone here. Let them do their job."

"And if she dies out there?"

"I promise that these men are going to do everything they can to find her. They're already coordinating boats and divers—"

"This is still a rescue operation."

"And no one is saying otherwise. But we need to be ready for anything."

"Please. Let me help. I'm qualified—"

"I can't take that risk."

"I need to do something."

"I've got two things for you to do. One, you're going to be looked at by the paramedics, and two, you're going to tell me exactly what happened."

He could hear the motor of a boat revving, casting a light across the water as it headed away from the shore. She walked him to a waiting ambulance, where a paramedic started cleaning up his shoulder.

"There was a truck that came out of nowhere, shooting at our car and trying to run us off the road. We were able to give dispatch a license plate. They shot out the back window. I lost control of the vehicle when they rammed the rear end and it plunged into the water. The last time I saw Gracie, she was headed for the surface, but with the current and the darkness . . . I couldn't find her."

"There's already a BOLO out on the vehicle.

We will find it. Were you able to see who was in the other car?"

"No. Everything happened too fast." A commotion caught his attention near the shoreline. "What's going on?"

"Stay here . . . I'll find out."

Panic washed through him like the swollen current in front of him as the paramedic finished wrapping up his shoulder. He was there again. Surrounded by the heat of the explosion. The acidic scent of death swirling around him.

The uniformed man finished working on his shoulder.

Nate spouted his thanks, then shot out after Paige. "Who is it?"

"It's Carl Macbain," she said, turning around and catching his gaze.

"Is he alive?"

"Yes, but they're going to take him to the hospital and treat him for hypothermia."

"And Gracie?"

Paige hesitated. "They haven't found her yet."

He tried to refocus his mind. He had no idea how much time had passed. Or how long someone could survive out there. He felt in his pocket for his watch, but it was gone. What did it matter? Nothing but seeing Gracie alive could help him now.

God, I can't go through this again. Please.

He'd shoved God into a box. Used him when

he needed him or wanted something. And now that he needed him, he was ready to bargain, or beg, or whatever it took to get what he wanted. Except that wasn't how things worked. Not in this life. He knew that. Prayers went unanswered. People died.

He knew because it was happening all over again.

19

Nate sat on the tailgate of one of the police vehicles with a blanket someone had given him wrapped around his shoulders while he waited. His hands shook as he took a sip from a steaming mug of coffee. He stared out across the water and at the lights reflecting in the darkness, unsure if he'd ever be warm again. He had no idea how much time had passed, but there was still no sign of Gracie.

Still no sign God was going to answer his prayer.

A wave of guilt pressed in around him. Maybe if he'd prayed more, gone to church more, somehow done more, maybe God would have heard him tonight.

"Nate?"

He turned at the sound of his name, then swallowed hard. "Pastor Rawlings."

One of the volunteer police chaplains stepped in front of him, favoring his good leg. Cameron Rawlings was thirty-three years old, with two little girls and a third one on the way. He'd lost his leg in an IED explosion on tour in the Middle East. He'd come home a changed man with a determination to make a difference in the world, despite what had happened to him. Which had always made Nate question his own response to tragedy. Like the fact that the last time he'd been to church had been before the bombing.

He had, though, gone to the pastor's office a few times after the bombing, trying to make some sense out of the world. But if he lost Gracie today, he'd know that making sense of his life was a hopeless cause.

"We were at my in-laws' nearby, and I heard about the accident on the police scanner," Cameron said. "When I heard you were involved, I had to come."

"She's gone." Nate stared out across the dark water. "One minute she was there next to me and the next . . . I don't know what happened."

"Who's gone?"

"Her name's Gracie. I hadn't seen her for years. Our paths crossed on this case."

"How did you know her?"

"Back in college we were pretty good friends."

"There's still a chance she's alive out there."

"You've always been an optimist, Cameron, but I'm so tired of life snatching away people I care about."

He knew he wasn't making sense, but he didn't care. What he really wanted to do was tell the man that he couldn't understand loss. But he knew that wasn't true. Cameron understood loss more than most people.

Nate bit the inside of his lip. He didn't need

to talk, he needed to do something. Everything about this situation reminded him of what he'd lost three months ago, and if he could stop this, maybe he could stop the helplessness and vulnerability he still felt.

"Sorry, I'm not exactly in the mood to talk," he said, cupping his hands around the hot drink. "I need to be out there looking for Gracie, but instead I'm stuck here, watching in the background."

"You've been through a lot these past few weeks. I imagine this is a reminder you'd rather do without."

"I don't need a babysitter, Cameron." He didn't even try to stop the flare of anger.

"Nate, I'm here to help. Nothing else."

"Then convince the captain that I should be out there helping find her. Not sitting on the sidelines."

"Those guys looking for her know what they're doing. They'll find her."

"You don't know that."

Nate glanced down at the man's prosthesis, regretting the sharp words as soon as they came out of his mouth. On the outside, except for his slight limp, a stranger wouldn't be able to tell what the man had gone through. Half a dozen surgeries and a year-plus of therapy had come with its own demons to tame. Nate knew that living in a fallen world meant tragedies would happen—his career choice had taught him that. But it couldn't ease the agony of the moment.

"I'm sorry," Nate said, setting his half-empty drink down beside him.

"You don't have anything to be sorry about. This can't be easy on you."

He wanted to blame God. Blame anyone. Or if nothing else, turn back the clock so none of this happened. His decisions had brought Gracie into this, and now there was a good chance she wasn't coming out of that water alive.

And it was his fault.

He shifted his gaze back to Cameron. "I should never have done this."

"Done what, Nate?"

"Come back to work."

"You weren't ready?"

"I'm not sure I'll ever be ready, but what's the point? I risk my life and for what? So a bunch of evil people who don't care about anyone can wreak havoc and end up ruining other people's lives. It doesn't matter how much we do or how hard I work to stop them. Because you know what happens when we stop them? Someone else takes their place. And then someone after that one and someone after that one. And for what? If she's dead, she died for nothing."

"I don't know how this is going to end, but you are right about one thing. There will always be evil in this world."

"Man's free will. I know. But that's an awfully convenient excuse for God to be able to blame man for something he could stop if he wanted to."

"Maybe you see it that way because you forgot one thing."

"What's that?"

"There's another side. We will escape the evil of this world one day. Jesus already won the battle on the cross."

Cameron's words threatened to seep past the hardened exterior Nate had formed around his heart. He'd grown up in church. Learned to sing the books of the Bible and quote dozens of memory verses. But all that wasn't enough at the moment. Today had placed him in the middle of a battle he wasn't sure he wanted to fight anymore.

He glanced up and caught Cameron's gaze. "What you're saying may happen in the distant future, but that doesn't erase the grief of right now."

"No, it doesn't. And yet while everything around you seems to be falling apart, I have no doubt that God is still working. He's still in control as he works out his plan for humanity. A plan that is so much bigger than you and me."

"And in the meantime, I'm supposed to what? Keep beating my head against the wall while people around me keep dying?"

"Maybe that's the problem," Cameron said. "Every day you see the worst of humanity. Then on top of that, the news cycle reflects more bad news. It's easy to forget that there's good out there as well. Not everyone's intent is evil."

"Maybe, but that won't bring Gracie back."

Nate stared out across the water. A boat light flashed in the distance, but so far none of them seemed to be coming back to the shore. Where was she?

"What happened to your shoulder?" Cameron asked.

He looked down at where part of the blanket had slid down his arm. "It's nothing. I cut myself on the back window of the car."

"You're starting to bleed through the bandage. I can call over one of the paramedics—"

Nate grabbed his arm. "Please . . . It's fine."

Cameron shoved his hands into his coat pockets and faced Nate. "There is something you've missed in all of this."

Nate sat quietly, waiting for him to continue. "What?"

"Every person at this scene right now is fighting to save a young woman's life. And they'll do it, even if it means risking their own lives. And you do make a difference." Cameron didn't wait for him to respond. "Every time you go out on the streets, you make a difference. You stop those who have broken the law from doing it again."

"But what about those I can't stop? Like the ones who killed Ashley and maybe Gracie?" He could feel the battle for his heart raging within him, pressing in against his chest. "Tell me where God is right now."

"Right where he's always been. It doesn't matter what is happening around you. He is here."

Nate shook his head. "I just don't know anymore. I've seen too much brokenness."

"So has he, Nate."

The pastor's words sent a chill down Nate's spine. He turned away and stared back out over the dark lake. If anyone was going to die tonight, it should have been him. Not her.

"She lost her daughter," he said, finally. "Her husband walked out on her. And now she ends up dying in the dark. Alone."

"You really care about her, don't you?"

He pulled the blanket closer around him. When did it get so cold? "She made me remember a time when I had faith in the world. When I believed I could take on the devil himself and win. But now . . . if I lose her, it's like all of that is lost again. Because what's the point of any of this? We live, we love, we hurt, we die, but in the end . . . there's just so much pain."

"You've been through a lot, Nate. You need to give yourself time to work through what you're feeling."

"That's what everyone keeps telling me, but

I'm not sure I know how." Some days he felt too fractured and broken to be able to move on. "What am I supposed to do?"

"What you've done all this time. Keep praying. Keep searching. I might be a pastor, but I'll be the first to claim I don't have all the answers."

"And right now?" Nate asked.

He knew the reality of the situation. The water temperature was probably around sixty, maybe sixty-five. If they did find her alive, there was a chance she could survive, but exhaustion or unconsciousness would come quickly. They needed to find her.

"I think it's time we both prayed for a miracle."

Nate bowed his head and felt a sense of peace surround him for the first time in days. A minute later, someone shouted from the shoreline. He opened his eyes. A boat was coming in fast. He started toward the water. They were pulling her out of the boat. Rushing her toward the ambulance.

"Nate . . ." Paige was there, running toward him. "She's alive, but they need to take her to the hospital now."

Nate turned to the pastor. "Do you mind giving me a ride?"

"Not at all, let's go."

An hour later, Nate paced the empty hospital waiting room. He was still so cold. Even with the dry clothes and jacket they'd picked up at Cameron's in-laws' on the way, he was still shivering and had yet to warm up. Or maybe it wasn't just the cold water he'd been in that had him shaken to the core.

A woman stepped into the room with a large canvas bag slung over her shoulder and a plastic water bottle in her hand. Nate worked to place the familiar face.

"Becca Long?" He stood up and walked toward her. "I'm Detective Quinn. We met at Gracie's house yesterday."

"Of course. I just got a message that she'd been in an accident. Something about her car going into the water. I had to have my husband drive me here, my hands are still shaking so bad. He's . . . he's parking the car." She drew in a deep breath. "Please tell me she's okay."

"I haven't been able to see her since they took her in there, but I do know that she was conscious and talking."

"Okay . . . wow. That's a good sign." She dropped her purse on the floor and slumped down onto one of the chairs. "This all seems so surreal. Seems like we were just planning my son's birthday party and now . . . She could be dead."

"I know." He sat down across from her. "They're working on warming up her core temperature and making sure all of her vitals are stabilized."

"So she'll be okay?"

"She has to be."

"How did this happen? She told me she had police protection outside her house last night, so I didn't need to worry."

Nate hesitated. "I took her with me to interview a witness in the case—"

"That homicide case? Are you crazy?" Becca bolted upright in her chair. "We're not talking about some misdemeanor. We're talking murder. Why in the world did you let her go with you?"

"Trust me, if I had known that taking her would end like this, I wouldn't have let her go with me. This . . . none of this was supposed to happen."

"Then why did it?"

He wished suddenly he hadn't told Cameron he could go back to his in-laws' anniversary party so the pastor could answer the woman's questions. But maybe it was okay if he didn't have all the answers.

"I don't know."

Her gaze seemed to pierce right through him. "She's not a cop. She's a psychologist. And after everything she's been through, she didn't need to be out there on police business."

"I know, and this is completely my fault." He had no desire to rationalize what had happened in the past twenty-four hours. There was no way to explain just how wrong everything had gone. But it had.

"I'm sorry." She waved a hand in the air. "I shouldn't yell at you. I'm just upset. I know Grace well enough to realize all of this was probably her idea. That's who she is. I just can't imagine losing her."

"How long have you known her?" he asked.

"We met at the gym before she moved out east. We ended up bonding over kale smoothies, and she became like a sister to me. I was going through a difficult time in my marriage, and she seemed to always know what to say."

"She's always been like that. I'm guessing that's why she became a psychologist."

She let out a low laugh, then pressed her lips together. "Seems like a lifetime ago."

"I met her in college. Back then, though, I was close friends with Kevin. I guess you knew him?"

"Yeah. He wasn't a bad person, but man, he made some bad choices. I guess difficult circumstances stretch people, make them consider doing things they never would have imagined otherwise."

"Tell me about it." He'd never even thought about walking away from his job. Not until tonight. Now, somehow, walking away had become a desirable option. Gracie had managed to become his breaking point.

Nate stood up as a doctor stepped into the room.

"You're the detective here waiting for Ms. Callahan?"

"Yes . . . is she okay?"

"She's going to be fine. I'm sorry to have taken so long. Her core body temperature is back to normal range. Any longer in that water could have been a lot more serious. We're going to keep her overnight for observation."

"What about Macbain?"

"He's going to be fine as well."

"Can we see Grace?" Becca asked.

"Your name?"

"Becca Long."

The doctor nodded. "She's in room 312. You've both been cleared to see her, just don't stay too long. She's going to need to get some rest over the next few days."

A minute later, Nate walked past the officer standing guard over room 312, then stopped in the doorway while Becca marched in. He stood, watching Gracie for a moment before he said anything. How had she managed to break through the walls of his heart in such a short time?

Gracie gave her friend a hug, then glanced up at the doorway. "Nate?"

"Hey." He moved to the end of the bed, suddenly feeling self-conscious.

"They told me that you and Macbain are okay."

"We are, though you had us worried for a while." He studied her face. It was pale and there was a bruise on her right cheek, but other than that she looked fine. "One minute I had you in my grasp and a second later . . . you were gone."

"The current dragged me out, but there were a couple guys out on a boat who found me struggling. Ended up saving my life."

"I thought I lost you." He felt his voice crack. "I never should have let you get involved in this."

"If I remember correctly, I was the one who insisted on coming. What happened to your shoulder?"

"It's nothing. Just a scratch." He glanced down at his stained shirt and noticed that his injury was starting to bleed again, but that was the least of his concerns at the moment. "You're the one I'm worried about. I'm so, so sorry this happened."

Becca held up her hands. "Why don't you both stop blaming yourselves and just be thankful that you're both safe. If you ask me, that's all that really matters right now."

He nodded at Becca. "You're right." Then he turned again to Gracie. He needed to change the subject. Ensure that nothing personal was said, because that wasn't a place he was prepared to go. "Listen, my boss told me I could stay until I knew you were okay, but I've got to go back to work and finish up some paperwork."

"I am okay. Really."

"If it's not too late when I'm done, I'll try to stop by on my way home."

Gracie smiled up at him. "I'd like that."

"Okay. I'll see you later then."

He rushed out, feeling more like a fool than a proficient officer following up on a case. Because somehow he'd already allowed this case to become too personal.

20

A couple hours later, Nate strode through the darkened halls of the hospital with a gift for Gracie in his hand. It was well past visiting hours, but the nurse at the desk had told him Gracie was awake, and as long as he promised not to stay long, he could see her. She'd also given him permission to bring her a surprise. He heard monitors beeping as he walked down the hallway to number 312. He'd checked with CSU at the crime scene, but they hadn't come up with any leads. Which meant they were no closer to finding out who'd shoved them into the water. It was always possible that a lead would turn up—especially come morning, with daylight, they might be able to find something.

But for the moment, it felt as if the death of Stephen Shaw had signaled the beginning of a chain of events that was rapidly spiraling out of control. If Macbain's assumption was right, and they were looking at someone trying to take down the grid, the impending result would be devastating, not just to the state of Texas, but to the entire country and beyond.

Pushing aside his concerns for the moment, he stopped at the door of Gracie's room, showed the guard his ID, then stepped into the room. She lay on her side in bed, and he was unsure if she was still awake or not. Her dark-blonde hair lay fanned out across the pillow. An IV was attached to her arm, and monitors quietly gauged her vitals in the background. Ten years had seemed to ground her, and even the losses she'd experienced hadn't completely taken away the spirited woman he remembered. And as far as he was concerned, she looked just as beautiful as she had back in college. But that wasn't the only thing that had his heart pushing him in a direction he had no desire to go.

He was reminded of how close he'd come to losing her today. How much it mattered to him personally that she stayed safe. And how a part of him was enjoying getting to know her all over again. He drew in a slow breath, trying to settle his conflicting emotions. Maybe he should wait to see her tomorrow. He turned around.

"Nate . . . ?"

He stopped and turned back toward her.

She pulled herself up to a sitting position, readjusting the pillow behind her. "Hey."

"Hey, yourself. I wasn't sure if you were awake."

"I'm tired, but finding it hard to sleep. I can't stop my mind from racing."

"Are you feeling up to a visitor for a few minutes?"

"Definitely."

"I know you should probably be sleeping, but selfishly I'm glad you're still awake. I just wanted to check on you. See how you're doing before I head home for the night."

"That's sweet of you. I'm fine, but as you know, they're making me stay overnight for observation, even after I insisted I'd be fine going home."

"They're right." He sat down next to her on the side of the bed and handed her two pudding cups. "I wanted to buy you some flowers in the gift shop, but it's closed. I did manage to talk one of the women running the cafeteria into getting me these."

"Chocolate pudding?" Gracie laughed. "You remembered my chocolate obsession."

"Has it changed?"

"Not at all."

Nate pulled off the lid, stuck in a plastic spoon, and handed the pudding to her. "I remember a lot of things, including your sweet tooth."

She took a spoonful, then smiled. "You must also have known that I'm hungry. They brought me some soup, but I'm still starving."

"An appetite sounds like a good sign. I'm sure I could scrounge up something more substantial than chocolate pudding, if you'd like. Or there's always a fast-food place close by that's open twenty-four hours."

"No. This is perfect, as long as you promise me that second one is for me as well."

He laughed. "It's all yours."

She took another spoonful of pudding. "Have

you found out anything about who hit us?"

"Nothing yet. I went back to the crash scene, but the crime scene unit hadn't found anything significant by the time I left to come here."

"What about Macbain?"

"He's going to be okay. They discharged him about an hour ago. The department put a detail outside his hotel, just in case." He caught the shadow that shifted in front of her eyes. "How do you feel? Physically, I mean."

"Honestly?" She tugged the blanket up around her. "Like I was hit by a bus. Lots of aches and pains I can't even explain."

He'd felt the same way after the bombing. He'd found bruises and cuts he didn't remember getting, and his entire body ached as if he'd been in a car accident. According to his shrink, it was all a normal part of the trauma he'd gone through and the wearing off of the adrenaline.

He shook off the memories.

"I just keep telling myself that it could have been so much worse," she said.

The thought was sobering. If whoever tried to run them off the road had fully succeeded in their plan, neither of them would be sitting here right now.

"You're okay," he said, "and that's all that matters. I'm trying not to think about what could have happened."

"I think the reality is hitting." She stuck her

240

spoon into her pudding. "I can't stop reliving the accident. The moment the car hit the water. Feeling the coldness that took my breath away, and the terrifying feeling of not being able to breathe. The moment I realized I had no idea where you were."

He wished he could erase the past forty-eight hours for her and make it all disappear. "I'm so sorry."

"I'm not blaming you, but you have to remember that while this is your job, I'm not exactly used to having my life in danger. I've never been so scared, Nate. I think it was even worse than the bank fiasco."

She dropped her empty pudding cup onto the bedside table, then pulled the blanket tighter around her.

"Your part in it is over, Gracie. And I'm going to keep you safe, no matter what that takes." He knew what it was like to be plagued by memories that haunted him, not only in his dreams, but while he was awake as well.

"Do you have any idea at all who is behind this?" she asked.

"Besides the fact that it has to be related to Stephen's death? No."

"We don't know who killed Stephen, who grabbed me at the bank, who's behind trying to take down the grid, or what information they have."

"The FBI is now officially involved, and we're going to find these people and put an end to this." Because they had to. There was too much at stake not to.

She pulled the lid off the second pudding. "I have to say, this is the best pudding I've ever had."

"I'm happy to be the one to bring it to you then."

"Kevin used to bring me boxes of chocolate when he traveled to Europe on business. He always claimed it was the best chocolate in the world, but I'm not sure." She shot him a smile. "You just might have him beat with this."

"Did you know that I had planned to ask you out before you and Kevin started dating?" He asked the question before he thought about it, then quickly shifted his gaze to his hands.

"Seriously?" She took another bite. "Did Kevin know that?"

"Yes, but when I mentioned it at the time, he told me he'd already asked you out, so I dropped the idea."

"And started seeing Kara Whitmore, as I remember."

Nate chuckled. "Now that's a memory I'd rather keep buried."

"She was . . . interesting."

"That's one way to describe her, though I can think of other ways. Too loud, too clingy, too entitled."

"But still, somehow I'm surprised neither of you ever told me you'd thought of asking me out."

"I'm sorry. I probably shouldn't have brought up Kevin."

She shook her head. "Please. You don't have to tiptoe around the subject. I know the two of you were close. I loved Kevin, but that part of my life is over, and I've accepted it."

"When I found out how he felt about you, I decided to back off. We were best friends. I didn't want a girl to come between us."

Gracie scraped out the last bit of pudding, then set the spoon and empty container on the bedside table beside the first one. "Hannah's death came between us. When she died, I couldn't find a way to reach him. He kept slipping away from me until I finally realized he was gone and not coming back."

He wasn't sure how she'd managed to handle losing both her daughter and her husband without it crushing her spirit and her faith. But that was a conversation he'd leave for another day. For now, she needed her rest and he needed to leave.

"Do you need anything before I go? A deck of cards? A book? Another pudding cup?"

She laughed and shook her head. "I'm good. But thanks."

"Okay. Then I should go. I just wanted to check on you one last time before I went home and grabbed a few hours of sleep myself."

"Good. I'm glad you're going home to sleep. I know you must be exhausted too."

"Fatigue comes with the territory."

"I hope not too often. At least not a day like today." Her smile faded. "What do you think the driver of the pickup wanted? If he wanted us dead, it seems like there are dozens of easier ways than running us off the road."

"I don't know, but what I don't want you to do is worry. You're safe here. We've got an officer on guard outside your room. And I'll be back first thing in the morning to check on you."

She brushed her hand across his arm and looked up at him. "Thank you."

"For what?"

"For picking this week to come back into my life."

Her voice managed to feed a fire that had already been lit. He pulled away from her touch. How was it that her presence made him feel like running and yet at the same time more alive? This was supposed to be just another case. Another day back on the job, but then she showed up and somehow managed to change everything.

"I would have thought you'd wished you never ran into me."

She shook her head. "No, though I'm already wishing I was in my own bed."

"You're not going anywhere until the doctors release you."

"I know, but you need me—"

"I need you to get better."

"I'm not exactly dying." She let out a low laugh. "I've been wet before and survived. I've been cold before and survived."

"I just need you to be okay. I thought I lost you."

He leaned forward, taking in those big eyes of hers. Everything that had happened over the last couple days vanished and all he could see was her. And somehow, she'd found a way to start piecing back together the fractured segments of his heart.

He tried to shake off the feeling.

"I'm fine, Nate."

She *was* going to be fine. He was going to make sure of it.

She lay back against the propped-up pillow, looking just the way he remembered her.

"Stop worrying," she said. "You could lock me up at some safe house, but that would make it harder for me to help you. And I'm not ready to quit just because of what happened."

"And when this is over? What happens then?"

"If the grid goes down, I'm going to wish I'd listened to my dad."

But he wasn't talking about the grid going down, or anything about the case they were working on, for that matter. "I agree, but I was thinking about something else. Like taking some time to reacquaint myself with this old friend I reconnected with recently."

"You mean that?" She leaned forward, face still pale, lips red, mesmerizing.

"I have this crazy feeling," he continued, suddenly wanting to kiss her, "that even after all these years, the two of us still have a lot in common."

He'd already clearly gone off the deep end. What did he have to lose?

"What would you say if I told you I wanted to kiss you?" he asked.

He tried to read her expression, regretting the words the second they came out. But instead of backing away from him, she leaned forward and brushed her mouth across his. His heart pounded at the sweetness of her lips. Her hand cupped his chin.

But was this really a good idea? They were both dealing with loss and grief. And this was going to take him to a place where he wasn't sure there was any way to return.

"Gracie . . . I'm sorry." He pulled back. "I never should have crossed the line. The last thing I need to be doing is taking advantage of you."

"If your hesitation has anything to do with Kevin—"

"It doesn't, but . . ."

What was he supposed to say? He knew this had nothing to do with Kevin. Instead, it had everything to do with himself. He'd lost people he loved, and the last thing he wanted was to lose again. And the only way not to let that happen was to guard his heart.

She looked back at him, confusion registering in her eyes.

"I need to go," he said, standing up. "Someone will come by in the morning to take your statement, but after that, I don't want you involved anymore."

"I'm already involved."

An awkward silence hovered between them. "Goodbye, Gracie."

Nate walked out of the room, then slipped into the elevator leading to the parking garage. What in the world had he been thinking? Gracie was an old friend, but that was it. Tonight's accident should have been a reminder not to involve his heart. Not to put it out there on the line to have it shattered again.

For a few moments, he'd been able to imagine what a future could hold for the two of them. No. How could he do that when he couldn't even imagine what tomorrow might hold? He'd stepped into a place he never should have. Kevin had been his best friend, and even though he'd walked out on Gracie, that didn't mean that now he had the right to take his place.

It was only a kiss. Nothing more.

But with it had come an unexpected yearning

for more of her smile and her laughter and her company. As he stepped outside, the brisk wind seemed to suck the air from his lungs. It was more than that. He was trying to make up for the past. He'd lost Ashley. Tonight, he'd almost lost Gracie.

He wasn't going to let that happen again.

21

A loud voice booming across the intercom system jolted Grace awake at seven. She opened her eyes to the bright light from the window and tried to decipher why her brain felt like scrambled eggs. She was certain she hadn't slept at all during what felt like a continuous barrage of vital checks and blood work throughout the night. But unfortunately, those disturbances hadn't stopped the vivid dreams or kept her mind from racing in the moments she had been awake.

She slowly sat up, then stumbled into the bathroom, thankful they'd taken out her IV at some point, unsure if she was ready to analyze her status. She looked into the mirror, surprised at how pale her skin was and how hollow her eyes looked. It was a face that was all too familiar to her.

When Hannah had died, the loss had been all-encompassing. Just getting up in the morning had taken more energy than she'd had most days. Coming back to life had been a long, slow journey filled with moments when she'd begged God to take her as well. And four years later, there were still days when she felt as if no time had really passed and she was starting all over again.

Somehow, though, in the middle of feeling as if no one understood, she'd begun to discover there was One who did understand this journey of grief. Sometimes she'd hear God's quiet voice in the wind. Feel his presence in the words of a song. She realized that he could feel her pain and that he understood the depth of her loss. Because he'd watched his own Son die as well.

But even in the times when she could feel God's peace and the scattering moments of joy, she'd never once imagined falling in love again. Not once.

Until Nate.

Somehow, he'd managed to sweep into her life in the middle of another tragedy and make her ask herself if maybe . . . just maybe . . . falling in love again could actually be a part of her future. He'd wanted to kiss her, and for a brief moment, she'd kissed him back. Wanted to kiss him back. His lips had felt like a healing salve that had washed over her and smoothed away some of the remaining ridges of pain and loss.

But was he right? That wasn't a place either of them needed to go right now. Had that moment been nothing more than an emotional reaction to a crisis situation? Had she wrongly interpreted his instinct to protect her as romantic feelings? As for herself, if she were honest, she didn't want to go down that road. Not with him. Not with anyone. When Kevin walked out on her, she'd told herself she'd never allow her heart to become vulnerable again. And that was exactly what was going to happen if she opened up her heart. She hated that out-of-control feeling vulnerability brought with it.

But while that might be true, a part of her was begging to explore what it might mean.

"Gracie?"

She drew in a deep breath and stepped back into the room.

"Hey." She shot Becca a smile. "I didn't expect you so early."

"I had John take the kids to school so I could come here early. I didn't know what time you were going to be able to leave, and I wanted to make sure you had clean clothes."

Becca set the bag on the end of the bed. "I have everything here from the list you gave me, but I threw in a few extras as well, just in case."

"You're an angel." Grace gathered her best friend into a hug and fought back the tears, tired of feeling so emotional. "Thank you so much."

Becca took a step back and caught her gaze. "You okay?"

"I'm fine. Really. Just a bit tired."

"I might be an angel, but I'm worried, Grace. I didn't want to upset you when I left, but I couldn't sleep last night. John and I ended up talking for a couple hours in the middle of the night, and we're both worried. I've barely seen you since the break-in, now you're in the hospital, and all I know is that one of your clients was murdered. But I have no idea how you're involved in all of this."

Grace hesitated, not sure how much she should actually tell Becca. "Stephen gave me proof of something he was involved in. Something that has the potential to hurt a lot of people."

"And now someone wants you dead?"

Grace sat down on the edge of the bed and rubbed her hands together. She still hadn't completely warmed up from last night, and trying to explain to Becca brought back that icy fear. "I don't understand everything myself, Becca. Someone is trying to make sure their loose ends are wrapped up."

"And you're a loose end?" Becca sat down beside her.

"I'll be fine. There's the police officer standing outside my door."

"Which is what has me worried. This isn't the plot to some movie where the good guys always catch the bad guys at the end of the show. This is your life we're talking about."

"Which is why I've given my statement and I'm finished helping."

But that didn't mean this was all over. She couldn't tell Becca just how high the stakes were. Or what was going to happen if the men who killed Stephen were able to implement their plan.

The truth would terrify Becca. She knew what would happen if the grid went down.

"Nate will make sure nothing happens to me." She squeezed her friend's hand. "I promise."

"I spoke with Nate for a few minutes yesterday."

Grace's eyes widened. "About?"

"He really cares about you. I can tell from his voice. And there's something about the way he says your name. I don't remember your mentioning him before."

"I knew him back in college. Before I met you. He was a friend of Kevin's."

"I was just wondering if I'd seen a spark between the two of you, or if I just imagined it?"

Grace pulled her gray sweater from the bag Becca had brought her, wanting to ignore the question. How could she even consider falling for someone she hadn't seen for so many years? Someone whose life was completely different from hers? The idea was crazy. They'd both changed and weren't at all the same people they'd been back in school. What had happened over the past two days wasn't going to change any of that.

"No . . . there's nothing there. Not really." She shook her head. How had their conversation switched to another topic she didn't want to talk about? "Too much has happened over the past few days for me to even consider my heart. But . . . there is something about him. Maybe it's because he makes me think about a time when things were less complicated. When I believed I could take on the world and actually make things better. We were invincible back then, but now . . ."

That was before she lost her family.

"Besides everything else that's going on, I'm not ready to think about a relationship."

"When will you be ready, Grace? I mean, if you keep waiting for the perfect moment, you might miss what's right in front of you."

"If you haven't noticed, we're in the middle of a crisis with a police guard outside my room. A relationship is not what I need to be thinking about."

"Maybe not, but if you ask me, he seems like the best thing that's come along for as long as I can remember. The problem is, you'll always have an excuse why not to get involved."

Grace pulled out the rest of the clothes Becca had brought for her and headed to the bathroom to change. "You need to stop."

"You're running."

"I'm not running." She closed the door partway and started changing out of the hospital gown.

"I just know that I saw the way he looked at you last night," Becca said through the partially open doorway. "Something's happened between the two of you."

Grace finished dressing, then stepped back into the room. "You're always trying to read between the lines. All I really want right now are these warm clothes, a big cup of coffee, and to go home and sleep in my own bed for the next twelve hours."

"You're changing the subject."

"Fine." Grace walked back to the bed. She'd never been able to keep the truth from Becca. "We kissed last night when he came to see me."

Becca let out an unladylike snort. "I knew it."

"Don't get too excited." Grace sat back down on the bed beside her friend. "It was awkward and passionate and crazy all at the same time."

Becca shot her a big smile. "So I was right."

"Maybe, but as soon as this is over, he's going back to his life, and I'm going back to mine."

"And you know that how?"

"I'm pretty sure he regretted the kiss."

"Did he? Or are you simply going by something he said? Because if you ask me, his actions tell a completely different story. Maybe the guy's shy. Maybe all he needs is a push in the right direction."

Grace frowned. She hated it when Becca decided to play psychologist and start analyzing everything. "Last time I checked, I was the one who went to school to learn how to read people, and as for his actions . . . he kissed me once, but we all know that statistically, relationships forged in the middle of a traumatic situation rarely last."

"Seriously, Grace?" Apparently Becca wasn't

buying her excuses. "You're going to pull that line on me? Sometimes you can't go by statistics when you're talking about love."

"Maybe so, but I'm not completely ignorant about men and relationships."

"What does your heart tell you?"

She reached into the bag and pulled out a tube of lotion. "That it's not going to come to anything. At least not now. He's lost too much to let himself care about someone again."

"That's what he told you?"

"Not exactly in those words." She squeezed a dime-sized blob of lotion on her hands and started rubbing them together. She couldn't let herself take an innocent kiss and twist it into something bigger. "Besides, I have no plans to give my heart away again either. I lost too much with Hannah and Kevin."

"Have you thought that maybe it's time to stop using them as an excuse?"

"I'm not like you, Becca. I don't have to have a husband and two-point-five kids to be happy." She dumped the lotion back into the bag, trying to ignore the sting in her friend's words. "I can't afford to lose everything again."

Her friend took her hand and caught her gaze. "You lost Kevin because he couldn't live with the pain of Hannah's death. It's time you stop blaming yourself for that. It's time you gave love another chance. Maybe Nate isn't the one, and that's okay. But you'll never know until you try."

"You're way too much of a romantic."

"If anything, having a couple kids and a husband who works too many hours has taught me that love and life and marriage aren't just about romance and happily ever after."

Grace knew that as well. Sometimes it was about doctors' visits, hospital stays, months of treatment, and horrible things like having to bury your little girl.

But maybe it was also about second chances. About taking a risk when it came to your heart, because you knew that no matter how much it might hurt, you wanted to take a chance anyway.

Becca squeezed her hand before letting go. "All I know is that there's this totally hot guy out there who I'm pretty sure is falling for you."

Grace drew in a breath, still not convinced. "And my heart? What if it can't take losing again? Because I'm scared. Scared of falling for someone again. Scared of the possibility of losing them. Of one day finding myself here again."

"I don't know what the future holds. I know that a piece of your heart went with Kevin when he left you. And maybe that's the kind of hole that can't ever be completely fixed. Maybe someone like Nate just might be the one to help your heart grow—if you'll let him."

22

Fifteen minutes later, Grace had finished getting dressed, eaten a fairly decent breakfast of a cheese omelet, whole wheat toast, and orange juice, and was anxiously waiting for the doctor to sign her release papers. She glanced around the starkly decorated hospital room, thankful—not for the first time—that she was alive. A shiver ran through her. There had been a moment in the water after her hand had slipped from Nate's that she was submerged in the darkness with no idea which way was up.

But not only had she survived, she'd realized how much she wanted to live.

That reality took her by surprise. How many times over the past four years had she wished she'd been the one who'd been struck with cancer instead of Hannah? Wished that she'd been the one they'd buried in the ground on that cold November day? She sat back down in the middle of the bed and pulled her legs beneath her. What had made yesterday different from all the days she'd begged God to take her home?

"Because God knows that sometimes, after you put the pieces back together, you end up with something stronger and even more beautiful than before."

The words Becca had reminded her of a dozen times over the past few years raced through her mind. Losing a child had changed her, and sometimes she did feel stronger. But strong enough to open her heart up again? That was something she wasn't sure she was ready for. And something she was pretty sure Nate wasn't ready for either.

The phone beside her bed rang. Grace reached for the receiver, then hesitated. Besides Becca, her parents were the only people she'd given the hospital information to, and they were never up this early. She let out a deep breath and shook off the paranoia. She was becoming like Stephen, who'd constantly looked over his shoulder. Except now she knew that his paranoia wasn't completely off base. Stephen was dead, and only hours ago someone had tried to take her life too.

She picked up the phone. "Hello?"

"Grace Callahan?" A deep, raspy voice spoke on the other end of the line.

"Yes?"

"We believe you have Stephen's security patch, and we're willing to pay you for it."

"Who is this?" She pressed her free hand against the bed.

"Two hundred thousand dollars. A simple trade."

She tried to place the voice, but it sounded like it was being digitally altered. "What makes you think I have the patch?"

"You've got fifteen seconds to give us an answer."

Grace's fingers tightened around the phone cord. Why would someone believe she had the security patch Stephen had written? She'd given the police the flash drive and had told them everything she could remember about her sessions with Stephen. But clearly whoever had the contents from the safe-deposit box needed that patch so the authorities wouldn't be able to stop them. Maybe they figured out that she'd snuck something out of the bank under their noses. However they knew, this wasn't going to be over until they were arrested and locked up in prison.

A patch could stop the grid from going down and was their only leverage against the hackers. What if this was their one chance to find out who was behind this?

Heart racing, she gave her answer before completely weighing the consequences. "Where do you want me to meet you?"

She waited for the man's response, knowing Nate was going to kill her himself when he found out what she'd just done. But if it got them closer to the men behind Stephen's death, it was worth the risk.

"There's a coffee shop two blocks west of the hospital. Be there in one hour. Give the flash drive to the redhead in the ball cap sitting in the corner of the room with a laptop, then wait for his instructions."

A shiver swept up her spine as she glanced toward the door. Whoever this was knew exactly where she was. They were following her, just like they'd followed Stephen. But what was going to happen when they found out she didn't have the flash drive? Try to kill her too? She had to find a way to stall them, so Nate and his team could figure out a way to handle things.

"There's a guard outside my door," she said. "They won't let me simply walk out of here."

"One hour. And don't tell anyone what you're doing. We're watching."

A second later the line went dead.

Grace felt her hand shake as she set down the receiver. She moved to the edge of the bed and pressed her hand against her heart. She could feel it pounding through her sweater. One hour to meet with whoever had tried to kill her, and she didn't even have what they wanted. What had she been thinking?

She was still trying to figure out how to tell Nate what she'd just done when he strode into the room. He'd missed a crease or two in his dark-green dress shirt and looked as if he hadn't slept at all, making her wonder if it was the case that had kept him up or the fact that he'd kissed her.

He stopped at the end of the bed and shot her a far-too-solemn smile. "Good morning."

She forced a smile back. "Good morning."

"I thought about bringing you a couple more chocolate pudding cups, but figured you'd probably already eaten by now."

"They brought me breakfast a little while ago. How's your arm?"

He reached up and touched his shoulder. "I had some pain during the night, but it's much better, thanks."

She suddenly felt awkward and self-conscious and hated it. What had happened between the two of them? Had everything really changed because of a kiss?

"You look a lot better than you did last night," he said. "Are you feeling thawed out yet?"

"Almost. They're supposed to release me soon. I'm just waiting for the final signature from the doctor, and someone to tell me I can go home."

"Are you sure you're ready to leave?" Any smile she'd seen, real or not, faded.

"I feel fine. Really. Still a bit cold, but really, I'm fine."

"You do understand that where you go at this point will be up to my boss. What's most important is making sure you're safe, which for the time being will include continued police protection. Okay?"

She nodded, wishing he didn't sound so businesslike. As if she were just another person of interest involved in one of his cases.

"No arguments?" he asked.

"After the past forty-eight-plus hours, I think I'd be foolish to argue this one." She tilted her head. "You look surprised, but all I want to do is go home."

He smiled, relieved at her answer. "I guess I expected you to put up more of a fight."

"I may be stubborn as a mule, but that doesn't mean I'm willing to pretend nothing could happen to me."

"Good. There's also one other thing we need to talk about." He hesitated, as if he also hated the awkwardness that had somehow been wedged between them. "About last night . . . I think it would be better if we put that behind us."

"Forget it." She waved her hand, hoping she appeared as if it were no big deal to her. "The last couple days have been crazy with both our emotions strung out on edge. It's fine."

It really was *not* fine, but she wanted things to be okay between them again, and if that's what he wanted . . .

"Just like I never should have let you get involved in this, I never should have taken advantage of you when you were in a vulnerable state," he said.

"Well, as for the kiss, I'll admit that I participated as much as you did." She let out a low laugh, hoping it masked the hurt trickling through her. Who was she kidding? She'd wanted him to march back into this hospital room and kiss her like he had last night. Tell her that he didn't regret what had happened between them, and tell her he wanted to see if they could make something work between the two of them.

But clearly that wasn't going to happen. And if he wanted to move forward with business as usual, she could do that too.

She swallowed the lump in her throat. "Helping Stephen has always been my choice, not yours, and I'd do it all over again if I had to. I'm not going to let Stephen die for nothing. He didn't deserve that. But what about Macbain? Do you have an update on him?"

"He's fine." Nate slipped his hand into his pocket, then frowned. "Just a bit frozen to the core, like you. He's on his way down to the precinct right now, and will start working with our techs there to see if he can do something to stop this."

She caught a flicker of something new in his eyes. "What's wrong?"

"Nothing. I . . ." He suddenly seemed distracted. "I just lost something in the water last night."

She didn't want to think about all she'd lost. Even if divers were able to find her wallet, she'd probably have to end up replacing her driver's license, credit cards, and cell phone. At least she had Hannah's memorial bracelet. It was one of the things Kevin had gotten for her right after

Hannah died. If she'd lost that in the accident . . .

"What did you lose?" she asked.

"It was my . . . my grandfather's pocket watch." He pulled his hand back out. "A watch can be replaced, though. A life can't. As long as all of us made it out of there alive, it's insignificant."

Except she could tell it wasn't. Not to him. And she understood why. "I'm sorry."

"It's nothing."

"There's something I need to tell you, Nate, though I'm not sure how you're going to take it."

He hesitated, then moved closer to the bed. "What's wrong?"

"I got a phone call right before you arrived."

"From who?"

She bit her lip. "Someone who believes I have the security patch Stephen wrote."

"Wait a minute. Why would anyone believe that?"

She shrugged. "Whoever Stephen worked for must have known he created the patch. They might have figured out one of the drives was missing and think I snatched the flash drive at the bank. And now they need to make sure their plans to take down the grid don't fail. But for whatever reason, they believe I have it."

"What did they do? Threaten you?"

She paused, avoiding his gaze. He'd fought her involvement this entire time. He definitely wasn't going to like what she was about to say. "They offered me two hundred thousand dollars for it."

He took a step forward, shaking his head. "Two hundred thousand dollars?"

"Either they're getting false information from somewhere, or they're trying to smoke me out."

He jumped up out of the chair and started pacing. "What phone did they use?"

"The hospital landline."

"If we can trace the call—"

"These are hackers we're dealing with. Do you really think that would work?"

"I don't know." Nate picked up the receiver and punched in *69 in an attempt to get the phone number of the last caller.

"You're right," he said, hanging up.

"Plus, they used voice alteration, so there's no way I could recognize the voice." She wadded up the sheet between her fingers and avoided his gaze again. "I told them I'd make the trade."

"What?" He stood in front of her, hands at his sides as he tried to take in the information she'd just given him. "You told them you'd make the exchange?"

"I know it sounds crazy, but if this gets us closer to whoever's behind this, it will be worth it. The fallout from this is huge, and we've got to find a way to stop it."

"I understand what the fallout is, but that doesn't change the fact that we don't have the patch. And now they think you've got it, so no matter what happens, they're going to try to come after you."

She caught the anger flaring in his eyes and the tension running up his jawline, but she still didn't regret what she'd done. They had Macbain's help, yes, which might pan out, but beyond that they were out of options.

"Where are you supposed to meet them?" he asked, his voice slightly calmer.

"At a coffee shop two blocks from here. I'm to give it to someone with red hair, a ball cap, and a laptop. I'm assuming they're planning to check out the flash drive before handing over any money."

"If they're actually even considering giving you any money. More than likely, they're planning on eliminating you."

"Nate—"

"What were you thinking? There's no way you're doing this."

Apparently, his rampage wasn't over.

"I know," she said.

He blew out a short breath. "You know?"

"I have no intention of showing up for the drop. But you can, or you can send someone in . . . that's up to you. I don't care. But whoever called me is desperate. Willing to take a chance to get that patch. They have to make sure we don't put in the patch before they can take down the grid."

She waited for him to answer.

"What do we do now?" she asked.

"I don't know. If you'd had a flash drive on you, it would have gotten wet, or even potentially lost in the lake." Nate was pacing, speaking his thoughts out loud. "Though the one you grabbed at the bank was waterproof."

"I can see Stephen taking that precaution."

Nate stopped in front of her, as if he was running through his options and didn't like any of them. She couldn't exactly blame him. He'd lost his team. Almost lost her. He wasn't going to want to handle going through that again.

He pulled his phone out of his pocket. "I'm going to get Paige here. The two of you are about the same size. She should be able to pull this off."

The ache in her gut intensified. "And when they realize she doesn't have the drive?"

"Don't worry about that. She'll have something to give them. This is what we do."

"Ms. Callahan. How are you feeling this morning?"

She looked up as Sergeant Addison stepped into the room. "Much better, sir. Thank you." She started to stand up.

"Please . . . you don't have to get up. I just came by to check on you. I hear the doctor is getting ready to release you, which means we need to discuss what will happen next."

Grace nodded. "Okay."

"Sarge . . . ," Nate said. "We need to talk."

23

Nate glanced back at Gracie before following his boss into the hallway, wondering why he felt as if he'd just made a big mistake. He'd caught her smile when he first arrived, but hadn't been able to interpret the expression hiding beneath it. Even he couldn't deny the chemistry he'd felt between them last night. Today, though, it had vanished, and in its place a sense of awkwardness had surfaced. But that was his fault. He'd told her that kissing her had been a mistake. What did he expect after that?

On the other hand, if he really believed what he'd said, then why had seeing her make him want to kiss her all over again?

Sarge strode down the hallway to a small alcove with a window overlooking the hospital grounds, then turned to face Nate. "Before you say anything, I've got something you need to hear, but you're not going to like it."

Nate shifted his attention fully back to the issue at hand. "What's going on?"

"I just came out of a meeting with the FBI. Six months ago, they opened up an investigation on a group of hackers called r06u3."

"R06 . . . What is that?"

"It's hackspeak for—"

"Rogue." The connection suddenly clicked. "The group Winters told us Jenkins was connected with."

"Exactly. We've now been able to confirm that there is a connection between this group and Stephen Shaw's death. They believe that this cyber group Rogue hired Stephen. Whether or not he knew what he was actually involved in from the beginning, I can't be certain. It's always possible he knew, and his conscience just got the best of him."

"What do we know about this group?"

"They've been behind a string of cyberattacks over the past year, all of which they've managed to execute under the radar. They started out stealing computer data from dozens of corporate networks, along with credit card and ATM numbers. With their last round, they did something called 'zero-day exploits.' "

"Which is . . ."

"A zero-day vulnerability is a hole in a program that the company or vendor doesn't know about. Hackers find it and write a code that will breach the vendor's security before the vendor is even aware of the problem. Your typical company concerned about security will hire developers who will look for these vulnerabilities as well as create software that will protect the security of the data. But if a hacker discovers that vulnerability before the developer even realizes there's a problem, he can in turn write a code that will exploit that vulnerability."

"That was Stephen Shaw's job. To find vulnerabilities and ensure that the clients his company worked for had security that couldn't be exploited."

"The flash drive that Grace managed to snatch holds pages and pages of binary data with corresponding details of recent attacks, and contained both the security vulnerabilities Stephen—we're assuming—found and the patches he designed to fix them."

"What about the supposed vulnerability in the grid security he found? Did the flash drive contain a patch for that?"

"The tech guys weren't able to find anything that seemed to be connected to the grid. Which is what has us worried. From what the FBI knows about this group so far, it seems to have international backing. If they have access to the grid's vulnerabilities and we don't have the patch, they could take down the grid and there would be nothing we could do to stop them. It could take days, if not weeks, for us to come up with another patch, and we don't have that kind of time."

"I don't think they have the patch," Nate said. "And I think they want it before they implement their plan to take down the grid."

Sarge stuffed his hands into his pockets. "What do you mean?"

"Someone called Gracie a few minutes ago. They believe she has the flash drive with the patch and offered her two hundred thousand dollars for it."

"Two hundred thousand dollars? But wait a minute. If she doesn't have it . . . and they don't have it . . . where is it?"

"I don't know, but here's our problem right now. Gracie arranged to make the exchange."

"She did what?"

Nate glanced at the time on his cell phone. "She agreed to meet them in about fifty minutes with the patch."

"A patch that we don't have."

"As much as I hate to admit it, she made the right call. If we can take advantage of this and find a way to use the situation to trace who's behind this—"

"She can't go in there."

"I agree. But we've got less than an hour to put a plan together. Paige is on her way here right now. She could pass as Gracie for someone who doesn't know her well. If tech could come up with a flash drive that would stall them—one that included some kind of untraceable malware so we could track them—it might be our one chance to find out who's behind this and stop them. And in the meantime, we can get Gracie out of here to somewhere safe until all of this is over."

Sarge still didn't look convinced. "All in less than an hour. We're going to have to pull a lot of strings to make this happen and even then—"

"The way it looks to me, this is not only our best option at the moment, it's our only option. How long do you think it will take them to implement Stephen's code? Twenty-four hours . . . forty-eight? And when they do take the grid down, are we prepared for that? We're talking about people running out of food and water within the first seventy-two hours. Within days, there will be nothing on the shelves of all the grocery stores. There will be no way to keep up with the increased crime as people begin to panic. There will be no communications, no fuel at the gas stations, and no functioning hospitals—"

"Okay, I get it." Sarge held up his hands. "We'll find a way to make this happen, but first I have to ask you one question. Do you trust Grace?"

"Why wouldn't I?"

"What if she actually has the patch? She had to know it was worth something, and she's just been offered two hundred thousand dollars for it. People have done a whole lot more for less money."

Nate shook his head, irritated at the direction his boss was going. "Yes, I trust her completely. Besides, if she had the patch, why would she tell me about the exchange?"

"I guess she wouldn't, but I need to make sure

we're covering all the angles. We can't afford to lose this one."

"She's told us everything she knows. Trust me on this, because it makes sense that Stephen wouldn't have wanted the two software programs together. Maybe a bit of insurance on his part. If black hackers managed to get ahold of the security vulnerabilities, he didn't want them to get the patch as well."

"Nate . . . Sarge . . . here you are." Paige stepped into the alcove, carrying her coffee. "What's going on?"

"While you were getting your coffee down-stairs," Nate said, "Gracie found out that someone believes she has the patch and wants to make an exchange. She set up a meeting to take place in about fifty minutes."

"Hold on." Paige held up her drink. "All this happened in the time it took for me to wait in line for my large caramel macchiato?"

"Pretty much," Nate said.

"And you're planning to send her out there to make the exchange?"

"Definitely not." Nate caught her gaze. "You're going to make the exchange."

"You know I'm game to do anything, but shouldn't we let the FBI take the lead on this one? I thought they were taking over the case."

"They are," Sarge said, "but we're here, and this is happening now. We'll give them what we have, once this is over. Then our primary job will be solving Stephen Shaw's murder. But at the moment, we need to move quickly."

"What exactly is the plan?" she asked.

"Biggest issue I see is what happens if they, one, realize you're not Gracie, and two, discover you aren't really turning over the patch," Nate said. "But we need to get Gracie—and Macbain—somewhere safe. I don't trust the setup here. We've got a safe house we can take them to."

"I'm going to get the ball rolling on the flash drive we need, so in the meantime," Sarge said, turning to Paige, "you and Grace need to prepare to switch roles."

A minute later, Nate headed back to Gracie's room, still worried that they wouldn't have enough time to put into place the details they'd just ironed out.

Gracie stood up as he and Paige entered the room.

"What's going on?"

"We've come up with a plan," Nate said.

"You and I are going to change places." Paige set her coffee down on the side table. "I think it'll work. We're about the same height and have similar hair color. If we switch clothes, and I let my hair down, I just might fool them."

"Gracie?" Nate caught her frown.

"I'm just second-guessing my rash decision," she said. "I don't want to do anything that could get any of you hurt. We know what they are capable of doing—"

"You did the right thing, Gracie," Nate said. "It's because we know what will happen if we don't stop these guys that we have to go through with this."

"Nate." His boss stepped back into the room and handed him an earpiece. "I want you to take Grace to the precinct. Make it look as if you and your partner are leaving the hospital. Business as usual. Paige, they need to think you walked out of the hospital on your own. We'll have a perimeter set up around the coffee shop, and a flash drive is on its way here now."

"And when he finds out that it's a fake patch?" Gracie asked.

"Our tech guys are working as quickly as possible to delay that. What we have to do is buy some time so we can trace it back to whoever's behind this," Sarge said. "We have one chance to get this right."

Sarge's phone rang and he moved to the corner of the room to answer it.

Nate stepped in front of Gracie, resisting the urge to pull her into his arms and promise her that everything was going to be okay. "Are you all right?"

"I don't know. I should have thought through what I was agreeing to. Now I feel like I've put everyone's lives at stake. They told me not to tell anyone, and like I said, we know what these people are capable of. I'm just . . . I'm ready for this to be over."

"I know, but this is what we do, Gracie. You did the right thing by telling me, because you might have just given us the one opportunity to find who's behind this."

"I hope so." She nodded, but there was still a glint of fear in her eyes.

"It will be over soon."

She glanced around the room. "They bugged Stephen's office. What if they bugged this room and know what your plan is?"

"The room's been swept several times. It's going to be okay."

He hated the inner turmoil raging inside, but he'd been right about one thing. Kissing her had been a mistake. He couldn't let any emotions get in the way. He was here to work a case, nothing more.

"We've got about forty minutes to pull this together," Sarge said, "but here's the plan we've got so far. Our tech team is working with the FBI to get us a flash drive that will look like legitimate code, but more importantly it will also install undetectable tracking software on the computer once it's plugged in." He turned to Paige. "Chances are the person you meet with will want to test the drive on their own computer to make sure they're getting what they're paying for. Unfortunately for them, they won't be able to fully test the code. If they ask where you had the flash drive, just tell them you had it in your pocket. If they know Grace has been in the hospital, they probably know why as well. The flash drive will be waterproof like the other one we have."

"So what we need now," Nate said, "is for the two of you to change. Paige will leave the hospital with the flash drive as Gracie, while Gracie will come with me to my car in the parking garage, like we're headed back to the precinct. I'll drive you to the safe house. Okay, Gracie?"

She nodded and this time he caught the determination in her eyes, reminding him once again of how strong she was despite her vulnerabilities. He waited outside the room while the two women swapped clothes. When he stepped inside a minute later, Gracie was wearing Paige's black pantsuit and bright-pink shirt and a pair of sturdy black boots, while Paige had on Grace's more casual sweater and black jeans outfit.

"What do you think?" Grace pulled her hair back the way Paige normally wore hers.

Nate hesitated, wishing she didn't look so stunning no matter what she was wearing. He wanted to tell her he was wrong about everything he'd said. That he wanted to see if things could work out between them. Instead, he put on his game face.

"Are you really okay about this?" he asked.

She smiled up at him. "If you ask me, I have the easy part."

"Personally, I'm happy you're not going to be caught up in the middle of this anymore."

"You make a great detective," Paige said, undoing her ponytail and letting her hair fall across her shoulders. "Watch the way you walk. Head up, back straight. Look confident. You'll do fine."

"What time is it?" Gracie asked.

Nate glanced at the clock on the wall. "Ten minutes to showtime."

24

Five minutes later, Gracie headed toward the elevator and the underground parking with Nate. She kept her head held high, making sure there was a note of confidence in her stride on the off chance someone was watching them. But the attempt couldn't totally mask what she was feeling. Inside she was shaking. In another thirty minutes or so, she'd be somewhere safe where the men who killed Stephen couldn't touch her. But until then? She'd seen how resourceful they were, and her gut told her she'd made a mistake agreeing to make the swap.

But it was too late to change that now.

She drew in a steadying breath. An undercover officer walked ahead of them. She'd been told there were three in total who were going to see that they made it safely from the hospital. Not that they were expecting anything to happen. At least that was what she'd been reassured. No one could make guarantees at this point. She still had a dozen questions. Like why Stephen had been killed if he had the answers they needed. Why they'd tried to run them off the road last night. Who was really behind this.

Nate walked next to her, hands at his side. Jaw tense. They were simply partners leaving the hospital. Nothing more than friends, as he'd been quick to remind her. But the high-stakes reality of what was happening wouldn't leave her alone. Part of her wanted to run into his arms. The other part of her wanted to stop where she was so she could call and warn her friends and family of some impending Armageddon.

But what would she tell them?

Hey, Becca, call your husband, grab your kids, and run, because life as you know it will never be the same.

Or, *by the way, Dad, you were right. I happen to have inside information and there's a good chance that the grid is going to crash in the next twenty-four hours. Drag out the toilet paper and beef jerky. You're going to need it.*

She could almost hear her father's I-told-you-so reaction. She'd always dismissed his yearly lectures, but he just might have been right all along.

She glanced at Nate as they stopped in front of the elevator and waited for the doors to open. She'd seen the relief in his eyes when she assured him she wasn't going to argue with him about having any involvement with the exchange. But she had no interest in playing this game anymore. The police had her statement, and she'd given everything she had. As far as she was concerned, she was finished.

They stepped inside the elevator with the officer. In another thirty seconds, they'd be on the bottom floor. Another minute, and they'd be inside Nate's vehicle. Taking her to the safe house was really just a precaution. Nothing more. She knew she'd be safe. Nate would make sure of that.

Then why did she feel so vulnerable?

The same sense of helplessness she'd felt when Hannah died swept over her. The feeling that no matter what she did, she couldn't escape the inevitable. She glanced around the elevator, needing to find a way to control her emotions that were quickly spiraling out of control. Needing to find that sense of stability in her life she'd worked so hard to create. Instead, the walls felt like they were closing in on her. She shifted her gaze to Nate, whose solemn expression reminded her of just how seriously he was taking the situation. Somehow, over the past three days, he'd become her shelter in the storm. Her rock when she couldn't figure out how to deal with the terror surrounding her. And yet just when she'd felt a small tremor of hope coming back to life inside her, he'd closed the door.

Do not fear.

Verses from Isaiah she'd memorized when Hannah had died surfaced.

I will uphold you with my strong right hand.

Nate could never be her rock and sense of security. There was only One who could do that.

The admission worked to slow her heart rate

and force a bit of balance into her thoughts. If the situation wasn't so serious, she just might laugh. Becca had told her she needed a distraction this week. Something to help her make it through the flood of memories surrounding Hannah's death. This was some distraction—she felt as if she were in the middle of a scene from prime-time TV.

"Did I ever tell you I thought about becoming a detective?" she asked, feeling the need to break the tension engulfing them. "Between *Magnum PI* and *Remington Steele*, I figured it would be the perfect career."

"What changed your mind?" he asked.

"For starters, my dad assured me that I would never make enough money to buy my own Ferrari."

Nate actually cracked a smile. "That had to have been a major letdown."

A second later, the elevator beeped and the doors slid open. Nate's hand was on his weapon as he stepped out of the elevator to the left and surveyed the area. The second officer moved to the right, doing the same thing.

"My car's one row over," he said.

Her black boots clicked against the cement floor as Gracie stepped outside the elevator and into the darkened garage. She might be dressed in Paige's clothes, but what she really needed was the detective's street smarts and a whole lot more courage.

Nate's radio buzzed and he snagged it out of the holder.

Sarge's voice came through. "An attempted ambush was just made on Carl Macbain's detail. They're fine, but watch your six."

Before Nate could respond, a bullet shattered the window of the car to their right. An alarm went off.

"Get her back inside. Now." The other officer ran forward, ducking behind a large cement support.

Nate pulled Grace back into the elevator, punched on the button to close the doors, then hit the button for the sixth floor. A moment later a second bullet slammed into the doors. She could hear men on the other side of the metal door shouting. Nate was yelling into his radio, securing backup to the garage. Her heart hammered inside her chest. Nausea washed through her. Three days ago, she was grieving the death of her daughter, while at the same time finding a bit of solace in the fact that life was slowly getting back to normal again. If there really was such a thing. She'd learned to thrive on keeping her life simple. Control the stress as much as she could. Find ways to take care of herself . . .

The elevator still hadn't started up again.

Today, she was running for her life.

"What is it about these people and elevators?" Nate jammed his finger against the button again.

"What?"

"Nothing . . . Just stay against the wall. I've got to get you somewhere safe."

Her heart pounded. She didn't want to ask him if it was possible for a bullet to penetrate the metal doors. As far as she was concerned, there was no place safe.

The elevator started moving.

Another question surfaced. If she'd agreed to make the exchange, why come after her now? Someone must have realized she wasn't the one who was going to be bringing the flash drive. But still, why come after her? This triggered another thought. What was going to stop them from coming after her again? They'd found her at her house. On the road. Knew she was here at the hospital. There was nowhere left to run.

She turned to face Nate. "What's going on?"

"Besides the fact that they attacked Macbain's detail, I honestly don't know."

"Why come after me here? I promised them the flash drive. Unless they found out—"

"I'm sorry, Gracie. I don't have the answers. Let's get you to safety and then worry about the rest."

"But where is safe? They're planning to take down the grid, Nate. Finding me—wherever I am—can't be that hard for these people."

Sarge's voice boomed over the radio again. "We've called off the plan. We'll try to grab whoever arrives to make the exchange, but this shouldn't have happened. Get back up here now."

"There has to be an explanation why they're targeting us," Gracie said. "Something must have changed on their end. I told them I'd give it to them. Paige hadn't even shown up yet."

He took her hand and squeezed it. "I don't know, Gracie. I just don't know."

The elevator stopped, and he pulled her out, still holding her hand.

"What's going on?" he asked his boss.

"Your guess is as good as mine." Sarge ushered them down the long hallway, past a dozen hospital rooms. "We're taking the stairwell and moving to plan B. We managed to catch a helo waiting on the roof."

"What about the officer who went down with us?" Nate asked.

"He's fine, but the shooter got away. Hospital is on lockdown and a full sweep of the building is being conducted. This seems like the safest way to get you out of here."

Grace tried to keep up. Nate still had her hand as they hurried down the hall. "Nate . . . Where are we going?"

He pulled open the heavy metal door, then stopped just inside the stairwell. "To the roof and then somewhere safe."

She hurried up the stairway with Sarge in front of them and Nate at her side. At the top of the stairwell, Sarge opened the door and stepped out onto the windy landing, where there was a helicopter sitting on the pad.

"You coming with us?" Nate shouted at him above the noise of the helo's rotors.

"No, just get her out of here and to safety. The pilot knows where to take you. Go to the fifth floor once you get there. An FBI agent will meet you. I'll be in touch as soon as I can."

Nate helped Grace up into the bird, then sat down next to her before buckling up his seat belt and checking hers.

"You okay?" he asked.

"Yeah."

For now, anyway.

The helo hovered above the rooftop for a few seconds, then swooped to the east over the city.

"I will say this, though." She leaned back against the seat and closed her eyes. "I'm not sure if this is a typical day for you, but if it is, I'd ask for a bigger paycheck."

"I think you're right." Nate laughed. "Though I'm not sure my boss would agree."

"Speaking of your boss, did he say where we're going?"

"They've switched the location of the safe house for security reasons, but even I don't know the location. The pilot has instructions."

She sat in silence the rest of the short trip. The city spread out beneath them, giving them a bird's-eye view of downtown. She'd only been on a helicopter one other time. She and Kevin had splurged so they could see Maui and Molokai from the air on their honeymoon. Views of the falls and the incredible green vegetation of the islands had taken her breath away. At the time, it had seemed the perfect ending to a fairy-tale wedding and honeymoon. Little had she known at the time that their happily-ever-after life was one day going to be shattered.

Her gaze shifted to Nate. He'd had his own struggles this past decade. He was, in a sense, a wounded warrior. A man who'd dedicated his life to making a difference for his country. First in the military. And now for the police force. But because of what he'd experienced, he was also a man who'd closed off his heart. She had no idea how much the bombing had played in changing him, but she knew how hard it was to heal sometimes. Life wasn't easy. She'd seen over and over in her own clients how loss had affected them, together with the guilt and blame that often came along with it.

But healing took time, and sometimes, people—like Nate—closed themselves off. She'd discovered, though, that it was always better not to take the journey alone. She'd had Becca. Who did he have?

Ten minutes later, the helo began its descent, then made its landing on a pad on the roof of another building. The pilot opened the door, and

288

moments later, they were ducking beneath the rotors and hurrying toward the stairwell.

A man in a gray suit met them in the hallway three flights down.

"Detective Quinn . . . Agent Mac Brown." The man flashed them his ID. "If you'll both come with me, please."

Three doors down, he led them inside an industrial loft that had been made into a safe house. Cement floors, brick walls with two-story vaulted ceilings. A loft took up a fourth of the room, with access by a metal ladder. Underneath the loft were two men working at a row of computers. There were a couch and chairs in one corner, but no pictures on the wall. Nothing personal.

"Where exactly are we?" Nate asked.

"An FBI safe house."

"FBI?" Grace asked.

"Because of the urgent nature of this case, the FBI has just completely taken control of operations. We requested both you and Mr. Macbain to come here so we can interview you as well as guarantee your safety."

Grace glanced at Nate, not sure she was happy with the situation. It wasn't as if she'd been given a choice, but she had no desire to go through another interview. She'd already told the police everything she knew about Stephen, and they'd taken detailed notes.

"If you'll wait here, Detective, Agent Fulton

and I will get started with the interview in the adjoining room."

Grace looked at Nate one last time before following the agent. She wanted to tell Nate how vulnerable she felt. How she wasn't ready for him to leave her in the hands of the FBI.

Instead she just nodded.

"Of course," she said. "Anything I can do to help to catch Stephen's killer."

And to stop the country's grid from going down.

25

Nate finished the call with Sarge as Gracie stood up on the other side of the room where the two agents had been interviewing her. He was unhappy with the fact that he wasn't the one doing the interviewing, but the agents had asked him to spend the day working as the bridge between the department and the FBI, and he'd agreed.

At least she was safe. For now.

Macbain was working with a couple of intelligence analysts on the computers, trying to decipher if they'd missed anything in the flash drive Gracie had managed to swipe. She walked over to where Nate stood in the living area and sat down on one of the worn, overstuffed chairs.

"How did it go?" he asked.

"I feel like I'm just repeating the same things over and over again, and I don't have the answers they want." She slumped against the back of the chair and closed her eyes.

He sat down across from her on the matching couch. "Are you done?"

"They're giving me a break." She opened her eyes. "In his phone message Stephen said he left everything I needed to end this. They're convinced Stephen said something to me or left me some kind of clue I'm supposed to know how to interpret."

"How can you do that if what we need was in the safe-deposit box, which we don't have?"

"I know, but if these people had everything they needed, why come to me, offering me money?"

He rubbed the back of his neck, wishing they had as many answers as questions. "And why try to grab you at the hospital before you even tried to make the swap?"

"Exactly. I feel like I'm on one of those merry-go-rounds at the park Hannah used to love. We're going in circles and not getting anywhere." She let out a low laugh. "And all I want to do is get off."

He nodded, understanding exactly how she felt. All he wanted to do right now was whisk her away from all of this.

"Here's something you might be interested in. I just got off the phone with Sarge," Nate said. "You remember the third guy, Eddie Sumter, who Stephen's sister told us about?"

"Yeah."

"We know he died about seven months ago under suspicious circumstances, but as of today there have been no arrests. Now here's the interesting part. Kelli's been looking for a connection between the two deaths and just found one. Remember when we were wondering if whoever was paying Stephen for the work he was doing had also been paying Eddie before he died? We were spot on."

Gracie's eyes widened. "All I can say is that whoever they are, they're definitely an employer I'd want to avoid working for."

Nate laughed. "Agreed. Kelli's working on following the money trail, hoping it will lead us in the right direction."

"I don't know how you do this. All of this"— she waved her hand—"chasing clues and killers just gives me a headache."

"You know, let's forget about all of this for right now." He glanced at the coffee table and the box of pizza that one of the agents had picked up for them. He didn't know about her, but he was starving. "What you need—what we both need— is a break, and something to eat. Pizza's still hot if you're hungry."

She shot him a smile despite the noticeable fatigue in her eyes. "Thanks, but I'm not sure I could eat. All I can think of is what happens if they don't find this patch. I've just gone over every conversation I can remember having with Stephen, and as much as I'd like to save the world, I don't think he gave it to me."

"Forget about it for now," he said. "You look tired."

"So do you." She pulled a pillow toward her chest. "When's the last time you had a good night's sleep? I mean a really good night's sleep."

"High school."

"I'm serious."

Nate reached for the box and pulled out a slice of pepperoni pizza. "So am I."

He saw her look at his scars, and he automatically pulled down his sleeves. It was a habit he'd gotten used to after the explosion, just like the habit he'd gotten into of wearing long sleeves to cover them. She understood loss. He knew that. But that didn't mean it was easy to open up about what had happened. The events of that day had been etched forever in his mind and followed him into his dreams at night. He'd yet to find an escape.

She set the pillow aside and ran her finger across one of the scars. "These are why you always wear long sleeves."

Nate stared at the brick wall behind her. There were so many things he admired about her. Her vulnerabilities coupled with her inner strength. She'd shared with him about Hannah and Kevin. But when it came to him sharing his story, something always managed to hold him back.

"You have nothing to hide," she said, leaning forward.

"Don't I?" He hesitated, then rolled up his left sleeve, revealing his forearm. The red markings, still raised, ran from his wrists to his elbows. A constant reminder of that day. "Keeping them covered helps to avoid questions and the answers they expect me to give."

She rested her hand on the back of his hand and caught his gaze. "Paige told me you were involved in the attack. It was all over the news, but I had no idea you were one of the victims affected by the bombing."

"To be honest, it's not something I bring up. 'Hey. I'm Nate and I was a victim of the Hyde Hotel Bombing.' Most of the time—okay, all the time—I just try to forget."

"Except that doesn't work, does it?"

"Are we talking about you or me?" he asked, trying to read her expression.

Gracie pressed her lips together. "Maybe both. This isn't exactly how I planned to spend the past couple days. And every time I start thinking about Hannah . . . I just miss her so much."

"I'm sorry, Gracie, so sorry, and I know that doesn't come close to helping."

"Thanks for being such a good friend," she said. "These last few days have been tough for you as well."

Friends.

Which was what he wanted. He'd always teased Kevin that if Kevin didn't end up marrying her, he would. At the time, he really had just been joking. At least on one level. Gracie had always seemed like the perfect catch. But Kevin had been one of his closest friends and there was no way Nate would have ever done anything to get between the two of them.

"Can I ask you a very personal question?" she said.

"Okay."

"I saw the details of what happened on the news, but what happened to you when the bomb went off?"

He pressed his hands together, emotionally back on the couch in his psychologist's office. How many times had she told him to stop running? "Are you asking as a friend, or a shrink?"

"You always were good at deflecting a situation with humor."

Nate caught the amusement in her voice. But the only person with whom he'd shared what had happened that day was his own shrink. He hadn't even talked to his brother or parents about the details, which meant they only knew what the news channels had reported. And what had happened physically to him. Now Gracie was wanting to see what was behind the solid wall he'd constructed around him, and for some crazy reason, a part of him wanted to let her in. Because ignoring what had happened, and continuing to push his feelings aside, hadn't worked so far.

"We'd been partners for just over a year. Ashley was smart and tough and knew how to handle herself. She'd just gotten married six months before the bombing, and at their wedding, her husband came up to me and told me he was counting on me to keep her safe. And even though it was a promise I knew I might not be able to keep, I told him I would. We were homicide detectives, not street cops. You know how it goes. In the back of your mind you know it could happen to you, and yet every day you go out there, with the goal to bring justice and make the world a better place."

But sometimes, that wasn't possible.

He squeezed his eyes shut, shocked at how clearly he could still remember the details of that morning. The smell of burning flesh. The heat scorching his arms. The crunch of broken glass beneath his shoes.

"We showed up at the scene of a homicide at eight thirty that morning at the hotel where CSI was busy processing the scene." He cleared his throat. "I stepped outside of the hotel to take a call where it was quieter and I could get some fresh air. As I left, I remember hearing this incredibly loud noise. People said you could hear the blast for miles. The ground shook, and at first I thought it was an earthquake. I turned around. One second the building had been there. The next second all that was left on one side was a blackened crater marking the site. I could feel the heat radiating from the blast. See the bodies strewn on the ground. Everything went deathly silent. I couldn't hear anything other than my heart pounding in my head. By the time first responders found Ashley and the others, they were all dead. Most of them were killed instantly by the blast. I was close enough to get hit by some of the shrapnel, but not close enough to be hit directly by the blast."

"I remember staring at the TV broadcast," she said. "Listening to how the bomber lured in the authorities, wanting as many casualties as possible."

He nodded. He reached for his grandfather's watch, then forced himself to dig back to the present when he remembered it wasn't there.

"Everything changed that day," he said.

She sat quietly across from him, her gaze fixed on his face. "And you can't stop feeling guilty that you were the one who survived?"

He shifted his gaze past her to a crack on the wall where the paint had chipped in a spot. It was as if she could read his mind. Her statement had hit its target, just as he assumed she knew it would.

"Yeah."

"In psychology, we call that a critical incident. Something that happens that's beyond your usual experience and out of your control. You spend every day viewing trauma, letting it numb you, until one day your brain can no longer process what happens."

His breathing quickened. "I had to identify her body. And then I had to go to her husband and tell him that she wasn't coming home that night."

He hadn't known how to tell her husband. He'd promised to take care of her. To keep her safe. But it had been a promise he couldn't keep. And he'd never forgiven himself.

"There was a second bomb that was found and disarmed," Nate said, "but it was already too late. Eighteen people were killed in that blast, including my team. It looked like a war zone, and we still have no idea who was behind it."

He hadn't planned to share with her what his own psychologist had to dig out of him, and yet for some reason Gracie was different. Talking to her came easy. Like she understood not just what he said, but what he didn't say. And while she was willing to tell him the truth, she did it all without judging or trying to force him into a mold.

"I'm sorry," she said.

"Don't be." He shot her a smile. "I think I know now why people like Stephen came to you."

"I think I just needed to hear from you today. Needed to hear from someone who understands loss."

He let the silence settle in between them for a moment. In the background, he could hear Macbain and the other agents working, their hushed voices echoing across the room in sporadic waves. The air conditioner clicked on. A siren wailed in the distance.

He turned back to Gracie. "Can I ask you something?"

"Sure."

"Since you lost Hannah, have you ever felt like you're going crazy?"

She pulled on the pillow tassel, keeping his gaze. "Honestly? More often than I admit."

"Because I can't sleep. I'm always irritated. Can't concentrate. It makes me wonder if I should be back on the job, but if I leave my job or get terminated, then what am I supposed to do? This job . . . it's all I know, Gracie. And I'm not sure I'm ever going to get back to normal."

"Can I switch and talk like a psychologist?"

He smiled, then nodded.

"How you're feeling doesn't mean it will be this intense forever, but you have to find a way to take care of yourself while you heal." She caught his gaze. "I know how PTSD feels, Nate. And I see it in you."

He sat silent, knowing she was right.

"It leaves you feeling that there aren't any safe places left," she continued. "You realize you have no control over anything that's going on around you. You lose what kept you grounded. Kept you together. It changes you."

"So you understand the guilt?" His voice was barely above a whisper.

"For months, I couldn't stop asking the same questions. What if I'd realized sooner that she was sick? If we'd tried more aggressive treatments. If I'd prayed more, or read my Bible more."

"I feel guilty for not protecting Ashley and the others," he said. "For not dying that day. And now . . . for not protecting you."

"Nate . . ."

"If I hadn't let you go to the bank with me, if I'd insisted you went into protective custody from the very beginning . . . none of this would have happened."

"You don't know that. Neither of us really know what might have happened. They would have found another way to get what they wanted."

"Maybe, but I almost lost you."

"But you didn't. You can't stop everything bad from happening to those you care about. And when something bad does happen, you can't always make things right again."

He studied her eyes that were rimmed with tears. She knew how hard it was for him to be vulnerable. For him to open up.

"I know. The feeling that you've done something wrong by being one of the survivors. That I shouldn't feel guilty because I lived and she didn't. That I just need to find a way to put it behind me and move on."

"I think you're wrong."

"What do you mean?"

"No one's asking you to ignore what happened. To just put behind you." She hesitated. "I'm sorry. I really am babbling on like a shrink, but I know what it's like to lose someone. To feel out of control when fate throws a wrench in your life and it all comes tumbling down like a house of cards."

"Like losing Hannah," he said.

"Yeah. Like losing Hannah."

26

Gracie felt her breath catch. Losing Hannah had changed her completely. That moment in time when everything she'd known and loved and expected out of life had shattered to the point that it had threatened to destroy her. There were no easy answers to grief and loss. No simple solution she'd discovered in all her years of studying. Answers that had always seemed perfect—answers she'd spouted off to clients— now seemed like a mess of clichés.

She searched for words to express the darkest journey she'd ever taken.

"When I lost Hannah," she said, "my entire life fell apart. I questioned God, agonized over the guilt, and felt completely powerless."

"How do you deal with it?" Nate leaned forward. "Ashley was my friend and my partner. I knew and cared about many of those who died that day, but you . . . you lost your daughter. And then Kevin on top of that. And yet there's this strength about you that doesn't make sense."

"How do any of us deal with loss and disappointment in life? We try to take one day at a time, doing everything we can to get through the next hour or minute. I know that Hannah would have told me to smile, and I want to make

Hannah proud. I want to live joyfully for the time I have left in life. Every day I try to find a way to hang on and make progress."

A phone rang on the other side of the room, reminding her for a moment where they were. Trying to find a way to stop not the death of just one child. Or the attack on just one location. But something that would change their way of life forever.

"You might not have lost a child," she said, focusing back on Nate, "but every day you're forced to show up at a crime scene and deal with the aftermath of something terrible. It doesn't matter who it is. A mother, a child, a criminal . . . you have to push aside your emotions and process the scene. And in order to cope, you have to numb your emotions so you can deal with it. But that numbness isn't enough to prepare you for the death of a partner, and everything else you experienced that day." She paused. "How close were you to Ashley?"

"She was like a sister. Her family invited me to their Fourth of July barbeque and Thanksgiving dinner, and I hung out with her brother watching the Super Bowl. It doesn't always work out that way with partners. You trust them with your life, though, which changes relationships. Watching her die that day along with others . . . All I know is that part of me died that day. And part of me wished I really had died. I still don't know how to get rid of that."

"Survivor's guilt is real, Nate. Do you know how many times I begged God to take me and not Hannah? It didn't make sense. She had her entire life ahead of her. She deserved to live. Or at least that was what I thought. But for whatever reason, God chose not to save her. At least not in a physical sense." She'd tried to work through her own understanding of healing over the past few years, and while she knew that she'd never completely understand it, she'd come to some measure of peace with Hannah's "eternal healing."

She touched his knee. "But maybe that's it. Who we are is made up partly of our experiences. You won't ever be the same again. You'll never be able to erase that part of your life. Both the experiences of having Ashley in your life and the grief that day brought. It makes you human, Nate. Just be patient with yourself. Give yourself the time you need to heal."

He reached out and laced their fingers together. "I feel guilty even comparing my loss to yours, but thank you."

"I haven't done anything. I'm still in the middle of the journey myself, which is why I'll never claim to have all the answers. But I do know what it's like to lose someone. Sometimes that's enough."

He pulled his hand away from hers and leaned back on the couch. "What about God?"

"What do you mean?"

"You said you found a way to hold on to your faith. Why is it that it's easy to run from God until something goes wrong? That moment when your life is hanging by a thread—why is that the moment you suddenly decide you need him? I'd done a good job of closing myself off from God, and now I find myself demanding answers from him."

His questions resurrected her own demons. Nights she'd spent questioning God, begging for answers and relief from the pain. Some questions were never answered. But she'd started to realize that was okay.

"I don't have an easy answer, Nate. I had to fight to find my faith again. And there were times when all I wanted to do was walk away. There are still times today when I want to yell at God and tell him I'm done. How could a good God let something like that happen? But I think he understands when we question him. I think he's there waiting for us to come back and realize he was always there."

"And the answers you found?"

"Sometimes there aren't any answers. Sometimes you just have to keep walking forward and holding on to whatever faith you have left. I had to let myself grieve. I know I'll never get over losing Hannah, but I know that one day I'll see her again."

"I think I'm finally finding a way out of the

306

darkness, but getting rid of the guilt, whether logical or not . . ."

"You have to let go of the guilt, Nate, or you'll never heal. What happened that day wasn't your fault, and nothing you could have done would have stopped what happened. And with Hannah, I did everything I could to save her, but sometimes everything you do just isn't enough."

"And the days you just want to quit?"

"We can start with today. There's usually another trigger, and before I know it, I'm drowning in self-pity. Sometimes pulling myself out seems just as hard as it did the first time we were hit with Hannah's diagnosis."

"Wednesday was my first day back on the job. I've been off for three months, waiting to get medical clearance. I was convinced that coming back would help me forget everything that happened. Like getting back into the saddle, and yet . . . I feel like it happened yesterday. Like it happened only minutes ago and not months. The images are that clear."

"What you're saying makes complete sense. I know how trauma can change a person. Sometimes it destroys them. But if we allow God to step in, he can take those broken pieces and turn them into something beautiful."

"I don't want this to destroy me, and yet sometimes . . ." He struggled to put his thoughts into words. "Sometimes I don't know how to escape the panic and anger that's always just under the surface."

"I know this sounds like a platitude, but give yourself time."

"Thanks for listening to me, though I feel like I'm the one who needs to be your rock today."

She leaned forward and pressed her hand against his knee again. "Stop worrying about me. I'll be fine. And all of this will be over soon."

She studied his face. He'd allowed himself to be vulnerable with her, something Kevin had never been able to do. She fought the urge to let him kiss her again. To explore what she couldn't deny was happening between them. But now wasn't the time. There would be a time and a place to discover whatever was happening. When all of this was over. Because first he needed to find out who he was on this side of tragedy. And in the meantime, find a way to put an end to this nightmare.

27

Grace glanced at the clock, then turned back to Nate. Even though she could sense there had been something about tonight that had brought a sense of healing to both of them, she could tell he was exhausted. And so was she. But there was also a part of her that didn't want this moment to end. She sat beside him, feet pulled up beneath her and her knee against his leg.

Am I really ready to take another chance with my heart, God?

"You need to go home and get some rest," she said.

"I'm fine. You're the one I'm worried about."

She shot him a smile. "You might need to rethink that, considering I'm the one holed up in a safe house for the night. You have to go out there and brave the bad guys on the street."

"Touché."

"Face it," she said. "We both need rest. If we're going to get to the bottom of this, we're both going to need to be at our best. And besides, you've got nothing to worry about. You're leaving me in a safe house with two guards. Not sure you could get much safer than that."

"But I'm not just talking about your physical safety. These agents will make sure you're okay, but I know this day has been emotionally draining as well."

"Actually, you won't get any arguments from me. I promise to get a good night's sleep."

"Good. We're going to figure this out, Gracie."

"Figure out the case . . . or what's happening between us?" She surprised herself with her bold words. Maybe the past couple hours had been nothing more to him than a free counseling session, but for her, it had made her realize what she wanted again in life. Someone she could share with. Could laugh with.

Someone to love her.

He smiled at her. "I think I'd like to figure out both."

"And the case? What if we don't find the patch?"

"Don't go there. There's too much at stake." His eyes seemed to pierce through her, all the way to her heart. He smiled again. "I'll be here early, and I'll bring breakfast. Bagels and coffee okay?"

"If you make them chocolate chip." She smiled back, knowing he was trying to distract her, but the fear had yet to disappear completely, safe house or not.

"I can do that. And one more thing," he said, pulling something out of his pocket. "I almost forgot, but since your phone is at the bottom of the lake, here's a replacement and charging cord for you in case you need to call . . . well, anyone. It's a secure phone no one will be able to trace."

"Thank you. I need to check in with my parents and a few other people. Let them know I'm okay."

"Anything else?"

"Yes. Go."

"Okay. The guards will stay out here, but you and Macbain each have your own rooms, so you should get a good night's sleep."

She watched him leave, marveling at the fact that the very day that marked her greatest loss had also brought her a possible chance for new love. Was that what God was giving her? A brand-new beginning?

What happened if the grid went down and everything she knew was suddenly ripped away, including any chance for something between her and Nate?

The fear started creeping in again.

She closed her eyes and pushed it away.

"You okay?"

She looked up at Macbain, who stood in front of her with a mug of coffee. "Sorry. It . . . it's been a long day, hasn't it?"

"I'm still trying to work my mind around the fact that I'm sitting in the middle of an FBI safe house." He let out a low laugh. "Not exactly what I had planned for the day."

"Me either. How was the interview?"

He sat down on the edge of the coffee table, then took a sip of his drink. "I told them the same things I told the police. I've also been working with the tech team nonstop for the past few hours, but without that patch . . . if we don't have it, there's no way to stop what could happen."

"Can't you develop another one?" she asked.

"Eventually." He set his mug down next to him. "But not only would we have to have access to what Stephen discovered about the grid's vulnerabilities, we don't have that kind of time. It could easily take a dozen programmers months to develop something like this. And they're estimating we have less than forty-eight hours before what's going on here is put into place. Stopping it is like finding a needle in a haystack."

"So there's nothing we can do?"

"I'm not saying I'm giving up. I told them I'd sleep for a couple hours, then get back to work. I can't help but feel like I'm missing something. Stephen said I could help, but I just don't know how."

"I guess all you can do is keep trying."

"What about your interview? How did it go?"

"I'm pretty sure I didn't come up with anything new either. Stephen told me he left me everything I needed to put an end to this. But how can I when I don't know what that means?"

"If we knew the answer to that, neither of us would be sitting here."

"I am sorry for the loss of your friend. I suppose you haven't really had any time to grieve."

"No. I thought I might go see his sister. I might even try to make it to the funeral, but I don't know."

"We don't have to make any decisions tonight. I know this has been hard. Get some sleep. I have a feeling we're going to have a long day tomorrow. Maybe something will click by then."

"Maybe."

He grabbed his mug and stood up.

"Good night then."

"Good night."

Grace yawned, then looked toward the room where they'd told her she'd sleep tonight. Macbain wasn't the only person who needed a good night's sleep, but as tired as she was, she didn't want to be alone. She glanced at the phone Nate had left her, tempted to call him. But she was going to have to get through this on her own for now. Two agents sat on the other side of the large room, laughing quietly over coffee and a game of cards. She told them good night, then headed to bed.

The room she'd been assigned to lacked any kind of personal touch. Just a bed and a dresser, and a painting of a dog on the wall that made it seem almost more cold and sterile than it already was. Someone had left a pair of red drawstring pajama pants and a long-sleeved T-shirt on the bed, the only real splash of color in the room. Nate had promised to bring her a couple outfits of clothes and a few other essential items in the morning, but for tonight she just wanted to forget that she'd almost died. Forget someone clearly wanted her dead. Forget that Nate had officially stolen her heart.

She'd call her parents, touch base with Anne, and deal with all of that tomorrow.

At one o'clock Grace lay staring at the ceiling like she'd done the last hour, and the hour before that. Shadows played in the room from the streetlight seeping in through the blinds. She pulled the blanket up around her shoulders and turned over, trying to find a more comfortable position to sleep. But she wasn't sure she was going to be able to find rest tonight. She was used to helping her patients deal with a laundry list of issues from divorce, to childhood traumas, to the pull of addiction. She'd learned over the years to keep her work separate from her personal life. To compartmentalize other people's issues so she didn't drag their problems home with her at night. And most of the time, it worked.

But this was different. This time she was the patient. She had no idea how to handle what was going on around her. She understood trauma, but not at the level of someone trying to take her life. That was something reserved for heroines in the books she read and the movies she went to see. They always ended up being saved by some dashingly handsome hero.

Like Nate.

His image hovered in front of her, playing with her heart. Except she knew there were no guarantees that everything would work out in this situation. They still didn't know who was behind the threats, or how to stop the grid from going down.

No . . . She didn't even want to go there.

Maybe she'd read too much into what he'd said. Into a kiss that never would have happened under normal circumstances. But there was nothing normal about Nate Quinn. She was used to a nine-to-five job where she did everything she could to make her clients' lives better, then returned home. Nate's work was completely different. High adrenaline . . . Life-and-death situations. Facing the moment in people's lives when everything spiraled out of control. For a few days she'd become a part of that life. She wasn't sure it was a place she wanted to stay.

Besides, romance—and even knights on white horses—seemed like a frivolous thought when someone wanted to kill you.

I need your peace, Jesus. And your protection. Because everything seems so out of control.

Like she was spinning in a great void. She hated feeling out of control.

She took a deep breath, hating that her nerves

were shot and her body was so exhausted. She needed to sleep if she was going to think clearly and be able to help Nate in the morning. But instead her heart still pounded like a sledgehammer and her brain refused to settle down and let her sleep.

She closed her eyes, continuing her prayer, and eventually felt herself slowly drifting off to sleep. When sleep did come, though, it was full of restless dreams of her and Nate, and Stephen's lifeless body.

She woke with a start at the sound of something rattling in the other room. The now familiar wave of adrenaline surged through her as she turned back over to face the door. The sound of muffled voices filled the adjoining room.

The last time she thought she'd imagined someone in her house she'd been right.

No. Not this time. She was in a safe house with guards. There was nothing to worry about. It was probably just Macbain getting a drink or the agents doing something to keep themselves awake. She was safe. There was no way for them to find her. No way for them to get to her.

"Grace?"

She opened her eyes. Someone was standing at the foot of her bed with a flashlight swung in her direction.

"Grace?" Macbain locked the door behind him. "You need to get up."

"Why?" She squinted against the light. She must still be sleeping.

"You need to get up now. They found us."

"Who found us?" She swung her legs over the side of the bed, still caught between the reality of the moment and the lingering memories of her nightmares. "What are you talking about?"

"I got up to get a drink and heard some commotion in the living room." He grabbed her shoes and threw them on the bed on his way to the window. "There are two men in the other room. They've taken down the officers, which means they'll be in here in a few seconds at the most."

"How is it possible someone found us here?"

"I don't know, but we need to get out now. There's a fire escape on the other side of this window. I saw it earlier. If we can get out and get to the street, we might be able to get away."

Grace tried to shove away the panic. If their guards had been immobilized, there was no way help would reach them in time. They were on their own. They wouldn't be able to go out the front door.

They needed to run. Needed to dial 911.

"I need my phone." She grabbed it off the dresser while Macbain ripped up the blinds and undid the window latch. She clicked the On button, then swiped the screen.

Nothing.

Macbain was tugging on the window, trying to get it open.

She pressed the button again. She must have been so tired that she'd forgotten to charge it.

This wasn't happening. Not again.

She could hear footsteps scuffling in the other room and a door shutting. They were close.

She threw her phone down.

"I knew I shouldn't have left my land. This would never have happened there." Macbain tugged at the window. "It's jammed."

"Let me try." She checked the lock, then tugged on the window. But he was right. It wouldn't budge.

The bedroom door slammed open behind her and two dark figures entered the room. One shoved Macbain against the wall and the other one grabbed her by her arm.

Grace let out a scream that was quickly muffled by the man's hand across her mouth. Seconds later, she felt something sharp pierce her arm. A fog spread through her as the room went dark, and she collapsed into nothingness.

28

Nate jolted awake out of a deep sleep. He glanced at the clock on the nightstand beside him, not sure what had woken him up. It was only three thirty. He didn't feel like he'd slept at all since he'd finally managed to fall asleep, but he knew he had. Gracie had filled his dreams, and no matter how much he wanted to push her away, she was still there, hovering in the recesses of his mind.

He didn't remember the last time a woman had affected him the way she did. He hadn't been able to ignore the connection between them, no matter how much he wanted to. Something about her smile, her compassion, and her grounded, no-nonsense way of looking at life intrigued him. And most of all, she managed to stir his heart in a way he couldn't simply dismiss.

But that didn't mean they were right for each other. Or that he was ready to move forward because of what his heart might be feeling. He still had to find healing himself before trying to make a relationship work. And he had to restore his faith again.

Without that in place, no relationship was going to work.

How did I forget how to trust you, God? How did I get so lost?

Gracie had encouraged him to open up to his grief and everything he'd been avoiding. He'd tried for so long to do it on his own. Tried to shake off the all-consuming guilt he'd taken on for failing his partner and team. Tried to find a way to justify the reality that he was alive while so many others had died. His job was to save and protect. Watching eighteen people die had shattered all of that. If he couldn't safeguard those around him, then what right did he have to wear a badge?

Even if there had been no way to stop what happened.

He blew out a lungful of air. Gracie hadn't been the only one to talk to him about survivor's guilt. His counselor had assured him that guilt was a common response to trauma. But she'd also told him that if he wasn't careful, he'd end up being eaten alive by its destructive lies. He'd watched the guilt affect his relationships with his family and friends. His relationship with God. It had pinned him down and left him feeling helpless because he hadn't been able to stop the evil taking place around him.

Just like Kevin.

He rolled over onto his side as his mind made the connection. Kevin had allowed the death of his daughter to immobilize him. It had stopped him from healing, and in the end he'd walked away from a relationship with the one person who completely understood his loss. But Nate understood why Kevin had bailed. The bombing had changed him too. Suddenly circumstances had shattered his normal life. It had affected his view of the future, his faith, and left him numb.

Loss often brought out both the best and worst in people. Gracie and Kevin would have grieved on a different timetable but, in the end, would have come out different people because of what they'd gone through. They'd understand exactly how much the other was hurting, and yet each looked at grief differently. A reality that had eventually pulled them apart.

Gracie, though, had shown him another side of grief. Her loss was still there, and time would never simply erase it. But he'd seen the strength in her. And a joy despite the pain. Instead of letting grief cripple her, she'd managed to take that loss and use it to help others. It was as if Hannah's death had become a reminder to her about what was important. What was real and meaningful.

"We try to take one day at a time, doing everything we can to get through the next hour or minute. I know that Hannah would have told me to smile, and I want to make Hannah proud. I want to live joyfully for the time I have left in life."

Gracie had been right. He needed to start living again. He knew there was no timetable. No quick fix. Knew that even his faith couldn't erase the grief. But it could give him hope. He wouldn't ever be the same again. He was finally beginning to realize that. But even Jesus lived as a man who understood grief.

When he closed his eyes, he could see her smile. Could hear her voice, telling him it was time to move forward. That it was time to take a chance.

Three hours later, Nate turned onto the street of the safe house with a bag of chocolate chip bagels on the passenger seat and two Styrofoam coffee cups in the cupholders. He'd managed to go back to sleep, and although his alarm had gone off before he wanted to get up, he was ready to get the day going and find a way to put an end to things. The FBI was holding a briefing at seven thirty, but first he wanted to see Gracie.

He slowed down at the sight of two marked cars sitting outside the apartment building. His mind immediately switched to alert. Something had happened. An ambulance was parked on the other side of the police cars. He jumped out of the car, leaving breakfast in the front seat, and ran across the lawn. Just because there was a break-in didn't mean it had anything to do with Gracie. There were dozens of break-ins every day in the Dallas city limits.

But his gut told him this was no coincidence.

He held up his badge as one of the officers

standing outside started to motion him back.

"Detective Nate Quinn from homicide," he said. "What's going on?"

"There was a break-in at one of the apartments. Neighbor called it in."

"Which apartment?"

"I'm sorry, but I was told not to talk about the situation. You'll have to speak with the agent in charge."

Nate glanced toward the building. Agent Brown was heading out the front door. His stomach churned as he ran to catch up with him. If the safe house had been compromised, why hadn't he been informed?

Oh God, tell me this isn't happening. Tell me nothing's happened to her.

"What's going on?" he asked, stopping in front of the man.

Agent Brown hesitated, then motioned for Nate to come with him inside the building. "I was getting ready to call your boss, but you might as well know what happened. A neighbor noticed that the front door was ajar. He went inside and found two bodies."

Nate stopped in front of the elevator. "Bodies?"

"Both my agents are dead."

The doors to the elevator opened, but Nate didn't move. He couldn't have understood the man correctly. "Dead?"

"And our witnesses are gone."

"What do you mean, they're gone?" Nate fought to process the news as he stepped into the elevator. There had to be something he was missing. Some mistake in the information he'd just been given. But from the look on the agent's face, he was dead serious. "Where are they?"

"I don't know. I showed up here a few minutes ago, responding to the call."

"I want a look inside."

"Of course."

He followed the officer out of the elevator and down the hall to apartment 612. They'd kept to a short list of people who knew where Gracie was in order to avoid something like this. The only explanation that made any sense was that somewhere they had a leak, but who? Everyone involved in the situation on his side he trusted completely.

But maybe he'd been wrong. The ambush at the bank. The accident in the car two nights ago. And now this. This was no coincidence. The only other options were that someone had somehow hacked into their communications. Which would make sense. They'd bugged Stephen's office. Probably hacked into the elevator he and Paige had taken. Someone who had the ability to take down the grid would find hacking into FBI surveillance a piece of cake.

"Our ERT is on their way, but it looks like whoever broke in picked the lock."

And managed to take down two trained agents? It didn't make sense.

Nate stepped inside the room where he and Gracie had sat together just a few hours ago. A chair was knocked over beside the first agent. The second one was slumped against the wall. Cards lay scattered across the table.

"They didn't have a chance," Agent Brown said. "Both of them were shot execution style."

"Looks to me like they didn't even know what hit them."

"I agree. They're here at the table playing a game of cards, someone managed to breach the property, then *bam . . . bam*. And there's no sign of the witnesses."

Where are you, Gracie?

They should have doubled the guards, he thought as they moved to Gracie's bedroom. Should have realized these guys would stop at nothing to finish their agenda. It was his job to take care of her. He'd promised to protect her and instead he'd let her walk right into a trap.

"Someone had to have seen or heard something," Nate said, standing in the middle of the room where she'd been sleeping.

"It's possible. Looks like she tried to get out the bedroom window when they realized someone had broken in, but the window was jammed. The blinds are pulled back and someone tried to get out, but couldn't."

"What about the neighbor who called it in?"

"He didn't see anyone."

"Can I talk with him?"

"I can arrange that."

"Thank you."

His phone rang, and he pulled it out of his pocket. "Paige?"

"Where are you? I just got the call that our safe house has been compromised."

"I know, because I'm standing here in the middle of it. Two FBI agents are dead—"

"And Grace and Macbain?"

"They're gone." He raked his fingers through his hair. "Paige . . . tell me how this happened. No one was supposed to know they were here."

"I don't know."

He didn't want to think about the obvious option that there was a leak. That someone on his team or in the FBI had been behind this. But how many millions of dollars were at stake? How easy would it have been to pay someone off?

The clothes Gracie had worn yesterday were neatly folded at the edge of the bed. He'd brought her some clothes from her house, thanks to Becca, who hadn't been particularly happy to see him. How could he blame her?

He picked up the phone he'd given her. Dead. That's why she hadn't called 911. The bag of things Becca had brought her in the hospital lay neatly on the small dresser next to the one set of clothes she had, a toothbrush, and a tube of tooth-paste.

Someone had taken her, and he hadn't been here.

"We're checking traffic cams, and we've got agents canvassing the neighborhood, but so far we have no idea where they are. It's going to take time."

"We don't have time." His instinct was to yell at someone—anyone—for their incompetence, but flying off the handle wasn't going to help. They needed to narrow down the information they had and lay out a plan.

Brown signaled him again and Nate stepped out into the hallway to speak with the man who'd first called 911.

"I'm Detective Nate Quinn. I know you've already spoken to one of the officers, but I'd like to know exactly what you saw."

"Not much, really. When I came out to walk my dog, I noticed that the door wasn't shut. I've always felt safe here, but my brother's house was broken into a couple of weeks ago. I think it made me a bit paranoid. Besides that, neighbors are supposed to watch out for each other, though I thought this apartment was still empty."

"What happened next?"

"I stepped inside the apartment, you know, just in case someone might be hurt. Called out, but no one answered. I started to leave when I noticed the two men lying on the floor on the other side of the room. I admit . . . I kind of freaked. It's one thing when you see a body on TV, but to see two actual bodies . . . That's when I called 911."

"What did 911 tell you to do?"

"When I assured her that they were dead—it was pretty obvious—she told me to go back to my apartment without touching anything, lock the door, and that she had people coming. That's it."

"Did you see anyone entering or leaving the building?"

"I looked out my window once I was back inside and saw two guys walking past the building. I don't know if they were involved or what they were doing." The man glanced back at the door to his apartment. "Can I go now?"

"Fine." Nate's panic escalated.

He rushed back into the adjoining loft to where Agent Brown was talking to another agent in the middle of the room.

Nate interrupted him. "I need to know how this happened. We turned our witnesses over to you barely twelve hours ago, and they've vanished, and two people are dead."

Agent Brown frowned. "Trust me, I wish I had answers for you. We're working as fast as we can, but right now we just don't have much. We'll scan for prints, but there isn't a lot to go on. The guards are both dead. The one witness didn't see anything, and so far, the building's security camera didn't get anything either. I've got someone going through the safe house's interior cameras."

Nate reached inside his pocket for his grandfather's watch, irritated when it wasn't there. He wanted to make a deal with God. Promise him whatever he wanted if he would just bring Gracie back. He'd quit running. Start going to church every Sunday, read his Bible twice a day . . .

He drew in a deep breath. He knew that wasn't how it worked. He couldn't make deals with God. Maybe because he wanted Nate to trust him instead. To realize that God was the One who was in control of the situation. That this world wasn't Nate's final destination.

I want to see you in all of this, Jesus. I want to trust you even when everything seems to be falling apart. I just don't know how to do this anymore.

"Detective?"

Nate glanced up. "Yes?"

"We just found a possible lead on one of the city street cams. I need you to come with me."

29

Grace's eyes opened at the sound of her name. She stared at the ceiling, trying to figure out where she was. The last thing she remembered was trying to go to sleep at the safe house. Someone had broken in . . . Macbain had come into her room, insisting that they leave . . . They'd tried to escape out the window, but then the window had jammed . . .

What else? And why did her body feel so . . . so heavy, and her brain like she'd just stepped into a fog? She needed to get up. Needed to find Nate.

"Grace. Can you hear me?"

She turned her head toward the sound of a voice. Macbain hovered above her.

"Grace."

"What happened?"

"A couple guys grabbed us at the safe house and brought us here."

Her mind fought to focus. How was that possible? They'd been inside an FBI safe house. Nate had promised her she'd be fine. Flashes of what had happened last night began to surface. Two men had come into her bedroom. One of them grabbed her. And then . . . nothing.

"I need to get up," she said. "We have to get out of here before whoever took us comes back."

"Just take a deep breath first, Grace."

He helped her sit up on the cot she'd been lying on, then waited as she put her feet on the ground. A wave of nausea spread through her. She pressed her hand against her stomach. What had they done to her?

She tried to get up, then stumbled, barely catching her balance.

"Whoa." Macbain grabbed her shoulders, then helped her sit back down on the cot. "Seriously. You need to slow down."

She glanced around the small room, waiting for the nausea to pass. There was a window at the top of one wall and a door. On the other side of the room was a row of computer monitors hanging over a long desk that was covered with processors, cords, and dozens of other computer things.

"Where are we?" she asked.

"A basement, but as for the where, I don't know."

"Have you seen anyone?"

"Not yet. I only woke up a few minutes ago, but I'm assuming they're waiting for us both to wake up. And by the way, if you feel a bit groggy and sick, I'm going to say it's because they drugged us. I felt the same way when I woke up, but it should pass."

It had to, because she couldn't think straight.

"Do you have any idea what they want?" she asked.

"Not yet, but I think we can easily assume it has to do with this whole mess Stephen was caught up in."

She glanced back up at the window. "We need to get out."

"The window's too small. Trust me, I've studied the place the past few minutes. And the only door's rock solid. I tried that too."

Maybe, but there was no way she was just going to give up. "And the computers? Can we use them to communicate?"

"There's no Wi-Fi or internet connection."

Great.

The door opened, and a man stepped into the room. Nausea shifted into panic. She recognized the bearded face and piercing gray eyes from the bank.

"You were the driver," she said.

"We meet again."

"You'll never get away with this—"

The man shot her a smile. "And yet I believe I already have."

Macbain stepped in front of Grace. "Just tell us what you want."

"It's quite simple, really. I need you to implement the code that Stephen Shaw wrote. He discovered a vulnerability in the grid, and we're going to use it to take it down. Everything you need is on this," he said, handing a flash drive to Macbain. "My investors are expecting this breach in the grid's vulnerabilities to be implemented within the next twelve hours."

Grace squeezed her eyes shut for a moment. This couldn't be happening. Not after everything they'd gone through. There had to be a way to stop the grid from going down.

Macbain took a step forward. "Wait a minute. Stephen worked for months on this project. And you think I can magically implement his code in a few hours?"

"He's already done all of the work, and you know more than anyone else about his procedures and methods."

"And if I can't . . . or won't?" Macbain asked.

"I thought you might say something like that." The man showed Macbain a photo on his cell phone of a young girl. "Then maybe you need to rethink things."

"Danielle?" Macbain grabbed the man's arm. "She has nothing to do with any of this."

The man jerked away from Macbain's grip, then pulled a handgun out of its holster. "Don't ever do that again."

Macbain held up his hands and took a step back. "I'll help you, if you swear you won't touch her."

"And I'll leave her alone, if you do what I say. In fact, if you can implement this code, I might be able to arrange safe passage out of the US for you and your daughter. Because, trust me, you won't want to be here once the grid goes down." The man's smile faded. "And if you don't come through, your daughter will die. If you try something funny with the code, she will die. Hopefully that's enough to motivate you to do as I say."

"You can't do this—"

"Sit down and get to work." He pointed to the other side of the room. "I'll be monitoring everything you do very closely, so be smart."

Macbain started across the room, then hesitated. "What about her?"

The man turned and caught Grace's gaze. "The FBI might believe you don't have the patch, but I'm convinced you know more than you're saying. You agreed to make the exchange until the FBI panicked and called off the swap. I want the patch. I was willing to pay for it. This time I'll simply consider not killing you if you give it to me."

Grace hesitated. Their belief that she had the patch was the only thing keeping her alive. Without it, they didn't need her. Or maybe it really didn't matter if she had it or not.

I have no idea what to do, God.

She'd spent so much time over the past three years fighting for the desire to live. Now she knew she wasn't ready to die.

"I don't have it," she said.

"I don't believe you."

"It's the truth. If Stephen left me something else, I have no idea where it is."

"Then start here." He grabbed a bag off a table and dumped out the contents. She recognized them from the safe-deposit box. "Stephen left this stuff for you for a reason. If you don't have the patch, then the answer to where it is has to be in here somewhere. Find it.

"And Macbain . . ." He held up the photo of Danielle again. "I'll be back in a minute. All you need to do is focus on your job."

Grace heard the click of the lock as he left the room. She glanced back at the table and the pile of papers Stephen had wanted her to have. But why? She couldn't read or understand code. How was she supposed to help?

"Find the Colonel. He can help stop this. I left everything you need to put an end to this with Oscar."

Oscar was supposed to have everything they would need to be able to stop them from taking down the grid, and the Colonel could help them stop it.

They had the safe-deposit box and they had Matthew. They also had the malware that could take down the grid, but not the patch that could protect it.

So where was it?

What were they missing?

"Do you know what's crazy about all of this?"

Macbain said, staring at the screen in front of him.

"What's that?"

"I've spent the past few years building up that compound, with my generators, solar power, fresh water system, and weapons stash, and now they're forcing me to implement Stephen's work and take down the grid."

Grace picked up one of the maps. "You know we can't actually take down the grid. You're going to have to find a way to stall."

He spun around in his chair. "He's threatening to kill my daughter."

"I know, but according to him, we've got twelve hours. Nate and his team will find us before then."

"I'm glad you're so confident in their skills, but I'm not. No one knows where we are, Grace. What if it was your daughter they were threatening?"

She took a step back and tried to fight against the rush of emotion. She wanted to believe that Nate and Paige would find her, but they had no idea where she was. But no matter what this man was threatening, they couldn't give them what they wanted. Taking down the grid would be catastrophic.

"All you have to do is add some kind of bug to the code or something," she said.

"You don't just add some kind of bug to the code or something. And besides, Stephen was the genius. This . . . this is way over my paygrade. I'll be lucky if I can actually add the code, let alone change it."

"What about your work in the military? Didn't you do this kind of stuff?"

"I wasn't exactly playing the role of a black hacker. I was fixing security issues, not breaking into the nation's infrastructure. And besides that, you heard what they said. They'll kill my daughter if I don't do what they say."

"Maybe they're bluffing."

"Did you see the photos of Stephen's body?" Macbain shook his head. "I'm pretty sure they're not bluffing."

She braced her hands against the table. "I don't want anything to happen to your daughter, but the alternative is that without electricity, food, and transportation, hundreds of thousands of lives are going to be at risk. There has to be a way to stop this."

Macbain looked at her for a long moment. "Do you really not have the patch, Grace? Because this guy clearly thinks you do. Maybe we could use it to make some kind of deal with him. If nothing else, it would ensure our getting out of the country."

"I'm not looking for a deal, and even if I were, I was telling the truth when I said I don't have it," she said. "If Stephen left me something else, I have no idea where it is."

"So telling them you'd make the swap was all just a ploy?"

"It was to buy time. An impulsive decision to try to stop whoever's behind this."

She continued digging through the diagrams of the power stations, infrastructure papers, and random notes Stephen had made, but none of it made sense to her. Why would Stephen leave her something she knew nothing about? No. If he had left her a clue, this wasn't how he would have done it.

She shivered in the cold, drafty basement. She was still wearing the red pajama pants and long-sleeved T-shirt she'd put on the night before. She wished she had a sweater. Her hand touched her wrist and her heart dropped as she looked down.

Hannah's silver charm bracelet was gone.

Grace glanced at the other side of the room where she'd been sleeping. It had to be here. She couldn't lose it. She tugged back the blanket of the cot, then checked underneath it. Nothing. She looked around the sides of the bed, making sure it hadn't fallen onto the floor. Something shiny caught her eye. She blew out a sharp breath of relief, then stooped down and picked up her bracelet. She started to stand up, then stopped. Something was on the other bed. A cell phone was peeking out from underneath the pillow.

She grabbed the phone, then glanced at Macbain, confused. If he had his phone here, then why hadn't he called for help? Unless . . .

The following thought left her queasy. Unless he was somehow in on this. But that wasn't possible. Stephen had told her to find him. Said he'd help.

She looked back at Macbain. He was still glued to his computer screen. She didn't have time to analyze the situation. She needed to get ahold of Nate. She quickly turned on the phone and searched the call history, looking for Nate's number. Most of the outgoing calls went to one number—she assumed it was Danielle's. There were four incoming calls on Wednesday that had to be from when Nate and she had called him.

"Grace? What are you doing?"

She quickly turned around.

"What are you doing?"

There was something in his voice that startled her. A coldness that hadn't been there before.

"I was looking for my bracelet and found a phone." She handed it to him, deciding to play innocent. "We can call—"

"You idiot!" He grabbed the phone out of her hands, then smashed it against the wall.

"What are you doing!"

"You're supposed to be looking for a clue to where the patch is."

"I said I don't have it, and if something is in the stuff he left me, I have no idea what to look for."

Grace's mind spun as the pieces started coming together, leaving a terrifying picture. Macbain had worked with Stephen in college when they'd

339

first started seriously messing around with computers and hacking. But Stephen had told her to go to him, which meant Stephen, as far as she could tell, believed Macbain could help.

She drew in a deep breath, determined to stand her ground. "This was you, wasn't it? You're behind all of this. You found a way to be on the inside of what was happening. Except your people couldn't figure out how to implement Stephen's code. Maybe he was never supposed to be killed. I don't know, but he's dead and now you're in a panic, because you're the one who has to do it now."

His whole demeanor changed.

"Get over here and sit down." Macbain grabbed a gun out of the drawer where he'd been sitting and aimed it at her. "I knew the charade would end eventually."

"Why play this game to begin with?"

"When you called, I knew I'd just stumbled upon the perfect opportunity. The police wanted me to be a part of the investigation. I was sure one of you had the patch I needed. I couldn't have planned it any better."

"And the accident on the lake?"

"It wasn't supposed to end that way. They were just trying to ensure you never guessed I was involved."

"And the phone call and the parking garage incident?"

"Apparently the people I work for believed I

had gone to the police and was working with the FBI. But I've straightened them out."

"But why try to take down the grid?"

"Do you have any idea how much other governments are willing to pay to take down the US grid?"

"Who's behind this?"

"Let's just say I discovered that some of these state-sponsored groups have far bigger budgets than even the companies they're hacking."

Stalling might not work, but she still wanted answers. "Why do they do it?"

"You name it. Political reasons, espionage, simple cyber warfare, revenge . . . As long as I'm on the receiving end, I really don't care."

"I might be able to understand why they are involved in this, but not you. You served your country. Why turn on everything you believed in? Why put the life of your daughter at risk?"

"I lost my wife serving my country. Lost my daughter because my ex-wife convinced the courts I wasn't fit to be a father. I woke up one day and everything I had worked for was gone."

"There are people willing to help—"

"You're a shrink. You should understand how hard it is transitioning back to civilian life. I couldn't get a job, so we had to live off credit cards until the benefits started kicking in, but it didn't matter. My wife had found someone else while I was gone and left me."

"So you found a job hacking for the wrong side."

"And I got Stephen thinking he was working for the right side."

"If you needed Stephen, why kill him?"

"He wasn't supposed to die. Not until he actually put his code into play anyway. But he found out the work he was doing wasn't what he thought it was and decided to let people know what was happening. And so what? Even without Stephen, I'm still good at what I do. As for the grid going down . . . it's going to happen eventually anyway. I figured I might as well get paid in the process, before I get out."

Her mind shifted for a moment to the guilt she and Nate had talked about last night. It was easy to give in to the loss. Somehow Macbain had let his own losses destroy who he was.

"And then what?" she said. "You go live in some third-world country the rest of your life?"

"I can do what I'm doing here, and live on the beach for a whole lot cheaper. Sounds like the perfect life to me. And have my daughter with me."

"You don't think your ex-wife will fight you on that one?"

"Shut up and stop asking questions. I've got very little time to finish implementing Stephen's code."

"So what happens now? You kill me?"

Macbain bound her hands behind her with a zip tie, pushed her into a chair, then sat back down where he'd been working. "I've learned over the past few days that I can't trust anyone to do what has to be done. Including taking care of my loose ends. And you're definitely a loose end."

30

Nate glanced at the ticking clock on the precinct wall. An hour and a half had passed since they'd discovered Gracie and Macbain were missing. They were running out of time. Time for finding Gracie and time for stopping the electric grid from going down. Unless the FBI could find a way to fix the vulnerability Stephen had discovered, the grid would go down. And without actually finding the patch he'd created, the odds of stopping whoever was behind this were slim.

And the cascading chain of events that would follow were going to change life as they knew it forever.

"Nate . . . I got you a pumpkin spice crème frappuccino," Paige said, handing him one of the cups she was carrying. "You might not need the caffeine, but I woke up tired, and I already know it's going to be a long day."

He took a sip of the drink. "Thanks."

"You're welcome."

He shifted his attention back to his desk where he'd been working the last thirty minutes. The street cam lead had been a bust. They'd caught a grainy photo of two men pulling up outside the building around the time the ME estimated the agents had been shot, but getting a close-up of their faces or license plate number had proven to be impossible.

Paige set her drink down on his desk. "You're lost in thought. What's going on?"

"Sorry." He rubbed his pounding temples. "I was just thinking."

"About Grace?"

"Yes, but more than that." He looked up at her, not sure if he was actually headed in the right direction, or if he was simply desperate for an answer. The FBI had an entire team of agents on this case, and while he believed in his own skills, he also knew that there was no way he could be completely objective on this case.

"We might not have been working long together," she said, "but I'm pretty sure I know that look of yours. You're on to something."

"What if Carl Macbain is the one behind this?" he said, deciding to simply throw out what he was thinking.

"Macbain?" Paige took a step back, the surprise clear in her expression. "Okay . . . I'll play along, though I'm not sure how that's possible. Stephen clearly trusted Macbain and even told Grace to go to him. And if he was in on it, why would someone try to kill him along with you and Grace?"

"Maybe he wasn't as indispensable to whoever he's working with as he thought he was."

Paige sat down on the edge of his desk and crossed her arms. "Wait a minute. How's that possible? Macbain has been working with us this entire time."

"Maybe." He grabbed a pile of papers from in front of him. "I was just looking at Stephen's phone records again. Macbain admitted that Stephen called him last week. But on the night he was killed, Stephen made a call to Macbain's number. Macbain was the unknown number that Stephen called in between his calls to Gracie."

"That's a good theory, but you're beginning to sound a bit like Stephen, if you ask me. Paranoid."

"Okay. What about this then? What's Macbain's greatest weakness?"

Paige hesitated. "His daughter."

"Exactly. If he is involved in this, not only would he have an exit plan, but I think he'd take her with him. Macbain's phone is waterproof and managed to survive the fall in the lake, but it wasn't found in the safe house. If he's planning to connect with his daughter before all of this is over, it would make sense he made sure he kept his phone with him."

"I thought we already tried to trace it."

"Kelli did, but the phone is off, so she wasn't able to pick up any signal."

"I don't know, Nate. I know you want to find Gracie and put an end to all of this. We all do. But this just seems like a bunch of random clues you're trying to make fit together."

"But if you put them together, it starts to make sense." He leaned back in his chair. "Let's look at motivation, then," he said. "Macbain lost custody of his daughter about a year ago. He petitioned the courts, but the judge refused to modify the child custody orders."

"Why? Because he lived off the grid?"

"I'm not sure how much that played into it, but according to the ex, he'd become paranoid. In one of her statements in the divorce case, she said he believed that the government was watching his every move, and he was always talking about moving to another country. We know Macbain had computer skills, maybe not as good as Stephen's, but enough that he ends up working as a hacker for hire."

"He's hired to take down the grid, but finds out it's above his skill set, so he finds a way to hire Eddie Sumter, and then Stephen," Paige said.

"Macbain believed Stephen had given Gracie the patch, and having that patch was the only way he could guarantee that no one could stop him."

"But running you all off the road? Don't tell me he planned that."

"I agree, that doesn't fit. Maybe there's someone else involved, or like I said, maybe he became a liability to the higher-ups. I don't know. But if he believed Gracie had the patch and was holding out, he needed someone to break into the safe house."

Paige's phone went off and she pulled it out of her pocket. "You might actually be on to something. An amber alert was just put out for a girl here in north Dallas. Want to guess what her name is?"

"Danielle." Nate stood up. "You believe me now? She's the one person he would worry about. He would do anything to ensure her safety. He's planning to flee the country with her before the grid goes down."

He strode across the noisy bull pen to Kelli's desk. "Kelli . . . I want you to try to trace that phone again."

"I've been monitoring the phone, but unless it's turned on—"

"Just try again. Please."

"Okay . . . I've got something this time. I can't guarantee he's still there, but he must have turned it on for a few minutes."

"Can you give me a location?"

"Give me a minute . . . I've got it," Kelli said. "I'm forwarding you the address right now."

"Notify the FBI and get a team there immediately. Paige and I will be right behind them."

"Detective Quinn."

Nate turned around at the sound of his name and paused as the uniformed officer walked up to him.

"I've got someone here who insists on speaking to you. She said it's urgent."

A woman stepped out from behind the officer. Nate worked to place the familiar face.

"I'm Anne Taylor. We met a couple days ago."

"Of course. Gracie's secretary."

"Yes. Is she okay? I haven't heard anything from her, and I'm worried sick."

"I'm not able to share with you the details of the investigation at this point, and I'm sorry, but I was just on my way out—"

"I won't keep you, but I have something for you. You're going to think this is crazy, but I went to feed Grace's fish tonight and try to clean up a bit—her office was left such a mess—and I found this."

Anne handed him a flash drive.

"Where did you get this?"

"Believe it or not, it was in the fish food. I don't know what it is, but after Grace found that key in the fishbowl . . . I just thought it might be significant. I can't see Grace leaving something like that in there."

"This is significant." Nate grabbed his coat off his chair. "I've got to go, but you might have just saved your country."

"What?"

"Long story," Nate said, slipping on his coat. "Kelli . . . I need you to get Agent Brown on the line and tell him what we've got and get tech working on it right away. If I'm right, we just found the patch."

"Where are you going?" Kelli asked.

"To find Gracie. We might have a chance to stop all of this after all."

• • •

SWAT punched through the front door of the ranch-style house while Nate and Paige stood outside the front door and waited for the signal that the house was clear. His heart pounded in his chest. If Gracie was in here, he could only pray that Macbain hadn't hurt her. If she wasn't here, he had no idea where to look for her.

I know you don't owe me anything, God, but if you can protect her . . .

Officers shouted from inside the house as they swept the rooms.

"Clear."

"Clear."

"Clear."

She has to be here, God . . . please.

Seconds ticked by. Adrenaline raced. He took in a slow, deep breath, then closed his eyes, but all he could see was Ashley's body in front of him. No . . . he opened them again. He wasn't going back there. Not today. He was going to find Gracie.

"We've got something."

Nate moved into the house as soon as Agent Brown gave them the signal and had them follow him into the basement. The dimly lit room was filled with computer monitors, a long desk on one side, and a table with a bunch of papers and a couple of cots on the other end.

But he was looking for only one thing.

Two of the officers had Carl Macbain on the floor,

while another officer was cutting off the zip tie around Gracie's wrists. As soon as she was free and saw him standing in the doorway, she ran to him.

"Gracie . . ." He pulled her against his chest, breathing in the smell of vanilla in her hair and feeling the warmth of her embrace. "Gracie, are you okay?"

"Yes, but I think it's too late. He's just finished using Stephen's source code to find the grid's vulnerabilities and implement—"

"We found the patch."

"What?"

"Oscar had it."

"Oscar . . . I don't understand."

"In Stephen's message, he told you that Oscar had everything you needed to put an end to this."

"But the patch wasn't in the fishbowl."

"He left it in the fish food. Anne found it. Those men that just came in here behind us have it and they're going to stop what Macbain tried to do."

"So this is really over?" she said, taking a step back.

"It won't be the last time someone tries to take down the grid, but yeah," he said, not ready to let go of her. "This is over, Gracie."

A wave of emotion rushed through her, and she blinked back the tears. "I wish Stephen had gone to the authorities with what he had instead of thinking he could handle things on his own. But his paranoia turned out to be legitimate."

"No guilt," Nate said.

She smiled up at him. "No guilt."

His phone rang, and he pulled it out of his pocket. "What have you got, Kelli?"

"Did you make it in time?"

"Are the lights still on?"

"For the moment," she said.

"We've got a team here making sure they stay that way," he said. "What about Danielle?"

"That's why I was calling you. A man was picked up about five minutes ago with Danielle in the back seat. She's fine and is on her way back to her mother right now. The officer who arrested the driver also found a pile of passports and cash in the trunk."

Nate glanced across the room where Macbain was now being led out of the room in handcuffs. "He was planning on skipping the country."

"Not anymore."

He hung up the phone, then turned back to Gracie. "The FBI is going to need to talk with you again about what happened."

"As long as this is finally over."

"There will be some loose ends to tie up," he said, "but yeah . . . I think this is finally over."

"We never had our breakfast," she said. "Maybe we can still try for those chocolate chip bagels and coffee some morning."

"I'd like that."

And he did. Wanted to see her again. Wanted to

see if something could happen between the two of them.

"But?" she asked, seeming to read his mind.

"I need some time to get my life back on track—both spiritually and emotionally—before I can even think about a relationship. It wouldn't be fair to you. Wouldn't be fair to either of us."

"No . . . You're right. You need time to heal. I totally understand that."

"And you? You've been through a lot this week, Gracie. Don't think it hasn't affected you."

"I don't. I've already decided to go talk to someone myself, to make sure I'm dealing with everything that's happened. I'm also going to steal Becca away for a couple days. We'll do a bit of antiquing, and I'll have time to eat that ice cream and do the binge-watching I'd planned for this week."

"Ms. Callahan, if you'll come with me."

Nate nodded at Agent Brown and stepped aside. Gracie smiled up at him before she left, making him wonder how he'd managed to lose his heart. But he couldn't expect her to wait for him, not with the tangled mess still inside him. They had no strings attached. No commitments made. She'd move on, and in the end, she'd be better off without him.

31

Grace leaned across the table and handed the four-year-old wearing Hello Kitty pajamas and a Santa hat a small container of glitter. Christmas had always been her favorite time of the year. After Hannah's death, it had become one of the hardest.

"Do you want a star on the top of your tree, Ella?"

Ella didn't even have to think. "The silver one."

"Here you go."

Next to her, Lily held up the construction-paper ornament she'd been coloring the past ten minutes. "Do you like it?"

Grace nodded. "I think it's going to look perfect on our tree."

Like Hannah, every child at the children's hospital had a story. Hospital stays had become the norm in a very abnormal life. But in the end, they were just children, trying to live in a world of uncertainty.

Friends and family had asked how she could stand coming back to the place where she'd lost so much. She simply asked them how could she not? She knew what these mothers and fathers were going through. Because she'd been there. It was a place where they understood her and she understood them. Just because she'd lost Hannah to a horrible disease, it was still a part of her life she couldn't pretend hadn't happened.

She glanced around the room that had been decorated with silver garlands, hanging snowflakes, and a ten-foot tree in the corner of the room. She couldn't help but smile. With the help of parents and volunteers, tables had been set up around the room, allowing the kids to work on making ornaments for the tree. In a few minutes Santa would show up with stockings filled with goodies for each of the children. The entire morning had been a success and worth every minute she and the others had put into planning it.

Ella's mom, Wendy, stepped up to the table and pulled her aside.

"Hey . . ." Gracie greeted her with a hug. "How are you doing?"

"I just wanted to tell you the doctor said that Ella's doing well and can go home. Probably tomorrow."

Grace felt her own tears surface as she pulled Ella's mother into another hug. "I'm so happy for you. She's looking good."

"I know. I also know there are no guarantees, but we've waited so long for this. If we can just get her home and start feeling like life is normal again."

Grace smiled, though she still wasn't sure what

normal was anymore. Was it normal to watch your child die? Normal for your husband to walk out on you because he couldn't handle the loss? If it was, she hated normal.

"Grace . . . someone's here to see you."

Grace turned around, then felt her breath catch at the sight of Nate. He stood in the doorway, hands behind his back, wearing that lopsided grin of his and making her heart race. She shoved aside a loose strand of her hair, wishing he didn't make her heart stir like she was a teenager with a crush. She hadn't seen him since the day SWAT had rescued her in the basement and arrested Macbain, before successfully securing the grid. Four weeks, three days, and five hours, give or take. It's not like she was counting.

She'd watched for updates on the news about the case, but she hadn't been able to find out anything. Apparently the authorities preferred to keep the near disaster under wraps.

She drew in a deep breath as he crossed the room to where she stood. Black jeans, a white button-down shirt layered with a brown sweater, and a long coat. She let out an inaudible sigh.

"Hey . . ." He stopped in front of her. "It's been a while."

Too long. "It's good to see you." *I didn't think I'd miss you so much.*

"I'm sorry if I'm interrupting," he said. "I didn't know you were having a party."

"No . . . it's fine."

"I couldn't get ahold of you, so I called Becca. She told me you were here. Assured me I wouldn't be in the way and told me I should come."

Grace laughed. "Sounds like Becca."

She wished it wasn't so good to see him. Wished her heart would stop pounding at the way he was looking at her. "It's our annual Christmas party. Right now, the kids are making cards."

He held up a red rose in front of her. "This is for you. You told me Hannah loved roses. And if I remember correctly, so do you."

"We did, and I still do." She held the rose and breathed in the subtle, sweet fragrance. "Thank you. It's beautiful."

Her heart stirred again. He wasn't afraid to talk about Hannah, and he didn't make her feel as if she needed to cover up her past.

"There was an update on the case," he said. "I wanted to tell you in person, before I head out of town, but if this is a bad time, I could always call you later."

Grace fought back the disappointment. She hadn't been able to stop thinking about him— no matter how many times she'd told herself he wasn't going to call and she needed to let go. They'd bonded under intense circumstances, but that wasn't enough to hold a relationship together. He'd told her he needed time to work things out, and she didn't think he expected her to wait for him.

This was just an update on the case before he left town. No matter how much she'd wanted to believe Becca, she'd been wrong. Nate—and their kiss—was something she was going to have to put behind her. She was going to have to let him walk away, for good this time. Something she knew deep inside. He wasn't ready to make a commitment. It would require more of an emotional payout than he could afford. She knew that.

"Do you have time to wait a few minutes?" she asked, shoving her doubts aside. "We're not quite done here, but if you give me another ten minutes I can give you my full attention—"

"Of course."

"In fact . . ." She glanced at a table of children. "I could use your help. We're making ornaments, and it looks like Micah over there could use some help with the glitter, if you don't mind getting your hands dirty."

"Glitter?" She caught the hesitation in his voice.

"You're pretty multitalented. I think you can handle the assignment."

Grace giggled as Nate sat down in an empty chair next to Micah, looking completely out of his element. For a man who spent his days chasing down the bad guys, how difficult could a handful of kids and a few bottles of glitter and glue be? Nate grabbed a piece of construction paper and a pair of scissors and began ripping pages out of a magazine. She saw one of the girls on the other side of the table laugh as he leaned forward and whispered something Grace couldn't hear.

"Who is he?" Wendy asked, nudging up beside her.

"Just a friend."

"Is he single?"

"Yes, but like I said. We're just friends."

"If you say so, but I saw your face when he walked into the room. It lit up. And so did his when he saw you. And on top of that he's a natural with kids. Look at him. Looks like he's cutting a Christmas tree out of those magazine pages."

It was impossible not to notice. She watched as he finished cutting, then grabbed a stapler and proceeded to staple the stack of trees together in the center. With all the kids now focused on what he was doing, he started creasing the pages at the staples so they fanned out and formed a 3-D tree.

"You sound surprised, but look at him. He'll make a wonderful dad one day."

"Enough." Grace busied herself with one of the tables, trying not to stare as Nate added glitter to his masterpiece.

She hadn't remembered him being so good with kids.

One of the boys reached out his paintbrush and dabbed a blob of red paint on the tip of Nate's nose. A tableful of giggles ensued.

"Hey." Nate laughed, then returned the favor with a dab of green paint.

Wendy was right. He was going to make a wonderful father.

"Why don't the two of you go talk," Wendy said. "You deserve a break, and there are plenty of parents to help out."

"I still need to clean up—"

"Go. And don't worry." Wendy shot her a smile. "I won't forget that you left me with the cleanup."

Grace grabbed two wet wipes and walked over to the table, wondering why she suddenly felt so nervous. "Looks like a couple of you have paint on your noses."

The kids all giggled as Grace handed Nate and the young instigator a wet wipe.

"I'm free, if you're done having so much fun."

"Are you sure?" he asked.

"Definitely."

He wiped the paint off his nose, then followed her.

"It looked like you were having as much fun as the kids," Grace said.

Nate laughed. "I have to say you're right."

"We try to give them something normal while they're here. Something to smile about." Grace grabbed her bag as they slipped out of the room.

"There's a garden just off the first floor. It's quieter there."

She walked down the hallway beside him, wondering if the garden had been the best idea. The last place she needed to be was alone with him. Because that meant dealing with her emotions.

"The kids loved you," she said, trying to fill the quiet between them. "You're great with them. And that tree . . . It was adorable."

"That was one crafty thing I remember my mother teaching me how to make. But if you're expecting to see an artistic side of me, that was all I've got."

She let out a low laugh. "Well, I'm still impressed."

"How are you doing?"

"I'm good," she said as they turned down another long hallway. Most of the children had gone to the party, leaving the rooms empty and quiet. "Mainly just glad I can put all of that behind me."

"I'm glad to hear that."

How had things become so . . . awkward between them?

What she wanted was for him to say something personal. Wanted him to gather her into his arms and kiss her like she'd dreamed the past few weeks. Wanted to hear that his heart was finally healed. And yet her head knew that wasn't going to happen.

They walked past a nurse in snowman scrubs. "Merry Christmas, Grace."

"Merry Christmas, JoAnn."

"How long have you been volunteering here?" he asked. "Everyone seems to know you."

"Maybe not everyone, but I started right after moving back here. When Hannah was in the hospital, I saw what a difference all the special activities made. Art therapy, pet therapy, holiday parties . . . Sometimes she was too sick to participate, but when she could, it was always the highlight of her day. There are dozens of volunteers who make it possible. I'm just one of them."

"It's got to be tough, I'd think. Spending time with families and children has to bring back your own memories."

They stepped through glass doors into the empty garden with a koi pond in the center. The well-kept space with sunlight streaming in from the windows gave patients a quiet place to enjoy outside the sterile feel of the hospital.

She dropped her bag on the ground and sat down on the narrow wooden bench overlooking the pond.

"It was pretty hard at first, but this is a place where people understand what I've been through. And if in the process I can help them, that makes it worth it. Honestly, though, I'm convinced that I get more out of it than they do."

"I'm glad it's helped."

"You said you had some news about the case?" she asked, changing the subject. "I haven't seen anything about this on the news."

He sat down next to her. "I'm not surprised, but that doesn't mean nothing's happening. In fact, this morning, the last of the team Macbain had working under him was arrested. And Stephen's program will actually end up helping security measures for the grid."

"So the case is closed?"

"There are still a number of unanswered questions that the FBI has. They believe that both the driver who ran us off the road and the attack in the parking garage were organized by a man named Rafael Bauer. He's connected to the men who originally hired Macbain. Bauer believed that Macbain was double-crossing him and working with the police. They're hoping that he eventually leads us to whoever was financing the actual takedown of the grid."

She listened to his explanation. There was nothing personal in his words or in the sound of his voice. It was as if he was simply following up on a case before he moved on to his next one.

"I appreciate your letting me know," she said. "Though you didn't have to come all the way here. Especially if you're leaving town."

"It's just for a few days of training in Houston."

"I know you're busy, but I have something to give you before you leave. I just wasn't sure when I'd see you again." She hesitated, then pulled the gift out of her bag. "Go ahead and open it."

"You didn't have to get me anything." Nate slipped off the paper and opened up the box. "Gracie . . ."

"It's a Hamilton pocket watch that was manufactured around the turn of the twentieth century. I know it isn't exactly like your grandfather's, but I know it was special to you. And after you lost it, well . . ."

"Wow." He glanced up. "I don't know what to say."

This time she caught the emotion in his eyes.

"You don't have to say anything," she said. "I saw it and thought of you."

"Actually . . ." He ran his fingers across the back of the watch, then looked up and caught her gaze. "I do know what I want to say."

She looked up at him and felt her heart stutter.

"Gracie, I've been so wrong."

She swallowed the lump in her throat. "What do you mean?"

"I really am leaving to do some training, but I'll be honest, coming to see you because of the case was an excuse."

"What do you mean?"

He moved closer to where she was sitting, then took her hand. Her breath caught at his nearness.

"I've never met anyone like you. I thought

I could run away after all this mess, because I didn't want to lose someone again. So I just pulled away. I didn't want to lose you, and yet that's exactly what I'm letting happen. I haven't figured everything out. I lost my team that day and failed to stop them from dying. You were a reminder of losing something I care about. I've tried to run. And yet everything leads back to you. I can't just walk away from you. Because . . . well, as crazy as it seems, I love you."

"Nate—"

"Maybe I'm completely wrong and I'm going to walk out of here feeling like a fool, but I don't care anymore. If there's even the smallest chance in the world that you might feel the same way I do—"

"Nate."

"What?"

"I love you too."

"Really?"

"Do I need to convince you?"

Nate laughed as he reached down and brushed his lips across hers.

"What happens next?"

He smiled at her. "We don't know what the future holds, but as long as we're together . . . that will be enough for me."

Lisa Harris is a Christy Award finalist for *Blood Ransom* and *Vendetta*, Christy Award winner for *Dangerous Passage*, and the winner of the Best Inspirational Suspense Novel for 2011 (*Blood Covenant*) and 2015 (*Vendetta*) from Romantic Times. She has over thirty novels and novella collections in print. She and her family have spent almost fifteen years working as missionaries in Africa. When she's not working, she loves hanging out with her family, cooking different ethnic dishes, photography, and heading into the African bush on safari. For more information about her books and life in Africa, visit her website at www.lisaharriswrites.com.